Quantum Avidya

By

Marc Gregory

Other books By Marc Gregory

Alternative Energy

Alternative Energy II - Blow Me

Price Per Barrel

Quantum Avidya

Banjo-rock music blasted through the stillness of the peaceful mountain morning. George Stanley looked up and used his index finger to push his thick-rimmed glasses back up his slightly bent nose as a rusted-out hillbilly truck tore into the campground, its tires spinning up rocks and dust. A surge of adrenaline flooded his body, sending his heart rate from calm to cardiac failure in the span of one beat.

The arranged meeting was set for that morning, at that time, at that specific site in that once-peaceful campground. To that point, George had been sitting quietly, washing down a granola bar with a bottle of water and enjoying his first morning of freedom in the scenic forest surrounding Metaline Falls, Washington.

His mind reasoned that in no way was this rowdy caravan the one he'd been waiting for. But instinct tensed his muscles and straightened the hair on the back of his neck.

The truck took a hard turn into his stall and skidded to a halt, sending a cloud of dust to hang heavy in the virgin morning air. In mid-stance, George stalled like a deer in headlights. His heart tried to pummel itself from his chest and run far, far away as his body remained frozen in a shock-induced paralysis.

As the veil of dust lifted, the music was muted and a man jumped over the side of the truck box. His weathered khaki pants hung low on his waist and the buttons on his floral print shirt were left undone, displaying his tanned, naturally muscular physique and hairy chest. His dirty-blond hair was long and shaggy with random dreads, and his beard was full and unkempt.

He swaggered up to George with a grin, tipped down his sunglasses, and gave him the once-over. A smouldering hand-rolled cigarette hung from his lips, and its smoke floated between their gazes, creating an almost sinister effect. As a silver tendril of the smoke tickled George's nose, the only category he could place the smell in was "illegal."

The man slid the sunglasses back into place and shot his hand forward. "John, I presume?"

George had used an alias for obvious reasons in these uncharted waters of humanity. Now, there, looking upon this man—this one he needed to trust to guide him in his quest to illegally cross over the border to Canada—he suddenly found himself missing the comfort and security of his structured life in the top-secret military think tank hidden deep beneath the plain-white brick façade of a pizzeria joint in Casper, Wyoming.

George's mind scrambled to pull together a response. John… the man had asked if he was John. John was him, George…

As the weight of the situation pressed on his analytical mind, his stomach clenched and he buckled forward and then heaved its contents into a chunk-spattered pile on the ground between them.

The stranger retracted his hand just in time. He met George's eyes with brows raised above his sunglasses. He pulled the cigarette from his mouth and exhaled a slow cloud of smoke, giving the impression of deep consideration.

George felt a trail of drool run off the edge of his slackened jaw.

"Y'know… *Johnny*," the man said, "I'm gonna take a wild stab at it and say you are John—the one Johnny I'm set to meet here." He looked back at his truckload of friends—two ladies in the box and another man behind the wheel—who broke from their fixated staring and bowed their heads to politely hide their snickering. He looked back at George and his hands became animated with his speech. "I'll just go ahead and say it, Johnny, bra… After our phone conversations, I was expecting someone more… hmm, say, composed?" He looked back at his friends to share a less discreet chuckle, then returned to George. "Y'know, bit more double-oh-seven." He shrugged his shoulders with a grin. "I'm thinkin' maybe you're not really into this, hey, bra? Got yourself some cold feet?"

George hung on the question for a moment, catching the irony of him—a highly respected young scientist with enough degrees and awards to paper a wall—not meeting the expectations of this vagrant. But maybe he wasn't ready? So far, all indications pointed to that conclusion. His mind raced back to the night before the last, when he'd stolen away from the shelter, leaving behind his security key with a note explaining that he just needed some time. Was going back an option? What would be waiting for him upon his return?

He blinked, closed his mouth, and straightened his posture. He reached for the sweat rag stuffed in his back pocket, then wiped the drool from his chin. It had taken too much of his will to get him that far, so he was not going back. Not yet.

"No-o," his said, his voice crackling. He cleared his throat and ran his fingers through his curly dark hair. His heart and mind joined to muster some courage, and when he had calmed well enough, he looked to the man. "I'm John, I'm the guy. It's all good, just a little queasy is all. Altitude maybe?" He stuffed the rag back in his pocket, then gave his hand a final rub on his pants and held it out to his guide. "You must be Jupiter?"

Jupiter slapped his hand into George's for a hefty shake and gave him a clever smirk. "Yes, Jupiter!" As part of his introduction, his gaze followed his other hand as it shot dramatically to the sky, then circled back down to the earth, as if he were cracking a whip. He laughed and let go of George's hand. "You like that? I've been workin' on it for a couple days." He rested his hands on his hips and looked at George standing meek and silent. He scratched his head. "Okay," he said and clapped his hands together. "We all decided to go with a planetary theme here with the names, so I'm Jupiter, mack daddy of all the planets. In the back there"—he began pointing—"the blonde, she's Venus, and the cute little redhead, she's Mars—you know, the Red Planet and all." He winked. "Behind the wheel is Your-Anus!" He bent over with laughter, slapping a hand to knee.

The driver shot his middle finger in the air and took a drink from a can of beer as the two lovely ladies smiled and waved.

When his laughter subsided, Jupiter got straight to business. "So, you got the money?" He held out his hand.

George's eyes widened and he looked around the campground. A few people were beginning their day, shooting the occasional curious glance in their direction. "Uh… yeah," he whispered. "H-here? You want me to just…?"

Jupiter didn't seem concerned about concealing anything as he nodded his smiling face and jutted his hand out farther.

George had the money bundled and ready in his coat pocket, and after another quick look around, he shoved it into Jupiter's hands. "Here," he whispered hastily, "half now and half when we get there, just as promised."

He was fully expecting Jupiter to thrust the money into hiding, but instead he laughed and lifted the stack of bills to his nose, breathing in while he fanned through it. "Ahhh," he sighed, then looked over at George. "Yeah, that's the deal— or we could just take you up into the trees, kill you, and take it."

George felt the colour drain from his face.

Jupiter laughed and slapped his knee again, then wrapped an arm tightly around George, drawing him close to his side. "I'm just kiddin', bra! Welcome aboard." He let George go with a playful shot to his shoulder and then led him to the back of the truck.

When they reached the side of the box, Jupiter held out his hand again. "Phone."

"Oh." George reached in his pocket and pulled out the pay-by-minute phone, his last point of connection to the world—and help. He slowly handed it over, looking in Jupiter's eyes and having second thoughts with every inch it drew closer.

Jupiter grew impatient and grabbed it. He tossed it on the ground between them and then put his hand out to the girls, who handed him a heavy chunk of firewood. He hammered the log down hard, smashing the phone to death.

To George, it seemed all their expressions flickered between those of happy-go-lucky hippies and happy-go-lucky satanic killers. He found himself questioning his yearning for freedom.

He nestled into a corner of the truck box, hugging his beefy backpack to him and keeping a close eye on Jupiter and the girls, who were talking, laughing, and being openly affectionate with one another while passing around a joint as they left the campground and headed through town, then took the bridge across the river and continued heading north for a while before taking a left onto a secondary gravel road.

The scenery was beautiful: crystal-clear rivers, towering cliffs, and gushing waterfalls. George wished he could enjoy it more, but he couldn't help continuing to question his decision.

It wasn't that he was angry, with his job or his life. He honestly couldn't give a reason for his decision to leave the think tank. It was something that had begun to pull at him a few years earlier, after the untimely death of his parents.

Till recently, he had been happy in his solitude. He would find an empty space with a whiteboard somewhere quiet and then sit in the safety of his own mind, numbers and symbols his selfish comfort. But lately, between dashes and deltas, thoughts of a soft touch and soothing voice tempted him. A curling smile on her lips and the smell of her skin. The sparkling little eyes of their child looking at him with love and admiration, the way he looked at his parents, once.

He snapped back to the present, displeased. Only one guy was supposed to be joining him on this excursion, not a whole band of hippie folk. He had pictured something a lot more Navy SEAL. The more he watched them goof around, the more vividly he imagined his picture appearing on the side of a milk carton.

He pretended to have no interest in them, but he couldn't help watching from the corner of his eye as they laughed and caressed. The ladies were beautiful, not only physically but also in their free-spirited nature. Laughing and giggling, taking turns tickling their fingers up Jupiter's thighs as he split his attention between them. The whole display swelled George's insecurities. This type of etiquette was alien to him, as make believe as the movies. George Stanley could construct a nuclear missile if he wanted—a damn good one too. But human intimacy was a complete mystery to him.

He tried to scoff at their behaviour as being immature and indecent. But in reality he was curious and even aroused. What was it about Jupiter that attracted these ladies? George found himself crafting a mental adventure log of Jupiter's penis. He bet if it could talk…

George had a penis, and it was used—used to transport waste fluid from his vesica urinaria to a receptacle of his choosing. Yep, George had himself some good times.

The gravel road eventually led to a narrow trail. The truck's pace slowed as it climbed up a steep hillside, its drivetrain whining and complaining as its box lurched and tipped heavily in every direction.

George peered over the side and found a steep cliff face dropping off right beside the path: one slip and that would be the end of him. Maybe he should have gone on some practice adventures first to warm up to this point—like maybe a wave pool or the New York subway system?

The trail levelled out and ended in a clearing with just enough room for a vehicle to turn around. They came to a stop and the driver announced that it was time to get out.

Jupiter puffed his cheeks as he exhaled an air of disappointment. He looked over at George. "Well, bra, now comes the hard part." He said goodbye to the ladies, kissing them each as they whined about losing his attention. He grabbed an overstuffed backpack and heaved it over the side before hopping out himself.

George followed Jupiter's lead but was slower and more careful in his dismount. He was grateful that the rest wouldn't be joining them, but he was a little less comfortable with the idea that three people who could identify him and knew of his plans were likely heading to some party, with a high chance of ending up in police custody at any given time. He would have to keep Jupiter motivated to get across that border as soon as possible.

He turned and looked toward a faint trail leading into thick brush, then at a snow-covered mountain peak in the distance. It wasn't too late to turn back. Really, what was he expecting to find on the other side?

The truck started up and Jupiter humped his pack onto his back, then helped George with his. The girls cried goodbyes and blew kisses as the driver turned the rig around, stopping for a moment to share a handshake with both the guys and wish them luck before heading back down the crooked trail.

They waited till the truck was out of sight, then Jupiter placed his hand on George's shoulder. "Well, now it's just the two of us, man. You ready for this?"

George checked the time on his old leather-strapped analog watch, his most cherished keepsake from his father, which told him it was almost 11:00 a.m. He traced the tip of his finger over its face and hoped his parents were keeping a watchful eye over him. He had brought no other electronics of any kind—no phone, no GPS, nothing he could be tracked by—just an old-school compass and paper map. He took a deep breath and nodded.

"All right, then." Jupiter reached over his shoulder and into his bag, then pulled out a machete.

The sudden mood change had George clenching up to avoid making a mess in his pants. His eyes burst open and his hands raised as he took a step back. "Uhhh" was the only dialogue he could manage.

"Yeah, right! She's sexy, eh? Just had her sharpened and polished. A guy I know made 'er for me, real old-school blacksmith. I stopped in after the last trip and had him shine her up. This bush in here is nasty thick, and grows back quicker than you'd think. You don't never wanna try any trek 'round these parts without a sturdy blade. So, c'mon." He stepped to the mouth of the trail and took a heavy whack at the first branch that dared get in his way, slicing it clean off. "Oh man! That's *so* sweet, ha!" He waved to George.

George took another deep breath and looked back at the trail that brought him there, the last glimpse at civilization he would see for some time. Then he turned and disappeared off the map, into the unknown.

Early that same morning, nestled deep in the Canadian Rocky Mountains a thousand or so kilometres north of George as the crow flies, Annabelle Jensen began her day.

The bald head of the sun was poking over the surrounding peaks of the Kootenay Valley when she opened the door of her small yurt in the quaint shanty village known as Beelieve. As she stepped onto the wooden landing, she closed her eyes and greeted the sun with her own radiant smile. She stretched her arms overhead, her tall and slender frame reaching toward the nourishing light like a forest tree. Then she let her hands fall to absentmindedly play with the long braids of her shimmering chestnut hair as she stepped to the earth.

When her foot touched down on the moist, grass-laden soil, she bit on her lip with a pleasured grin, savouring every kiss of mother earth's sweet lips on her skin. She moved slowly and gracefully, like a heron navigating the slippery rocks of a river bottom as she went where she went every morning: down the gentle slope, just past Granny and Cappy's place, to the grassy knoll that overlooked the forest stretching far below, till it drowned in the glacial valley lake. Griz, the local carpenter, had built her a wooden platform there so she could perform a yoga ritual she had choreographed to welcome the birth of a new dawn and to give thanks to everything and everyone in her life.

Annabelle had run away from a troubled home, full of addiction and abuse, as soon as she felt she could fend for herself. Travelling around for some time, she'd walked a dangerous line between light and her own darkness until she'd fallen upon this small off-the-grid village of makeshift dwellings in a patch of paradise, where she was welcomed by the local hippie tribe, who taught her the beauty of spirituality and a minimalist lifestyle.

That is where she found herself, found her own inner beauty. She had never felt quite right in the city, with all the prim-and-propers. Her large clown feet weren't designed for heels, and her lack of chest could never fill a dress the way the girls on magazine covers did. She remembered the hate she had felt for herself years back, when she dressed for the part and then looked at her reflection. Her mother was always cursing at her when she found her concealer empty—freckles are so hard to hide. But Annabelle had found peace and happiness in the forest, where she blended seamlessly.

The village habitants were truly a happy bunch. The weather in the valley stayed mild year-round for the most part, so they could work a patch of garden big enough to supply food for themselves and then sell the rest to some of the shops and tourists in town—in addition to fruits and vegetables, they sold silly-weed, wine, and their most prized product: honey. They even blew their own glass jars to hold their products, and everything was labelled with the village emblem, consisting of a blooming lotus flower inside a single honeycomb. They also made fine arts, crafts, and clothing constructed from natural fibres. They didn't like to have to rely on money at all, but it was a necessary evil of the modern world.

Annabelle did her part by tending to the garden and taking food and wares into town for sale. The villagers all but insisted on her being the one to take the run to town as it seemed her innocent charm fetched a few more dollars. She was a delight to her little village and the surrounding towns. Everyone knew and welcomed her. Her powers within the spiritual community were of legend in the area; she could heal the sick and communicate with universal energies. She would chuckle at the whisperings, modest in her beliefs. She liked to think that her presence and happy nature helped those in need to feel hope.

Life to her was simple, magical, and almost complete, except for her want for a happy family of her own. Living in a shanty village hidden from the public made it hard to meet new people. As for tourists, well, they were there and then they were gone. At times she would remember her abusive family and ask herself why she would ever want to bring children into such a place. But she could never convince herself otherwise. She yearned for a charming, intelligent, and loving partner, along with the pitter-patter of little feet.

Finding her suitor might mean she'd have to leave, but she couldn't stand the thought. She'd lived in some of the possibilities out there.

Finishing her morning routine, Annabelle blew a kiss to the sun and returned to her yurt to get ready for a trip to town. She freshened up, straightened her braids, and put on her favourite yellow spring dress, gifted to her by Stella, the village tailor.

Then she was off to see Cappy and Granny. They were the elders of the village, wise beyond their years and tender and loving. Like the lighthouse on a rocky outcrop on a stormy night, they'd guide you inside and wrap you in a blanket and warm you with a cup of milky cocoa… Safe, loved.

She could see Granny watching her from the doorway of their place—an old wooden shed-like structure, added on to by another… and another. Granny was smiling as always, in a white robe with colourful beaded accents, her silver hair shimmering in the fragmented beams of morning sun. Cappy would no doubt be enjoying his morning coffee in his rocker around the side.

"Good morning, Granny! Good morning, Cappy!" she sang.

Granny's smile grew as she approached. "Oh! Good morning, Annabelle, m'dear."

Cappy came around the corner holding his steaming mug. "Good morning, beautiful." He smiled a sweet, toothless grin, and the morning rays shone off his scalp through the comb-over he always maintained. *Gotta do the best with what you got,* he would say with a wink. "What do you have planned for the world today?"

"Just the usual, going to town to sell what needs to be sold. What do we have for today's run?"

"Oh, not much new, really." Cappy began sorting through the wicker baskets saddled up on their loyal village steed, Dennis the mule. "Batch of vegetables, some flowers Stella picked from the field, and a few nice paintings she did— y'know, the ones she does on the birch bark. You going to be back for dinner, my sweet? Munch has some new tricks he's going to show."

"Oh, really? Well of course I'll be back for it. I wouldn't miss it for the world!" Annabelle stepped up to her travel companion with a smile. "Good morning, Dennis." She scratched him under his cheek the way he liked as she leaned down and gave him a kiss on his nose. "Light load today, buddy," she said and gathered his reins.

Granny held her hand softly. "Yes, it's not much, m'dear, but it should fetch a few dollars. And you know…"

"Every dollar counts, I know." Annabelle gave Granny's hand a gentle squeeze and kissed her cheek. "I'll be back in time for the show."

"Take care, m'dear," Cappy called.

As she turned to leave, Annabelle almost ran right into the slender-framed Gwyn, dressed as usual in her flowing dark robes, with her lightning-white hair hanging straight to her waist. Gwyn caught Annabelle's gaze and stared until Annabelle felt a little discomfort. It was the usual greeting from Gwyn, who was a self-taught reader of sorts.

Gwyn flinched, her eyes widened, and she grabbed Annabelle's hand. Looking down, she traced her fingers over the creases. "Oh… ah yes… yes!" She nodded and lifted her gaze. "There is change coming! I see it! It's money! You will get some— No, wait… Sickness. There is a sickness in your family!"

"Oh? Oh dear." Annabelle politely fetched her hand back. She looked back at Granny, whose eyes were lifted to a hanging basket of flowers, ignoring the conversation as she usually did when Gwyn began one of her uninvited readings. She smirked and turned back to Gwyn. "Well, I best keep up on my vitamins and make sure to stay warm and dry for the next few days. Thank you, Gwyn, you're always such a wonderful help to all of us. I don't know what we would do without you, honestly."

Gwyn accepted the compliment with a proud smile. "Yes, if only the rest of the world would be as accepting. It would be a much better place, I say." She gave Annabelle a gentle hug.

Annabelle nodded and bid farewell to the group, then continued on her way.

"Goodbye, Annabelle," Granny called from behind. "Travel George."

Annabelle stopped in her tracks. She shook her head, then turned back. "George? What?... What was it you said, Granny?"

"Huh?" Granny replied, equally confused. "I said travel safe, m'dear."

Annabelle pondered for a second. *Of course that's what she said, just as she always does. Must be games of my dizzy mind.* She corrected her smile. "Yes, of course. I, I will travel… safe. Thank you."

The trip to town was on a broken path at best. As the crow flew, Nelson wasn't far, but the forest in that area was dense and lush, and so walking there took careful navigation of animal trails and riverbanks, and one stream required crossing via an old uprooted hemlock tree. But the gorge it spanned wasn't deep and the tree was as thick around as it was tall. It would take a person of considerable intoxication to not be able to manage it, and while it would be amusing to see most mules manage the course, Dennis had made the trip more than any other villager.

Annabelle loved her forest walks, with the sound of the birds and the rushing water and the friendly visits from furry friends.

It was in society where she felt somewhat out of place. It wasn't all bad—Nelson was a very beautiful hillside town stretching up out of the pristine, glacial Kootenay Lake, in the valley of the same name. It was well back from any major highways, so one would need to go off the beaten path and cross by ferry or over a mountain pass to get there. The civilized part of the area had a heavy European influence, and the people in the hills were mostly descendants of those who had escaped the draft back in the days of war. But walking the engineered surface between Nelson's brick buildings flattened Annabelle's smile as much as her feet. And while she enjoyed the company of the few locals and shopkeepers she dealt with regularly, she had learned to steer clear of the wealthy seasonal tourists who came for some carefree adventure, knowing they would be leaving any consequences behind in a few days' time.

With tropical summers attracting the cottage families and snowy but mild winters for the ski junkies, it was a little piece of hidden paradise. The exhaust and electronic waves polluting the air during those seasons confused Annabelle. She would watch it all—the luxury automobiles, Rolex watches, and designer handbags passing by the lone man playing guitar on the corner to earn enough for a meal. The differences between classes was cosmetically vast, but only as thick as a dollar bill. Land developers and corporations looking to cash in had made several attempts to make the area more mainstream over the generations, but the locals had fought hard to keep it a quaint mom-and-pop community.

Annabelle thought back to her family and the trials they had faced in pursuit of what they thought would be their happiness, then she caught herself and stuffed the thoughts back where they belonged: in the past.

Down the main street she strolled, bidding good morning to all the workers placing out their patio furnishings, spraying down the sidewalks, and watering the plants. "Good morning, Annabelle!" chimed the polite welcomes along the street.

She pulled up to the corner grocery to find Mr. Mulland putting out potted plants and giving them a morning drink. "Good morning, Mr. Mulland, what a beautiful spring day."

The short, round man with olive-toned skin and a wreath of grey hair wrapped around a bald cap looked up. "Uh-huh, good morning, Annabelle." He shot her a forced smirk.

Annabelle returned her brightest of smiles. He was always terse with her when she first arrived. It was business to him, and pleasantries would be exchanged only after business was complete. Even if the transaction was only worth a few dollars.

"So, whatcha trying to sell this morning, huh?"

"Oh, just the usual for you. Peppers, tomatoes, and cucumbers—all one hundred percent organic, you know."

"Yes, yes, organic, of course," he mumbled while rummaging through her offerings. "It looks okay, I s'pose. I'll give you six dollars for the lot."

"Six dollars? Oh, Mr. Mulland, surely you could do eight, at the very least."

"Eight? That's thirty percent more!" He waved a hand at her.

She picked up a pepper. "But look how big this is, look at the colour, and here"—she held it to her nose and breathed in softly—"so fragrant." She pressed it to his nose.

His face scrunched as he gave a short sniff, then he raised an eyebrow as he contemplated her . "All right, eight."

Annabelle smiled and clapped her hands lightly. "Thank you so much, Mr. Mulland, you're such a dear." She wrapped her arms around his shoulders and squeezed.

He tried to hide his blush as always, then invited her to join him for an early-morning glass of chilled tea. He opened two folding chairs and set them on the sidewalk so they could sit and watch the morning ramblings.

The bustle was light. In town there were basically two directions: uphill and down. This morning, it was mostly just townsfolk walking their dogs or heading for an early breakfast at one of the many quaint cafés.

They passed the short time with some idle chit-chat and laughs, then they said their farewells and Annabelle continued her route up to the craft store, where she greeted Ms. Baumhauer with a friendly hug.

Ms. Baumhauer held her at arm's-length, looking her over. "Oh goodness, child, is it possible you get more beautiful every time I see you?"

Annabelle blushed. Ms. Baumhauer was always so sweet to her.

"Is this a new dress? Maybe it's a new dress?"

Annabelle looked down and pulled the bottom of the dress out to the sides. "No, not new. Stella made a few subtle alterations, but it is my same old dress."

Ms. Baumhauer walked around her slowly, studying the tailor work. "Hmm, this Stella, she is very good. I will have to talk to her about doing some work for me."

"Yes, well, she'll be in for the festival, as always."

"Yes, right, the festival. Please tell her to stop by. Now, dear, what do you have for me today?"

The women went through the items, including a few small paintings, a wooden bear carving, and a pretty blue dress. The two quickly agreed on a price. The craft sale was always the money-maker for the village because of the top quality and originality.

"Okay, my dear, now you'll return to your trees? You know how I worry about you living this way you do."

"The village? Oh, Ms. Baumhauer. You're sweet to worry, but the village is the most beautiful place in the world to me."

"Yes, yes." Ms. Baumhauer sighed. "A beautiful place, I know. You know if you ever need anything, Annabelle, you are always welcome here with me. I have a room and work waiting for you anytime. Maybe we can find a good George for you?"

Annabelle's smile faltered. "A… what? I'm sorry, what was it you said, Ms. Baumhauer?"

"What?" I said I have a room and work for you anytime." She shrugged her shoulders.

Annabelle's head tilted. "Yes… right, that is what you said."

Ms. Baumhauer shot back a look of concern. "You don't look well. Ugh! Why don't you come stay with me, let me care for you. The forest is no place for such a lady."

"Yes… no, it's fine. Maybe you're right. Maybe I'm not well." She pondered Gwyn's warning of illness. "Maybe I should return and lie down for a bit. Thank you so much, Ms. Baumhauer. I'll see you again in a few days—at the festival for sure!"

"Yes, the festival. You go straight home now and get some rest." She gave her a strong hug and a kiss on the cheek.

George? This was now two times that day someone had randomly said the name George. Was it coincidence? She didn't know of any George. Her spiritual sense was tingling… *George?*

And it got worse as she made her way back to the village. Stopping in at the bakery to grab one of her favourite pastries, a couple in the corner used the word *George* out of context multiple times. She escaped into the trees, but even there the birds whistled *George* and the grazing deer grunted the same.

By the time she reached the village, her smile had faded, along with her colour. She dropped the basket and the money off with Granny and Cappy, who expressed their concern between words of *George*.

Annabelle hurried herself back home, fell onto her bed, closed her eyes tightly, and welcomed rest to take her.

"All he left was this note, General." A sheepish man in slacks and a shirt and tie known as Tardy handed over the paper.

General Mathis was a very large man—tall, with broad shoulders. He wore his dark hair in a short military cut and had a thick moustache streaked with silver. He was a man whose masculinity could be literally felt.

The general looked down upon his assistant. "Did you do a thorough sweep of his room?"

"Yes sir, we turned everything over and didn't find anything suspicious."

He read through the short letter. "Says he just wants some personal time? All he had to do was ask, we allow for personal time."

"Yes sir, that's correct. That's what makes this all a little strange."

"Yes," he drawled, pacing the floor and stroking his chin.

"What do you think we should do, sir? Should we call it in?"

Mathis knew George Stanley as well as anyone. He knew of George's past, and of the unfortunate incident with his parents. George was a good man by the general's standards. This little stunt he was pulling seemed completely out of character.

But George had the highest of security clearance in the scientific division. Normally this kind of reckless behaviour from someone of that status would be unacceptable. What the general had to decide right then was how much of a threat George Stanley was to the military, and to their secrets.

He stopped pacing and headed up to the pizzeria, then lifted a napkin holder and found George's security card—which meant the man couldn't be logging in to anything confidential. Security checks were already being run on the computer systems and nothing was turning up as being tampered with.

The general knew George to be a man of his word, but he suspected that the reason he offered was not the whole of the story. George was one of his best men, but he had seemed a little off since his parents' tragedy, so maybe it would be best to give him his time, and when he returned, he'd be rejuvenated.

Tardy followed the general out as he stepped into the dark street, took a breath, and scanned the neighbourhood. He pulled a cigar from his pocket and lit it up. He puffed a couple times, then watched the smoke float through the still night air and then dissipate into the stars. *Where are you, George Stanley?... Why?*

Tardy chose that moment to break the silence. "*Ahem*, sir? Sir? Do you think we should put out an alert?"

The general exhaled another cloud before dropping the cigar and rubbing it out with his boot. "No, no alert, not right now. If George Stanley wants some personal time, I think we should let him have it. He's a good man, a loyal man, and he's earned at least that. We'll keep our eyes and ears open and see how this plays out, for now."

Trudging through the forest took more effort than George was accustomed to. It wasn't that he was grossly out of shape, as could be expected from a guy who spent the majority of his life running formulas at a desk. Fitness was a focal point of George's life: *Healthy body, healthy mind,* he always told himself, and he made good use of the state-of-the-art fitness centre in the bunker. But in a gym, it was hard to replicate nature's steep inclines over rugged terrain at a high altitude in the hot sun and humidity. He owed much to Jupiter for clearing the path of branches and lending a hand when they had to make short scrambles across rocky faces. George was impressed by how Jupiter could keep idle chit-chat going through it all, without missing a breath, whereas George had to concentrate to keep his wind and so couldn't risk any length of conversation.

Jupiter's knowledge of the land also impressed George. He could state the history of certain areas and facts about some of the plants and animals that crossed their path. It became apparent that he was passionate about his profession and was not just some mindless hippie making money by smuggling people across international lines.

But George still had his guard up. He kept his pack close to his side and maintained a respectable distance from Jupiter, one eye on him at all times.

The sun passed long overhead and they took very few breaks. For lunch, they stopped at a landmark Jupiter used to keep his bearings: a rock bluff with a beautiful view of the valley. With no time to waste on building a fire, lunch consisted of the juice and egg salad sandwiches Jupiter had packed, which again,

George had to admit, exceeded his expectations.

Jupiter had taken off his sunglasses while he ate, and when George looked into his eyes he saw a very human honesty.

"So… how did you end up here, in this lifestyle?" George asked between mouthfuls.

Jupiter finished chewing his food while looking over the land, as if thinking about where to start his answer. "Well…" He took a sip of juice and swallowed his food. "Not much of a story, really. I was raised by my mom, in a trailer park not far from where I picked you up. I never knew my dad—never met him, to be honest. At least, I don't think I did. Mom… well, I know she had a good heart. But y'know, she hung around with the wrong type… wrong type of *men* mostly. None took care of her the way she deserved. And it was just one bad decision after another, lots of yellin' and screamin', none of them cared much for me. She ended up in the hospital a few times. People in the park were always helpin' each other—there's lots of kids in the park—so I always had somethin' to eat and somewhere to crash when Mom was away dealin' with whatever. She got worse over time, and then there were all the prescription drugs the docs were givin' her. I got older, and started comin' around less. School was never much of a thing for me, so I just got on doin' what I do. And she drifted away. Got hooked on them opiates. Came home one day to an eviction notice and a big lock on the door, and heard she ran off to the coast with some other junk man. Seattle, I s'pose." He shook his head. "I never went lookin'."

Jupiter had suddenly become very human to George. He wrapped his arms around his knees and watched him as the two sat in silence for a moment. "I'm sorry to here that, Ju—"

"Na!" Jupiter waved it off. "It ain't nothin', man. I just figure we all get that hand, right? Some get gold and some get shit. But I'd rather be tryin' to turn shit to gold than have gold that turns to shit. 'Cause at least that way I got somethin' to look forward to, ya feel that?"

"*Hmph*… Yeah, I do feel that." George grinned at the simple wisdom.

Jupiter nodded and put his shades back in place, then looked at George. "You? What's your story? Whatcha runnin' from? Seems everyone I bring through here is runnin' from somethin'. But I don't expect you to say nothin' of it. They never do… none of my business anyway."

George wasn't interested in telling Jupiter his whole story, but he felt he should at least share something, now that the guide had shared a piece of himself.

"I… My parents are dead."

His parents had been a couple so full of life and love, so strong in their commitments, he had been convinced it would take nothing less than a giant meteor strike to wipe them from this life.

But there was nothing spectacular in their passing. A silent killer had come as they shared a bed in the basement spare room one night to escape the summer heat. Like the wings of a butterfly, the spent energy of four AAA batteries in the carbon monoxide detector changed George's life forever. He had no other family, no siblings—now there was just him and his work.

"They were good people," George continued. "Died of carbon monoxide poisoning. Not suicide, just the wrong place at the wrong time."

"That's sad to hear." Jupiter crossed his arms. "They should've had one of them detector things."

George dropped his head with a puff and a grin, then nodded and looked back at Jupiter. "I've lived a very sheltered life. My parents were both professors, Mom with English, Dad with science, so education was a priority in my home. I graduated from high school at fifteen and moved on to university, majoring in science. Had multiple job offers from some big corporations—big money—but I felt the military had better resources. So, I've been hiding underground for most of my adult life… all of it, I guess. This trip… I'm really not sure that I'm running away from anything—at least that's not how it started. I feel like I'm going *to* something. At least I hope there's something at the end of this. But I have no idea what, if anything. There's just this memory of my Mom and I on a Sunday morning. This movie would come on, a funny romance where this guy with a huge nose is trying to get the beautiful woman… Anyway, it's set in this beautiful mountain town, and Mom loved the scenery, so she looked it up one day and promised that we would go sometime. So… I might be throwing away my whole life because of nothing… because I'm stupid, or maybe crazy."

Jupiter smiled as he threw his backpack on, and then he stepped up to George and placed a hand on his shoulder. "Well, Johnny, that's the nice thing 'bout up here. You can be as stupid-crazy as you need, and no one's gonna take no special notice, ha!" He gave George's arm a friendly pat and continued on his way.

They scrambled up the hills and down the valleys and hiked through the marshes. George grew anxious as the time for the actual border crossing grew closer. Would there be a wall? Armed military? Maybe a tunnel labyrinth haunted by ghouls and trolls? What if they got caught? What would become of them?

But as he grew more and more tired, those thoughts faded to concern about how he would make it over the next slope, and as the sun began to fall, they morphed into wondering when they were finally going to stop for the night. Or would they?

It wasn't much farther till they hit a clearing beside a creek in the valley, where there was a fire pit and enough room to set up a couple tents.

Jupiter let out a sigh as he dropped the pack from his shoulders. "Ahhh, man, that hike never seems to get any shorter." He stripped naked without any kind of warning to George, then walked waist-deep into the water and splashed it over his body before submerging himself entirely, then popping back up. "Wooo! Johnny, bra! You gotta get in here, man! Nothin' like it after the day we just had."

George wasn't at the same stage of comfort in their relationship yet. But he did roll up his sleeves and wash his face at the water's edge, finding it ice cold, refreshing, and much welcomed.

Jupiter put his pants back on, then dragged some deadfall from the forest and had a fire going in no time.

The fire made George quite nervous. "Jupiter, uh, do you really think that's… smart?"

"Huh? What's that, Johnny? What's smart?"

George motioned toward the fire, which only seemed to confuse his guide further. "The, uhhh, the fire? Do you think that's something we should have going right now? I mean, with the whole border-crossing thing? The smoke?… The light?"

"Oh yeah, right. Well, there's been a lot of rain this year, so there's no fire bans on yet."

George wondered if Jupiter really understood the illegality of their excursion, but he decided there were better uses for his energy than that conversation. And the warmth of the fire was comforting as the mountain air cooled with the sunset.

Jupiter pulled an unexpected amount of food from his bag, including two large vacuum-sealed salmon fillets. He worked to get the food served while George put up his tent. Then the two feasted like kings. George couldn't help kicking back with a smile after the meal, impressed once more by his guide's efforts.

"John… Johnny!"

George looked over to find Jupiter trying to pass him a smouldering joint. "Uh, no… No, thanks, Jupiter, I've never really been into that stuff, honestly."

Jupiter shrugged it off and put the joint in his mouth, but a second later he was calling to George again. "Hey, John! *Psst*, Johnny!"

George looked over again to find a cracked can of beer being pushed on him. He wasn't much for beer either. He'd only had one once before, on one of his nightly strolls with a co-worker when they'd snuck into a neighbourhood pub. George could barely stomach it then, and he didn't have any higher hopes for this round, but he was on the run, sleeping under the stars. Besides, if he didn't accept it, he was scared of what would be thrust upon him next.

"Ahhh." Jupiter finally kicked back on his blanket and relaxed, sipping his beer between strong tokes that filled the still night air with a spicy aroma. "Man, look at those stars out tonight, Johnny. That's one thing I love about being up here. Nothing—no pollution, nothing—to block the view of all that's pure, bra."

The stars were brilliant that night. Most would look up at the twinkling lights and see nothing more than that, but George was beyond the ordinary in the way he looked at the world. He was on the frontline of quantum science, the study of the very smallest of particles that make up our universe, where science discovered that the universal equations could only be calculated to a probability, rather than certainty, and was indeed more chaos than fact. His studies took centuries of scientific theory, crumpled it up, and tossed it in the wastebasket. He was kicking down big doors to a very mysterious and fascinating world that functions very differently from the one we know. He had an ability to see and understand life on the smallest of scales, to the point that when in deep thought, the world became pixelated.

There under the stars, his mind was allowed to drift and theories and calculations began to swirl before him. As he fell into a trance, he saw the air moving through the leaves, and the leaves displacing particles as they fluttered. Like grains of sand, space flowed around the planets, comets, and satellites. It was all connected, all of it tiny particles of matter. The breath from his mouth and the beat of his heart constantly created waves through space and time—zillions of waves, of every size, coming from countless directions in an endless ocean of mayhem.

George sniffed at his beer, took a sip to wet his palette, then took a bigger gulp and sat back to look up at the theatre in the heavens. Stars were a part of his work, always measuring distances and calculating masses. He couldn't remember a time when he had kicked back with someone and just… looked. He didn't know anyone who could just sit back and appreciate something strange or beautiful. They were always looking for the "whys" or "hows."

He had that instinct as well—to start dissecting everything to try explaining it. But at that moment, somehow, he was able to stop the formulas spinning in front of his vision and just watch.

Must be the beer. He grinned. "Yeah, it really is beautiful. I admit, I was pretty hesitant about taking this trip with you when we first met. But I'll tell you, you're doing an excellent job. The dinner was fantastic. You really go the extra mile for your clients."

"Yeah, haha, 'Jupiter Tours.'" He raised his beer to the sky, clouded in a puff of smoke. "You gotta leave a review on the travel sites, hahaha. Glad you're having a good time, Johnny bra. That's what trippin' with Jupiter's all about. AH! Haha! That's it, man! That's the new name! 'Trippin' with Jupiter'!"

George shook his head, finding a laugh for the first time in a while. It was a good name.

But then the smile faded as he reminded himself just how far he'd come in such a short time, and how crazy it all was. Why? It was a question George had asked himself countless times throughout the planning stages of his journey. He knew there wasn't always an answer. People understand a leaf in a current being guided wherever the flow desired. To believe what you see is easy.

Waves… waves of motion, waves of your breath, waves of your heart, and waves of your thoughts—constant, continual, everything in life has its own distinct vibration.

So… why? Why was he doing what he was doing? It was one of those questions without answer—not yet, at least. The breeze had changed and the currents had shifted. He didn't know why, but he knew it had to be.

Annabelle woke from her afternoon slumber to find her room cloaked in darkness. She blinked her eyes and gathered her thoughts. She had slept away the day, and what a strange day it had been.

She took a deep breath and relaxed in her bed, the shapes and silhouettes of her room appearing as her eyes adjusted to the light.

She couldn't help the name echoing through her mind… *George.*

Annabelle knew little about matter, waves, or particles. What she believed in were the ancient teachings of the spiritualists, the Buddhists, and the Mayans—the ancient beliefs that people had complete control over their lives and destinies. One could transform their world and path within it through belief and focus.

But it was a hard wisdom to stay true to. On one hand you can transform your world through energy of thought, but on the other, things were as they were and you should accept them… and breathe. Always remember to breathe.

She was very thankful for her life. She was healthy and she was loved and adored. But she wanted more. It was human greed, and she was guilty of it. She knew she had caught the eye of some men in the surrounding areas, the regulars in the hills who would stop in to trade wares—but none of them were him, the one she had outlined in her mind. Nothing was distinct about him, but she had a basic mould, and she knew that her heart would know immediately when she saw him. But impatience questioned when and if that day would ever come. It was more possible than not that this man would never cross her path… not hidden as she was in the backcountry.

George… She drifted back to sleep.

***

George startled in the middle of the night to find himself lying in the same spot, the half empty can of beer in his hand splashing him when he jumped. What was it?… He could have sworn he heard someone call his name. The fire had burned down to glowing embers and Jupiter, who hadn't moved either, was snoring softly.

He looked around and tried to calm himself. The full day of exercise and fresh air, finished off with a beer, must have knocked him out fast.

"*Whu-whoooooo!*"

That must be the sound that had woken him.

"*How-howlllllllll!*"

One after the other, calling from everywhere around them, was a full orchestra… and what big teeth they have.

George's heart raced; some were very close, and he hated to raise his voice or draw any attention.

"J-Jupiter!" he whispered. "Jupiter!" He tossed a small stone toward him to get his attention. But Jupiter only rolled onto his side and snored louder.

"*WHOOOOOOOOOOOOOOO!*" The howl came loud and crisp from just beyond the edge of the campground.

George wasted no time ripping open the zipper on his tent, crawling inside, and zipping it shut tight behind him. He looked at the nylon walls, knowing they would stop nothing from getting him if it truly wanted. Then he thought about his friend out there, by himself, in the sinister darkness. What kind of man was he to just leave him there?

"*Whu-whooooooo!*"

He'll probably be all right—yes, perfectly fine. He's a confident man of the woods and he stinks like beer and grass, so he should be fine.

He pulled the blankets around himself and lay down, staying low and quiet, and listening. It took a long time for him to settle again. The howling became more distant and less frequent over time, and eventually exhaustion conquered him again.

A faint glow began to soak through the white canvas walls of Annabelle's yurt. It was happening earlier every morning on the build up to summer solstice. She usually wouldn't get up quite that soon, but she felt she needed some meditation time in the twilight before the sun crested.

On her platform, she laid out her mat and sat down cross-legged, straightening her spine and looking at the purple horizon as she took a deep draw of the crisp, dewy morning air. She closed her eyes and exhaled.

She followed her normal path into mindfulness: slowing her breath to deep draws from the belly, focusing on the cool air as it entered her nostrils and expanded her lungs, then on the warm exhaust as it exited. In… out… The dizzying thoughts in her mind ceased, the much-needed calm coming to her as stress left her body, as she came to exist in that moment. In… out… Peace settled into her.

There existed nothing but the feel of her body and the emptiness of her mind, and she sat motionless, a beautiful statue on the bluff. And if she had opened her eyes, she would have seen the variety of woodland creatures basking in the tranquility emanating from her.

Then the first rays of the sun peeked over the mountaintop, casting a warm glow on her face. A songbird chirped along with the dawning of the day, beckoning Annabelle back.

Slowly, her fingertips began to twitch, then her toes. She raised her arms slowly over her head. Her eyelids fluttered and opened to the sun. She lowered her arms gently, and with a deep inhale, she planted her hands on her mat and pushed to her feet to begin her ceremony.

Her aura was captivating, and many mornings during this time, some of the villagers would be lucky enough to catch her salutation. This morning Granny and Cappy held hands and watched from their chairs. They could tell Annabelle was more focused than usual. Her form was a little sharper and her stretch a little longer, her balance stronger. Exhausting the bad to soak up the good. They knew she became more focused at times when she was struggling with emotions, and that made the ritual even more passionate.

As Annabelle came to the closing, she sat back into her starting position, raised her hands to prayer, and whispered appreciation in her mind.

Namaste.

She opened her eyes to the sun.

GEORGE!!! boomed a voice in her mind, like a hard slap to the face.

***

Cappy's and Granny's hands broke, and their coffee mugs fell to the ground as they watched Annabelle collapse into a heap.

George's lungs heaved in deeply as his eyes burst open. Light was filtering through his tent canopy, morning birds were chirping, and it was hot!

He rubbed at his eyes and took a mental trip through the night's events. He paused all movement to listen for anything outside the tent, wondering if his guide had been devoured in the darkness… He heard nothing.

He coughed and cleared his throat to warn unwanted guests that he was about to make an appearance. He found his glasses, then unzipped the tent and stuck his head outside, sucking in the cool morning air.

And… no Jupiter. He turned his head in either direction, listening but hearing only the babbling of the creek and the chirping of the birds. There was no sign of struggle where George had left him—the blanket was still laid out—so he gathered himself and stepped out of his hideaway.

Confused but less concerned, George stumbled away from the camp area so he could transport waste fluid from his bladder—but not into a receptacle, not this time. George was peeing on a tree, so wild and untamed. He was smiling to himself about walking on the wild side when he caught movement down by the water. He turned and saw Jupiter stepping out of the creek, buck-naked.

"Hey, bra!" multiple appendages waved at George. "I was wonderin' when you were gonna make an appearance. Was just gonna come kick your ass up, actually." He stretched high overhead and then reached back to wring the water from his long hair. "Man! Did I sleep like the dead, ha! Nothin' like a good night in fresh mountain air, bra."

He continued toward George till he stood within arm's reach. George stopped his quest for relief and began fidgeting, raising his arms for a stretch, and then running his fingers through his dark curls, then crossing his arms, and then shoving his hands into his jacket pockets, all while his face found many creative new expressions.

Jupiter seemed to tire just watching him. He scratched at his head. "Uh, yeah, so, anyway, you best get ready for the crossing. Get everything packed up tight. It's really not that big a deal, but you want to keep your stuff as dry as possible. So"—Jupiter gave him the once-over—"you're likely gonna wanna strip down aaaand, yeah…" He puffed out his cheeks, gave George a look that suggested he was losing it, then returned to camp.

George fidgeted a bit more, then called up to Jupiter, "The… the crossing? What, uh, what crossing are you talking about exactly… Jupiter?"

Jupiter waved an arm overhead. "That way, bra! We gotta cross that river, first thing."

"Oh." George looked at the water. It wasn't so bad, maybe a little bigger than a stream? Somewhere between a stream and a river, really, although the current didn't look overpowering. But it did look as if it got a fair bit deeper past the halfway point. George smiled and shrugged; it wasn't such a big deal. He returned to watering the tree.

When he got back to camp, Jupiter already had his gear rolled up and packed—dressed in nothing more than his hat. He stood tall, carrying his pack by the straps. "I'm gonna head on across first 'cause that bank can be a little tricky and I wanna be there to help you up."

George smiled and gave a thumbs-up. He quickly changed into some water friendly shorts and a T-shirt, then packed up and went down to the water's edge. Jupiter was already lounging in the sun on the other side.

"Oh, dude. Johnny man, you gotta shed the clothes, bra. I told ya to strip down—you gotta get wet for this one, and you don't need all your clothes soaked, man."

George looked up and down the stream. He didn't care for walking around naked, or even half-naked, and really had no interest in finding any sharp rocks with his bare feet. He hadn't skimped on his gear, and his hiking boots were guaranteed to be waterproof. "Nah, you know, I think I'll just hike up to that point there where the river flattens out, see? It gets wider, so it'll be shallow, you know? You can see the water churning over the rocks there, so it should be shallow enough, no problem."

Jupiter rubbed his hand over his face, "Dude. Johnny, bud, if you just... I mean, at least take your boots off and come across here..."

"Yeah, I got this, Jupiter. Just give me a second, it won't be any problem. It'll be better, really, you can use this way on your future crossings."

George got to the wide section and walked the bank a bit before committing to a line. The water was so clear, he could see every pebble. He found a path where he could hop across exposed rocks and hardly touch the water at all, so he ventured out.

Things were working as he had planned until he reached a point where the next perch was a little beyond his reach. He looked for a rock that was only slightly submerged, and when he stepped on it, he found the rock to be covered in a clever slime and the current to be much more powerful than he expected. He fell into the freezing water at the deepest part in the rapids, and the current dragged him downstream.

"Johnny! Awe, man, hold on! Hold on!"

George was an exceptional swimmer, and even with the pack on, he was able to keep his head up. It was his pride that stung the most—especially when a naked Jupiter fished him out at the exact spot where he was first advised to cross. It was hard for George to take a hand from his naked guide, but in his defeat, he let Jupiter drag his drenched mass onto the bank.

They both lay in the sun catching their breath.

"Well, Johnny man. Hate to say it, bra, but the rest of the day is gonna be nasty for ya. I have other appearances to make, so we don't have time to dry your gear out."

George lay on top of his pack, nodding to the sky. "Yeah, I get that. It's my own stupidity."

Jupiter finally got dressed and cinched his pack, then reached down and helped George up, with a heavy groan.

"Don't worry, I won't put this on your review." George smiled.

Everything on George was soaked and chaffed against his skin. His pack leaked water down his body, like a loaded sponge. While he sloshed along, he found that his fancy boots held the water in just as well as out. Now he would be forced to tackle the border while waterlogged and thirty pounds heavier.

They hit a thick bunch of bushes as they climbed down a steep rock face, and as they pushed through the last bit at the bottom, they came out to a rest area on the side of a highway.

"Ha!" Jupiter turned to him. "And there ya go, Johnny bra!" He gave a proud smile and held out his hand.

"Wha?... There I go? There I go what? Is this... is this the border? Can we just be standing out here like this?" He was ready to run back into cover.

"Huh? The border?" Jupiter's face scrunched. "What, man? We're here! This is it, as promised."

"What! What do you mean, 'This is it'?" George looked around in disbelief. "This is what?"

"What-what? Colorado, just as promised."

It suddenly all made unfortunate sense. "Wha? C-Colorado!"

Jupiter laughed. "Oh, man! Bra! Y-you should've seen the look on your face! Ah-haha! That... that should be on the review for sure! Trippin' with Jupiter, oh yeah! I'm just joking with ya, man—look!" He pointed to a large green traffic sign on the side of the road. "See, *km*—Kanada-miles, man, just as promised."

He was right, the distance on the sign was measured in metric. George's jaw dropped and he turned around, looking back. "But... how... where's the... There's no fence? No wall? There's no secret tunnel?"

"The wha?... There's no none of that, Johnny man, it's Canada." He thrust his hand out to George again.

George gave one last look around, having a hard time accepting it to be so simple. But he reached into his pocket and pulled out the other half of the payment, then handed the sopping wet bundle over to Jupiter.

Jupiter snatched it from his hand and immediately began walking toward a running pickup truck just down the road.

George called out to him. "But how is it so easy?"

"Wednesdays, Johnny man! Always cross on Wednesdays. It's shift change!"

"So... you just cross whenever you want? Just like that?"

"There are no borders in my world, Johnny bra. But I will suggest you get moving. Either hitch a ride or get back in the trees 'cause them Mounties will be asking questions if they find ya." Jupiter jumped in the truck box and slapped his hand on its side, and the truck pulled away. "See you on the other side, Johnny! Good luck to you, man, ha!" He smiled and waved till he disappeared from sight.

Annabelle woke to the smell of something nasty. She pushed away that nasty something in Granny's hand as she began coughing and heaving. She leaned over the edge of her bed as Cappy raised a bucket.

"There, there," Granny said as she rubbed Annabelle's back. "I know it's awful stuff to smell, m'dear, but we had to getcha to come 'round." Granny was a wizard with herbal remedies and many claimed there was no illness she couldn't cure. "What in goodness happened to you? I've been noticing a change in you lately—something strange. Now, you better start talking before it festers into something of more trouble." She pried each of Annabelle's eyelids wide, staring deep into each one. "You're not out partying with those town boys, now, are ya? You getting yourself into some trouble, missy?"

Gwyn shoved her way in between Granny and Cappy, then fanned a deck of cards in front of Annabelle. "Go on, pick one now."

Annabelle sighed and rubbed at her face, then put a half-hearted effort into picking a card so Gwyn would give her some space.

Gwyn took the card and disappeared to a small table at the side of the room.

Granny placed a damp chilled cloth on Annabelle's forehead. "Now, what's going on?"

Annabelle groaned. "It's nothing. No, no boys from town are giving me trouble. I've just… it's… just these things have been happening. Nothing over-crazy, but there's this energy that's been messing with me the last couple days, just really random… thoughts. They weren't much to begin with, but now, this morning, it's getting overbearing."

"Yes, yes, the voice!" Gwyn chanted from her table of cards. "The voice is danger… Unless the moon is in your house—then it might be something happy."

Granny sighed and looked to Cappy.

After all their years together, Cappy knew every hint in Granny's book. He leaned down to Annabelle and gave her a gentle kiss on her forehead. "You get better, my lady. Don't be scaring me like that no more. You give ol' Cappy a heart attack." He smiled sweetly, then touched his hand gently to Granny's shoulder and turned to Gwyn. "C'mon, Gwyn, we gotta leave these two for some alone time."

"Yes, ye-e-e-s." Gwyn's head was tilted back and her eyes were closed as she waved her hand over the cards. "I'm close, the answers are coming…"

"Not close enough, and you're coming with me." Cappy swept the cards from the table and into Gwyn's box and carried them out the door.

Gwyn was quick to follow. "Cappy, wait, I know!… She's going to be handed a big promotion at work."

"That's good, Gwyn, I was planning on sending an extra cucumber on her next trip to town." The two faded out the door.

Granny turned back to Annabelle, taking her hand in hers. "Now, my sweet. You wanna tell me what this is really all about? You know I won't say nothing to no one."

"*Pfff!*" Annabelle blew out, lying back in her bed and staring at the ceiling. She grabbed one of her pillows and slammed it over her face. Something that sounded like "gorlage" filtered through the down.

Granny pulled at the pillow till Annabelle finally let it go. "Say it!" she commanded.

"George."

"George? Who's George?"

"I don't know!" Annabelle exhaled her frustration. "All I know is that every time I try to have a conversation with someone, it's *George* this and *George* that."

"Who George? When you talk to George?"

Annabelle squeezed the pillow to her face again and screamed, then slammed it back down to her lap. "I don't know what *George*. I've been searching my brain for anyone named George, and I don't know—and have never known—anyone named George! But everyone keeps saying *George* to me! The people in town, everyone around here, the deer and the bunnies—I hear it everywhere. And this morning, after my yoga, this all-powerful voice shouted *George* like it punched me in the face… and I must've fainted."

"You did faint, sweetie." Granny continued to dab at Annabelle's forehead with the cloth. "You fell right to the ground. It's a good thing you weren't standing, or lord knows what shape you'd be in. So, *George*… People are saying *George* to you? Have I ever said *George* to you?"

"Yes—you, Cappy, people in town. It wasn't very often at first, but then it happened more and more. Then the animals began, and now the name is, I guess, just popping into my head whenever it wants. And now I'm fainting, and now… next…" Annabelle started to sob. "I guess it will just keep going until it kills me." She rolled into Granny's open arms and buried her face into her chest. "What's wrong with me, Granny? Can you make it stop? Am I… Am I going crazy?"

"Shhh, my child, oh-ho-no…" She rocked Annabelle gently. "No, you're not going crazy. We'll get this figured out. There's a good chance all you needed was to talk to someone about it. Now that I know, it wouldn't surprise me one bit if it all just goes away. You know the mind can be an awful trickster if you let it go off on its own. We'll beat this together, now, don't you worry about it any longer." Granny squeezed her hard and kissed her cheek.

When Annabelle had calmed, Granny lifted Annabelle's face and looked at her. "You know what I think the best medicine is for this right now? The whole village is gathering out there, and some of the hill people have come down to help us prepare for the summer festival in town—it's this weekend already. We have costumes to prepare and a float to build and magic shows to work on. Everyone is waiting for you out there; they're all concerned. And I can't think of anything better to distract you from these voices in your head. And if they start to bother you again, the second they start, you come and see me, okay?" She looked into Annabelle's flooded eyes.

Annabelle nodded.

"Okay, honey, we have so much to do, and no time to waste. So let's get out there!"

Annabelle agreed with a sweet smile, feeling better now that she had a friend in the know.

Granny helped her get presentable. Then, with one last hug, they stepped outside into the bustle.

And a bustle it was.

They walked around a greenhouse that sheltered Annabelle's place from the view of most of the village and made their way toward two other shanty homes. The first one belonged to Gwyn and her partner, Munch. The name drove him mad, but it was much more convenient than the name he preferred: the Great and Marvellous Marvin Munchousin the VI. He was a practised—or practising—magician, and you would never see him without his flowing cape.

Munch's act left much to be desired for those wishing to be whisked away on a journey full of awe and wonder, but anyone looking for some fun would never be disappointed. Many in the audience would argue that his blunders and follies were all rehearsed, but the ones behind the scenes could promise you they weren't. Though it bothered Munch that he rarely got it right, it was hard for him to accept it as failure when he saw all the smiling faces at the end of his show. And his loving partner Gwyn, who was also his assistant, was there through every good time and bad, pushing him onward to be the best he could.

Stella and Griz were the couple in the final dwelling, situated between the greenhouse and the field of flowers where the beehives were kept, beside the pond. Stella was an artist with no boundaries. From paintings to dresses, baskets, and rugs, she put a little bit of herself into everything she created, and it showed. Griz was a highly skilled carpenter, and there was nothing she couldn't build.

That day the couples had joined forces and were working on some elaborate costumes and a small but magnificent float that would need to be taken to town in sections.

"Annabelle!" They all waved to her as she walked up the slope.

Munch approached her with his dark hair flowing over his shoulders and his beard collected into a pair of elastics. "Annabelle," he said, his voice dark and mysterious as he took her hand, raised it to his lips, and kissed it gently. "I hear you have been giving the village some concern. But I see your smile is back now. Perhaps we can lift your spirits with one of our new tricks?" He winked and stood aside to reveal Gwyn standing beside a cloaked structure. She righted herself with a smile, then waved her hands over it.

"We are working with doves this year." He winked again, then turned to his assistant and waved the wand. "Acra-babba cantoosa!"

Gwyn slid the cover off a large bird cage.

"Yeeeeessss." Munch's movements mimicked something serpentine. "Now the cage is empty." He waved his wand back toward Gwyn, who needed multiple attempts to get the sheet back over the cage as it was a little too tall for her.

Munch blushed slightly. "Yes, just… okay, we'll have to get Griz to cut a couple inches off the legs." He turned back to Annabelle, who held her hands before her lips as if in prayer to hide her laughter.

"Now… Bumble-bee-mumble-fantasta!"

Gwyn ripped the sheet from the structure once again.

"There we have i—" Munch did a double take at the cage. "Wha?… Who?… Honey… Gwyn?" He seemed to forget about Annabelle as he walked back to Gwyn. "Where are the birds?"

At the question, Gwyn broke from her splendid pose and realized the birds were missing. She shrugged her shoulders and began to examine the prop for defects.

Annabelle giggled to herself, then called, "I think it's amazing, you two! Just a couple bugs to work out, and I know it will be the talk of the festival!"

They stopped to smile and wave back to her, blowing kisses and wishing her well.

Annabelle continued up to see Stella and Griz.

Stella broke from her work when she saw Annabelle and ran over with a hug and kiss on her cheek. "My Anna, are you okay?"

Annabelle had always been a little envious of Stella's beauty and talent. Her strawberry-blonde hair glowed in the morning light, draping flawlessly all the way to her waist, and the blue in her eyes was as pure as the sky.

"Yes, I'm much better, thanks. Granny worked her magic, of course."

The women joined hands and turned to Griz, who was the more masculine female in the relationship with her large frame, broad shoulders, and short dark hair, but who was equally as kind and beautiful.

Stella walked Annabelle over to the base of the float they were decorating with wooden sculptures of mountain sheep and colourful tapestry. "What do you think? Do these colours work? Griz thinks maybe it's too much blue."

Annabelle whispered, "I think it's perfect, Stella, absolutely beautiful. You have such a talent. Let Griz work the hammer, the colours are your job."

The two giggled and hugged, till Annabelle was startled by an aggressive shove to her lower back, followed by a familiar snort.

"Ooh!" She turned, knowing well who was there for some attention. "Hello,

Dennis." She smiled and scratched his cheeks.

He snorted again and pushed himself harder into her, almost bowling her over.

"Oh-ho-ho, yes, I know, I know. I haven't been feeling well. But I'm better now. Are you hungry for some treats? Let's go see what the garden has for us today."

She scratched behind his ears again and then waved goodbye to her friends, and Dennis followed her closely.

Annabelle smiled toward the light wisps of clouds in the sky. She was feeling much better. And though her mind was not screaming the name to her anymore, it was still there in her wonder.

George.

In the days winding up to the first festival of summer, Nelson was always full of merriment, with people from all walks of life coming together in a celebration brimming with wonderful food, music, and colour. The villagers scrambled to get everything ready in town, where they were allowed to store supplies in a secure yard used for civil equipment.

This meant that Annabelle and Dennis were joined at the hip, which suited the mule just fine. She would load him up to full capacity and head to town, where she helped the others with decorating the streetlamps and buildings, erecting the stage, and preparing the float as well as all the props Munch needed for his magic show.

Granny's advice that Annabelle keep herself distracted was solid as always. As the week passed, she had little time to think about anything besides the festival.

But in times of stillness, she would sometimes allow the name to seep back into her mind like a fog. Where had it gone? What had it meant? It was once so present and so powerful. It must have been a sign... for something. The mind is funny, and as time passed and her loneliness continued, she realized she was becoming more desperate to find her purpose. She knew what she wanted, but as the universal wisdom goes, what you want isn't always what you get.

At the end of the day, she led Dennis out of the bustle to a favourite bench where she had a view of the sun setting behind the mountains across the lake, which was calm as glass except for a couple kayakers enjoying a lazy evening paddle. Their wakes fanned behind them in the reflection of the sky, like two merging flocks of geese. Lovers, she guessed as she watched.

Dennis nudged at Annabelle's sweater pocket, knowing well that's where she kept his treats. She smiled at him and took out a chunk of carrot, then rubbed his nose. "You behave now." She cradled his cheeks and gave him a kiss.

She had been guilty in the past of manifesting signs in her subconscious to justify feelings or deeds of greed or selfishness. She had learned hard lessons because of it. But if this was another attempt at that, surely her subconscious could do better than the name *George.*

Oh, here comes my saviour, my knight in shining armour, riding in on his white stallion... Oh, save me, noble George!

She couldn't help but snort a laugh, which prompted an immediate nudge to her pocket from Dennis.

She looked at him and chuckled. "Yes, Dennis." She rubbed his nose again, then pulled him to her as she fed him another treat. "Is that how it will be for me, hmm? Maybe you will be the magnificent steed? Here comes George-the-fearless and... Dennis!" She laughed harder, massaging his cheeks deeply and giving him another kiss. "His feet would drag on the ground riding you... At least, I hope they would!"

Her laughter subsided as she turned back to the valley. The kayakers had disappeared behind the cliffs and their wake had faded to little more than a ripple across the other bank. The sun had fallen behind the mountains, leaving behind a brilliant orange sky.

Annabelle's smile disappeared, and as she looked on, a single tear tracked down her cheek.

It didn't take George long to find a lift with a trucker who took him to the intersection where he needed to head north. There, he managed to find another ride with a senior couple, who took him as far as they could.

Since then, though, finding a ride hadn't been as easy, partly because the traffic had thinned but also because he was still nervous about being along the road. A run-in with the law wouldn't bode well for him. And ultimately, he wasn't comfortable with hitchhiking. He didn't like people being able to identify him, and with most of his gear still wet he feared the odour would be unbearable to outsiders.

At the next traffic marker, he hiked down into the trees, found a nice log for a seat, and enjoyed a snack and some water while he did his best to figure out his location on the map. He didn't have far to go, as the crow flew—but beware the path of the crow. According to his map, it was just over that hill across the road. Not even over the top of it, really—he could just skirt along the side, out of sight from everyone, and cut his time on foot by half.

He dreamed of life with warm running water and toiletries. He'd like to get himself straightened and then figure out what to do from there.

The slope across the road looked tame enough. He had his compass and the sun, and he felt he had enough supplies to make it. By his calculations, he should be there before dark. It would be no sweat. So he quickly folded his map back up, crossed the highway, and disappeared into the trees.

At the beginning of the hike, he climbed steadily upward—the slope not steep enough to make him scramble but steep enough to keep his heart pumping and the sweat running beneath his load. Then the terrain got more challenging. Although the slope levelled out at times, he sometimes had to scramble across cliffs. His calculations were failing him, which was incredibly rare.

Then came a heavy "*Huff!*" and some movement in the brush to his right. A beast emerged, and it didn't look happy. George had never seen a real bear before. Maybe in a zoo when he was young, but this was not a zoo bear, this was a big bear, a wild bear. It bared its teeth and snorted hard enough to stir the dirt on the ground. George felt suddenly faint. The bear growled loudly again, scratched at the earth with its massive paw, and reared on its hind legs.

Bear safety wasn't a topic they had covered in the think tank. But George was fluent in several languages, and this display translated to "bear doesn't like George." It would be a smart decision for George to get out of there, as fast as possible.

And George was a smart guy.

He slid down the steepest part of the hill he could find, and ran. Ran faster than he had ever run before, his feet barely having time to touch the ground with each stride. It might have been his imagination, but he felt that bear's breath on the back of his neck and heard it chuffing in his ear, heavy and loathing.

He raced even faster, to the point where it was no longer possible for him to adapt to the terrain. So, by his calculations, the probability of him having a wreck was a matter of when. And it happened just then.

He bounded over a short, bluff rock face and his ankle buckled and twisted below him. He screamed and folded into a high-speed tumble down the rocky face.

Over and over he tumbled. Free falling at points before smashing against rocks or trees, he continued his cartwheel. The world spun so fast he was never able to get his bearing, certain it was only time before he found the edge of an endless cliff or an impaling branch. Each blow took a bit more of his wind and he became weaker.

With one final crash, all the life was knocked from his body and George Stanley's world faded to black.

***

"Hey… Hey, look, over there—oh man!"

George heard a voice calling.

"Hey! Hey, man! Man, hey… You all right?"

He felt a hand shake him gently.

"Hey… Oh! I think he's breathing!"

He managed to slowly open an eye, just a crack. Twinkling sunlight filtered through the leaves, and as he strained for focus, a snaggle of curly hair materialized.

Realizing he was still alive, he sucked in a huge gulp of air. "H-help… help me." He was barely audible with his parched mouth so stuffed with dirt and grass. "B-bear, there's a bear." He tried to sit up, and everything in his body creaked and groaned as if he had been sentenced to torture on a medieval rack, then run over by a truck.

"Whoa! Whoa, dude! You just gotta chill, bud. Take your time." The stranger looked up the almost-vertical slope as he rubbed George's back. "There's no bear, just relax. Man, if you just did what I think, and totally plummeted off that cliff and smashed into this nasty old tree, and survived… that's *so* awesome, dude! You're supernatural. Hey, babe? You seeing all that?"

A young lady peered around the man and brushed a lock of her dark hair over her ear, then waved politely and smiled. "Oh man, you all right, guy? Did you say a bear? A bear made you do that?"

George lay still for a minute, just breathing and looking at these two new people in his life. He was not convinced they were the qualified medical experts he was in need of.

George himself was trained in first aid, and so he began going over the vital preliminary checks, wiggling his fingers and toes. Surprisingly he had no signs of paralysis. His right eye was swollen shut behind his battered glasses, that he knew, and as he started to take back control of his arms and legs, he didn't notice any breaks. He felt around his face and found patches of dried blood, which led to some cuts, but nothing he felt was life-threatening. He sat up on one elbow and pointed to his mouth. "W-water… Do you have some water?"

"Oh man, yeah. Yeah, for sure." He reached for the dented-up old canteen he had hanging around his neck. "Here, man, have some, definitely."

The water was warm and stale, but George took enough to wash the dried goop from his throat. He could feel it absorbing into his cells, like rain being slurped up into crusted desert earth.

He held the last gulp in his mouth as he closed his eyes and let his head fall back, giving thanks to any higher power that may have been listening. He sighed, then looked at the bystanders. "How do I look?"

The man stood wide-eyed, staring down at George. "Man, you look like hell! But if you just done all that, you… you're like a god! That's gotta be, like, thirty feet, straight down, dude!"

The lady stood beside the man, nodding while twirling her hair around her finger. "Yeah… yeah."

George sighed. *Oh, god.* "Yes, well, that's great, I guess—thank you. I'm happy you're impressed, but I mean… how do I look? Does anything seem to be out of place? Any bones sticking out, or, say, big pools of blood anywhere? Ground? Clothes?"

"Man!" The stranger wiped at his eyes. "There is a reason for you, dude!"

"Yes, well… th-thanks, as I'm sure there's reason for us all. But, uh, I think maybe part of your reason now could be to help me up?"

"Oh man! Dude, totally… Absolutely." He grabbed one of George's arms and nodded to his friend to grab the other.

When George felt the pressure of their hands, he begged, "Okay! Okay! Niiiice and careful now, easy does it. Okay…" As they pulled him to his feet, he felt the weight of the pack dragging him down. He was weak and his body tremored, and he braced himself against the man.

He stayed that way for a minute, looking up at the cliff he'd fallen from. "Jesus!" he muttered. "What time is it? How long was I out?"

"Oh, we don't keep time much, dude." The man looked at the sun high overhead. "But it's close to midday."

George looked the two over, noticing their casual clothing and wild hairstyles. He had read about the hippie culture in the area, for which these two were poster children.

Then George remembered his watch, and he checked it to confirm the man's estimate—but a day later than when he had met the bear. George had lain there overnight. He realized just how lucky he was to be alive, and that renewed his appreciation for these two travellers.

He took another deep breath, coming to terms with everything. "Where are we? I was trying to get to Nelson. Is that anywhere close to here?"

"Oh, yeah, man! We're going there too. You heading for the festival, eh?"

"The what?"

"The festival that's going on there, happens every year this time, when they have the bands and the market. Everyone from around these parts knows about it. But you don't really look like you're from around here, dude." The man held out his hand. "I'm Friday, by the way, but people call me Fri. And this here is Daffodil." He pointed to his friend.

She smiled. "Call me Daffy."

"Uh, okay, Fri and Daffy." George shook their hands. "I… I'm John, or Johnny."

"Ha!" Friday gave George a friendly pat on the shoulder. "Sure, Johnny, that'll work as well as any." He winked. "S'all right, man, we're all hiding from something up here."

George guessed that the pause before his introduction had given it away. But obviously Friday and Daffodil weren't their real names either… maybe. They were all hiding from something.

"Well, we'll make sure and get you safe into town. How you feel? Think you can walk?"

George pushed away from Fri slowly, taking ownership of his weight. He was a little wobbly and very stiff. "I, I don't think I can do this slope on my own."

"No sweat, bud. We'll help you down, no prob." He wrapped George's arm around his neck. Babe"—he motioned to Daffy—"get under his other arm there."

She did, and the three of them took their time managing their way down. Every muscle and joint of George's ached, and he sensed some areas would take time to heal, like his badly bruised ribs. But he slowly began to loosen up.

About an hour down, the thick brush cleared and their feet hit the asphalt of a winding road. They came across many people out hiking with day packs and walking poles. George was aware of how he must look. Despite Daffy's attempt to get him somewhat presentable along their journey, there were still many battle scars on display. But for the moment, he was happy to be alive and looking for some quality rest.

They soon came to a roadside parking area that was packed with cars.

"I can't thank you two enough, honestly. You know, all I need is a hotel room and some rest. Could you get me to an area with some hotels?"

They invited George to head downtown with them, and it took only a second for Fri to scrounge up a ride in the back of a beat-up old pickup truck.

Along the way, the trees began to part, opening up to splendid views of the lake valley.

Beautiful, just like in the movie.

The sun was hot and the air was thick, and George lifted his face to welcome it. Broken but not beaten, he had arrived.

The truck pulled into a parking stall in front of a hardware store, and Daffy and Friday helped George out. The streets were packed with festival-goers, and folk music and the sweet smell of street vendor food wafted from between the mountain town's old brick buildings.

George turned to his companions. "Friday, Daffodil, I really… words can't say enough, how grateful I am." He shook both their hands. "I just, I would have been dead… You saved…"

"Aw, man." Friday drew Daffy tight to his side, and both their smiling faces bowed bashfully to the ground. "It's nothing, right? You'd've done the same. Just the way we do things around here, Johnny boy."

"Yeah, well…" George searched through his coat pockets and found a crumpled wad of cash. He flipped through it quickly to figure a couple hundred bucks, then handed it over to them without hesitation. "Here, take this, please. It's the least I can do."

Friday's eyes popped as he looked at the bills. "Aw, man. I mean, you don't gotta—not at all, Johnny."

George pushed the money forward. "Take it, I insist. I wouldn't feel right not offering."

"Oh, wow! Johnny, bud. It's like we caught a frickin' leprechaun in the woods, dude. Lucky Johnny, that's your new name." He grabbed on to George with a gracious hug, nodding at Daffy to join in.

George wheezed and flinched, then pushed them back softly. "Really, you two, you saved me. I wish I could do more. Please, go enjoy the festival, and thank you so much for everything."

Friday directed George to a street with some hotels before saying their final farewells, then George watched them wave back at him as they disappeared into the crowd.

George sighed, then looked around the bustle. The population was a vast mix of cultures and ethnicities. Many fit the traditional tourist stereotype. The ones who stood out were the flamboyant hippies. One could have easily assumed they were all street performers, but from the research George had done on the area, it was the culture of these people—so colourful and free from the stresses of the daily grind, living naturally off the land.

Of course, the stereotype came with mixed reviews. Some might say they stink, and they steal, and they take advantage of government social programs, living off the tax dollars of hard-working Canadians.

But George couldn't help but find interest in them. The ones he had met to date seemed decent; he could even credit his life to them.

He gathered himself carefully, fitting his pack to his shoulders for what he hoped would be a short walk to find a room. His mind and body grew excited for soapy warm water, fresh sheets on a soft bed, a cool pillow against his cheek, and a large pepperoni delivered to his door.

But George's mirage began to fade as, one by one, he discovered the hotels were booked solid. Some of the clerks even took pity on him in his state and called around for him, but nothing could be found. Not even the hostel could squeeze him in.

He walked out of his last chance and found a bench along the sidewalk. He slid his pack off carefully and eased himself down. *So,* he thought as he looked at the celebration around him, *this is freedom.* During all the travelling, he hadn't actually taken the time to think about how free he was, like never before. He had imagined something more magnificent. Like holding hands with a beautiful woman, spinning through a field of flowers.

But in reality, freedom was a painful beating. Freedom was hunger, dirt, chaffing… and loneliness. He leaned back in his seat, raised his face to the sky, and watched the clouds pixelate in front of his eyes, then turn to numbers and equations. He closed his good eye, took a breath, and thought about how nice it was back in the bunker, with everything neat, tidy, and scheduled. He'd had an adventure—a true and honest adventure—that few would ever face in their lifetime. But it was silliness, and there was nothing here for him. He would rest for a moment, then find a phone. It was a magical place, but he just didn't fit in. He clenched his jaw as a single tear rolled down his cheek.

***

As tiny a tear as it was, it caused massive waves of disturbance in the quantum realm. Because in the quantum realm, feelings and emotions that were normally invisible carried massive weight. More weight than an inanimate semi-truck rolling down the highway. Passion of the mind and heart could bring down mountains and shift the planets. Rolling like a tsunami, it washed over everything in its path, displacing gas in the atmosphere, and so on and on and on till the tiny wave grew bigger, covering distance faster, crashing and breaking through the crowds of people.

And one single ripple made it through the obstacles as a soft whisper in her ear…

George.

Annabelle was busy discussing displays with Ms. Baumhauer when she heard it, sudden and intimate as breath on her skin.

She started, clutching her hand to her chest and turning her head to the side. She hadn't heard it in days, and though it was subtle, it was definitely there. She peered through the mass of faces passing by, looking for someone to catch her eye, but found nothing.

Ms. Baumhauer gently touched her hand. "Annabelle, dear, are you okay?"

The tension in Annabelle began to ease, but just as she was turning back to her conversation, the sea of people parted and she caught a glimpse of curly dark hair in the corner of her eye that made her turn back.

Why? She immediately began to question. *Why him? Why this guy?* This wasn't someone she would feel safe approaching. In his battered state, he reminded her of the transients who came through at times. And his puffy GORE-TEX vest, designer khaki shorts, and fancy backpack loaded with only the very best in camping equipment were all products of the billion-dollar corporations the people in the area had united against on several occasions to keep their dirty money out of their valley.

The rich kids, trust-fund babies. Looking for excitement away from their flat-screen televisions and country clubs. They run away to rebel against Mommy and Daddy. Come to the hills with all their designer drugs and end up way over their head. The locals weren't too friendly with ignorant outsiders, and this one looked like he had pissed off a few of them enough to take a nasty round out of him. So… *Why him?* She had no sympathy for his type.

But although he looked the part in many ways, she sensed there was something different about him. He honestly looked as though he'd had a run-in with a bear rather than the local barflies. And there was no arrogance or entitlement in the way he held himself. He didn't even seem aware that the arm to his glasses was broken and hanging from his ear. He seemed… lost. That, she could feel.

She looked at Ms. Baumhauer, forgetting where their conversation had ended. "I, uh, I gotta go, Ms. Baumhauer. I have to help Gwyn with her booth. I'll come back as soon as I can, okay?" She patted the woman's hand, then gathered Dennis's reins and stepped into the river of people.

She made her way slowly closer, watching him but ready to look away before he noticed. He didn't move, just sat with his face toward the sky. She stopped when she stood across the street, trying to blend in as much as she could, with her portly ass in tow.

She could see that he wasn't a kid, but he was too old to be a runaway delinquent. He might even be somewhat cute, after a shower and some TLC… maybe. He looked kind of nerdy-cute. She grinned to herself, trying to make something out of this peculiar circumstance, this potential George.

With still no sign of movement, she became more daring and stepped closer, until she could see the cuts on his hands and that one of his eyes was swollen shut, quite badly. Every detail made her more curious, drawing her closer still.

She was almost standing right in front of him when he jerked to life, sitting straight with a wince and a soft moan. She jumped and disappeared quickly around the corner, pulling hard on Dennis to follow as she slammed herself up against a wall, remaining still and silent.

***

George held his side, the sudden jerk reminding him of his condition. He'd had an overwhelming feeling that he was being watched, very closely. His glasses fell from his face and as he picked them up, he noticed the break in the arm, and he cursed… But had someone been there? He looked around. The image had been blurred, of course, but he'd heard a voice… he'd heard *her* voice.

Though he hadn't gotten a clear view of her, she'd seemed awfully close and a little too interested. He needed to be more cautious about resting on crowded streets full of vagrants. Though his pocket was empty of cash, his pack most definitely wasn't. And he hadn't taken out any travel insurance. He pulled his pack closer.

As he shook off the sadness, he decided it was time to make that call and apologize to the department. He was sure they would be glad to have him back safely. They may even send a chopper. He could be back within hours, with a shower, bed, food, and professional medical attention.

He looked up and down the streets, and he managed to see the romance in his turmoil. Someday he would return. Someday soon, on a scheduled vacation, maybe drive up in a vehicle and book a five-star suite in advance. He managed a grin. As he placed his hands on the bench and began to gently push himself up, there was a strange squeak and a snort from around the corner, and then he felt a nudge in his side.

He winced. "Ow, Jesus!" He jumped at the sight of his assailant: a large mule. His glasses fell from his face again and he fumbled to find them, then held them in place and looked again, down at the donkey's curled lip and bared teeth.

"Ah!" he shouted.

"It, it's okay, I'm really so sorry."

George kept his finger pressed to the frame of his glasses right between his eyes. He saw the reins and then followed them up to a slender hand, to a long arm, to her blushing cheeks beneath large eyes filled with a kaleidoscope of hazel and emerald… and pain, and passion, and trials and wisdom of life well beyond her years. He was instantly entranced.

"I, I…" he stammered.

The lady had an urgent frustration about her as she tugged at her stubborn friend, who seemed not at all interested in giving up on George's pocket.

"I, I'm really very sorry. He means no harm, honest. That's just the way he says 'please.'" She pulled on the donkey again. "He's just like a big dog, really—a very big and very stubborn dog right, Dennis?" She clenched her teeth and yanked, the mule not budging a nano. "I'm guessing you must have something in your pocket that he wants, like a treat maybe?"

Stunned, George continued to look blankly at her till the conversation caught up to him. "Oh, uh, that's possible, I guess." He relaxed a bit, looking down at Dennis, who was still curling his lip and squeaking in that odd donkey fashion. George searched through his pocket and found the source of Dennis's infatuation. "Uh, well, I have this old smashed-up granola bar, is that of any interest to you… Dennis?" He smiled.

"Is it apple by chance?" she asked.

"Ummm…" George examined the wrapper. "Yes, it so happens that this is an apple-flavoured one." He looked down at the donkey. "Is this it, Dennis? Is this what's driving you so crazy?" He smiled again.

Dennis brayed.

"Okay, buddy, I think I can spare this one." He held out the bar toward Dennis, forgetting about his swollen eye till he found that his depth perception was lacking. He made a couple of attempts to get the bar to Dennis before the mule lost patience and snatched it from his hand.

The reminder of his state and how he must look to others pushed him back into a shell. He turned his attention from Dennis-the-Donkey and his lovely sidekick and began to secure the straps on his pack.

But she persisted. "I… I mean, are you from around here?" she asked. "It's just, I live in the area and spend a lot of time in town here. I can't say that I recognize you."

George continued his preparations, avoiding looking at her. "No, I'm not from around here. I'm just a tourist. Thought I'd check this place out. I've read so many nice things about it. It is really beautiful here. I unfortunately don't have time to look around much, but maybe I'll come back someday."

"Oh, so you travelled here but have to go already? When did you get here?"

"Just today, actually, but… I got a call from work and there's an emergency. I have to return." George felt the story snowballing and was hoping she would walk away before he tumbled into some tale of alien-abduction. He'd seen enough to understand she was beautiful, and for a guy like him, conversation with a beautiful woman never came easily. Any confidence he did have had been rolled down a hill and tossed off a cliff.

"Oh, work? What is it that you do, if you don't mind my asking?"

George sighed, continuing to keep his head low, trying to show disinterest without being too rude. But she was proving slow to take the hint.

"I'm a programmer—computer programmer."

"Oh, well, that's a good job I suppose. But couldn't you just do your work here? There's internet."

George's posture slumped with another sigh.

He pushed himself from the bench and shouldered his pack, doing his best not to let on to his many aches and pains. "Yes," he said and nodded, "I normally could, but I didn't bring my computer."

"Ah, well, that seems a bit strange for, well, pretty much anyone these days, let alone a programmer. Is it something you could take care of in the café? They have computers there."

George shook his head slowly and wiped at this face.

"My name is Annabelle, by the way." She held her hand out to him.

George snorted a laugh at how ridiculous this encounter had become. But he acknowledged that he wasn't getting away without being rude. He accepted her hand and turned to face her. And his feelings changed.

Standing in front of her, he was able to see her true beauty. Maybe she was no centrefold model, but he found something very naturally warm and inviting about her. The attraction was instant, and the micro particles between their hands warmed and tingled with excitement and wrapped around them, squeezing them together just a little harder.

The sun became trapped in her hair and sparkled in her eyes. The energy between them was all-consuming.

She tilted her head at him, her smile brightening a little more. "Uh, I'm Annabelle."

George stumbled over his tongue. "I G-G… John."

He shook off the fairy dust and collected himself. "*Ahem*, sorry, I'm John." He released her hand and nervously scratched the back of his head. "Uh, yeah, the café. I mean, it's pretty frowned upon for me to do work on an unsecure network. I don't have my computer because, well, ha! The idea of the trip was for me to totally disconnect, and soooo, no electronics, computers, phones. And I was taking this back-to-nature kind of tour and tried to take a shortcut through the woods and ran across a bear that scared the hell out of me. I had a really bad fall, but these two people found me and helped me get into town. So, here I am, and this is why"—he held his hands out to the side and gave himself the once-over—"I look like this."

"Well, John," she said and smiled again, "that's a very crazy story. I'm sorry to hear that your travels were so troublesome. But maybe I can be the first to welcome you to our little town? Welcome to Nelson." She grinned. "I hate to hear that you're thinking about leaving us so soon."

"Well"—George looked up and down the street—"all the hotels are full. That's another thing I didn't do before I left. I also didn't know there was a festival this weekend."

"If I had to guess, I'd say you don't travel very much, John. You know, it looks like you've had a pretty rough introduction. Why don't you come with me? See if we can get your sense of adventure back?"

George scratched at his head, suspicious of her motives. It was hard for him to buy into her being genuinely interested in getting to know him better. He was just a broken-down tourist, sitting on a bench. There were plenty of more handsome men walking around the streets.

But he did fit the profile of an easy target, especially to a beautiful young lady. The donkey, though, didn't really fit in with someone wanting to do the grab-and-dash. His radar was up, but she seemed genuine. And the romantic in him felt there was a reason. There was a reason for him to travel all that way to be there right then. And she was definitely a good argument to be that reason. The air between them warmed with her smile, and as he took a breath, the molecules entered his body and calmed his nerves, and he nodded to her.

"Okay."

She walked over and reached for his pack, but he resisted.

She looked at him. "It's okay, John." She touched his arm softly. "You can stay right beside your pack. I just thought, why should you carry it when we have Dennis here? After all, he's gotta work off that treat. Can't have him getting fat and lazy now, hey Dennis?" She set the pack on Dennis's back and secured it with a couple straps. "There, that's a load off your shoulders."

He smiled, pulling up beside Dennis as Annabelle took the reins out front.

There was something between them. She could feel it, a magnetism of sorts. He had potential for cuteness, would maybe even be handsome once the swelling went down. He was a slight bit taller than her, which was a hard find for a lady of her length. And there was a soft, boyish innocence in his eye, when she happened to catch it. But this was John and not a George, and she had heard that name very clearly in her mind. She worried that while tending to John, she may miss George. As they walked in idle chit-chat, she kept her sensors on high alert.

Granny's old-school covered wagon was in its usual spot beside Ms. Baumhauer's store. She'd had Griz do the needed modifications to turn it into a roadside sales display for her various apothecary products, like soaps, cleansers, scented oils, and homeopathic cures. She always drew a steady crowd of new and returning customers.

Granny gasped as she saw the trio heading toward her. "Oh my, what have you brought to me now, Annabelle? Another stray?" She smiled sweetly. "And who might this young fellow of misfortune be? Who had the light of Annabelle shine on him in his time of need?"

They pulled to a stop in front of her, and Annabelle waved her hand between them. "Granny, this is John. John, this is our Granny."

John reached out his hand to greet Granny, looking a little ashamed of his state.

"John, m'dear, what has happened to leave you in such a mess?"

"Well, uh, ma'am, I had an unfortunate incident, I guess, up in the hills."

"Hmm." Her eyes questioned. "I detect a slight accent, John. Not from around here, eh?"

"I, uh…" John took a step back and began to fidget.

"It's okay, son." She snuck a quick look to Annabelle. "I don't expect any more of an explanation than you're willing to offer—for now." She winked. "Cappy!" she called toward the wooden cart.

"Huh?" came the response from inside the wagon. It began to creak and groan, and then Cappy made his way down the rickety steps. "What is it now, Gra— Oh?" He looked at John with surprise. "Well, I say, what have we got here?"

"Cappy, this here is John, a new friend of Annabelle's. Seems he's had a bit of a fall and I want to go fix him up enough so he can maybe enjoy some of the day. You need to watch the sales for a moment."

"Oh, well…" Cappy made his way to the sidewalk and gave John the once-over. "Well, I think he'll clean up good. Hey, young fella?" Cappy shook John's hand with a warm smile.

"Yes, well, I haven't time to waste, so watch the cart. Come with me, young man." Granny took his hand and led him into Ms. Baumhauer's shop. Annabelle handed Dennis's reins to Cappy and followed.

***

With permission from Ms. Baumhauer, the two ladies took George to the bathroom in the back of the shop and sat him down on the toilet. They got him to remove as much clothing as possible without making him uncomfortable.

He followed Granny's instructions as she checked for any signs of breaks or concussion. Then she opened the small bag she had brought and set out a variety of vials along the sink. She rubbed some nasty-scented stuff right under his nose and then held a cool cloth on his swollen eye for a spell before rubbing it down with some salve. She was applying the salve to his other wounds when Annabelle brought him some tea.

Interestingly enough, he was starting to feel better—nowhere near new, but any bit of attention helped. And he couldn't help remembering how he had felt an hour before, when he was about to make that phone call; couldn't help comparing that to how he felt now, looking at Annabelle as she stood in the doorway. He was mesmerized by her, and he was aware that he was looking at her more than anyone should. But there was something powerful about her, beyond her physical beauty—something much deeper. At times she would meet his eyes, if only for the briefest of a second, and he knew that she could feel something too. But was it the same magical feeling he had? Or was she getting ready to blow on her "creepy guy staring" whistle?"

"Now, John, do you have a fresh change of clothes in your pack?" Granny asked as she finished up.

"Uh, yes, ma'am, I do."

Granny snapped her fingers toward the door. "Annabelle, go fetch John's pack and give us a moment in private so I can check the rest of him, m'dear."

"Yes, Granny." Annabelle left, closing the door behind her.

Granny grabbed George's hand and turned it over in hers. She applied pressure to the middle of his palm with her thumb, placed her other hand firmly on his shoulder, and peered into his eyes, pushing deep into his discomfort zone.

"John…" She looked deeper. "Where you from, John? Why are you here, John? That pretty young lady that brought you here is like my own daughter, and I need a little more information on you, son, before I let you go walking around with her. You understand?"

George's forehead ran with sweat. "Y-yes, ma'am." He gulped. "I, uh, I'm a computer programmer and I went on one of those… those adventure—"

"Don't play me for a fool, son! I'm not interested in your lies and secrets. I'm interested in your heart. Show me your heart, John."

He began to panic even more, till he broke and slumped in his seat, his good eye flooding with tears. "I… Granny, I have no intention of harming Annabelle in any way. I didn't even approach her in the first place. She… well, I guess it was Dennis…" His face contorted as he tried to recall exactly how they'd met. Then he looked her in the eye. "I'm from a ways away. South of here. I'm not a criminal or anything. You could say that I'm running from something, but, really, I just needed to see something else."

"Uh-huh. You married?"

"What? Married? No… No, I would never. Let me just say that I've lived a very sheltered life. I just needed an… an adventure, I guess. I really have no intention of hurting Annabelle in any way. I just can't believe… You know, an hour ago I was about to find a phone and make a call to… to take me home. And then…" He shook his head and grinned. "Now I'm here. I can't thank you and Annabelle enough for everything you've done to help me. I was maybe the loneliest person on earth an hour ago."

"Hmm." Granny loosened her grip, but she wasn't done yet. "Why here? Out of all the places, why here?"

"Well, there's this movie my mom— Huh!" He slumped some more. "I don't know why."

Granny let his hand go, then gently patted his cheek and winked at him. "Yes, you don't know. That part of your story I believe, John." She smiled, seemingly satisfied with his lack of answer. "All right, let's see the rest of you!"

George's eyes bulged.

"C'mon, I don't have all day. Cappy ain't selling nothing out there. If anything, he's scaring all the customers away 'cause he doesn't want to deal with nothing. Down to your shorts, now, c'mon."

***

Annabelle waited outside the door with the pack, as instructed. She could hear muffled voices inside and knew Granny was doing her thing. As much as Annabelle and Gwyn and everyone else from the village and in the hills wanted to say they had that special ability, no one had it like Granny. If there was something off with John, Granny would sniff it out.

The door opened a crack and Granny's arm poked out. Annabelle passed her the pack and waited again after the door closed. A second later, the door opened just enough for Granny to fit through, then she closed it tightly again behind her.

Granny looked sweetly up at Annabelle, cupped her hands around her cheeks, and drew her down for a motherly kiss. "John, eh?"

Annabelle's frowned. "Yeah, John."

"There's a very strong energy about the two of you when you're together. I could feel it before I even seen you coming, you know it?"

"Yes, I know, I can feel it. But I've been resisting it." She looked up at the ceiling and sighed, then faced Granny again. "It's just... the voice!" She shook her hands madly at either side of her head. "It's *George*! It's always *George*! It's very much a George, not a John. I like John, he seems nice, but I'm afraid that I'm missing the one, you know? *J*... *G*... I guess they sound the same. It's a start, at least. But what if...?"

"Well, he's a good man—I know it, and he has my blessing. I also know there's more to him than either of us know—a lot more, Annabelle. Sometimes in life, all we get handed to us is the 'J-G.' Something brought you two together. Don't block it, sweetie. He's a fine young man and it's a beautiful day for celebration. Go have fun. You'll figure it out." Granny kissed her cheek again, then left.

Annabelle considered Granny's words of wisdom. Maybe she was right. After all, she wasn't supposed to try to force anything, just follow the signs as best she could. But was she right to follow the signs toward John? She shook her head free of the uncertainty, just in time for the door to creak slowly open.

John's head popped out first, his wide eye looking around, no doubt on the lookout for Granny-the-Interrogator. But his guard appeared to drop when he saw Annabelle standing there on her own.

He cleared his throat. "Did I... I guess I passed the Granny-test?"

He looked cleaner in his fresh light-blue shorts and white button-down shirt—actually quite stylish. He'd also made his hair more presentable, and with everything put together, the scrapes and swelling didn't seem so bad. The white first-aid tape he'd used to fix his glasses wasn't sexy, but he'd done pretty well with what he had.

One thing he couldn't hide was his nerdy roots, which ran very deep. No amount of rugged outdoor wear or expensive cologne could hide that. He didn't need a computer to prove it. He was a math geek, beyond doubt. But to Annabelle, intelligence was attractive.

"Yes," she said and giggled. "You're safe, she left. And you should be very proud to know that she gave you her blessing. I can't remember her ever doing that with a man who was chasing me... I mean, not that you were... I..."

He blushed. "No, I know. I get what you're saying." He stepped out into the hall and let the door fall behind him. "So"—he held his hands out to the side—"will this work?"

"Haha, yes, Geor-ohn," Annabelle, said, catching her slip just in time. "John—*ahem*—yes, you look very handsome."

"Great…" The conversation stalled for a moment. "Listen, Annabelle. I honestly… I can't thank you enough for everything you and, and Granny… Wow! I mean, you really have no idea. But, I mean, I can understand that maybe you're busy with other things and…"

She watched him fidget as she waited. He was very flattering, in his own way.

"No, I'm not busy, John. I was going to ask if you'd let me show you around our little town. There's lots going on at the festival. And we could get to know each other better."

***

Though no one could see it, at that moment, their heartbeats increased at the same time, pumping waves back and forth till they found the exact same beat and rhythm. The air between them grew a fraction of a degree warmer, photons and neurons clashing and rubbing, polarizing and magnetizing, until a warm and energized field grew around them, pulling them together.

***

George stood breathless while he listened to her, watching her. The way her lips moved when she spoke. The natural glow radiating from her. She made him feel as though one look at her would turn his worst day ever into his best day ever. Which was pretty much what had just happened. And this woman of such incredible fantawesomeness was inviting him, George, to spend the day with her in this picturesque mountain town.

"*Bwuh*, I… I, uh, yeah. I… that sounds really great. Umm…" He looked down at his pack.

"Oh, don't worry about your pack. Granny and Cappy can keep it in their wagon. No one will touch it, I promise."

The thought of leaving it was a little unnerving. He had already taken some money out to keep on him, but there was still a lot left in there, not to mention all his identification. But he really felt he could trust them, and he really didn't want to lug it around, so he agreed.

They stepped out into the warm late-afternoon sun, which was slowly starting to sink. But at the peak of summer, there were still many light hours to be had. Annabelle handed the pack to Cappy, who was sitting on the stairs leading into the wagon, drinking his own home brew. He secured the pack away for George, ensuring him it was safe, then got a kiss on the cheek from the young lady for his efforts.

George and Annabelle walked around to the front of the wagon and stopped in to see Granny, who reached for one of each of their hands and…

CRACK!

They all pulled back from the zapping shock sent between them all.

"Ouch!" Annabelle rubbed at her hand. "That was a big one. Weird, out here in the street like this."

Granny didn't bat an eye, just responded with a wise grin. "Yes, m'dear, it was very strong, wasn't it?" She chose then to give her farewell affections to each of them—separately this time. "I think Dennis would like to join you," she added.

"Yes, of course, Granny. What's a celebration without Dennis, haha." Annabelle grabbed the donkey's reins and the three set off down the hill.

***

The town was vibrant. Everywhere they turned there was a band or performance. Wild people were dancing in the streets of a little town nestled deep in the mountains that time seemed to float past, like a wisp of cloud.

George's nerves were tight and he could feel the perspiration beginning to run. This day had presented a lot of firsts for him, without any time for him to prepare or ease in at his own pace. And he was not used to being around women to begin with. There were a few in the think tank, but there had never been anything in the form of sexual tension between him and any of them, at any time. For George, Annabelle was a fantasy straight out of a movie. To complicate it further, he couldn't let the conversation flow toward anything about his past, or present, or anything George-related. Even his name was false. How could he, in good conscience, carry on with misleading this lady? So, he planned to keep the conversation focused on her.

"So-o-o…" His voice quivered. "Are you from here, Annabelle? Is Granny really your granny?" He dropped his head and shook it, feeling completely stupid. "I'm sorry, of course she's your granny, why—"

Annabelle snickered. "No, it's fine. She actually isn't my granny. That's just what we all call her."

"Oh… 'We all' as innnn the whole town?"

"Well, yes, I guess everyone I know calls her that. But I was talking about everyone in… in the village."

George caught hesitance in Annabelle and noticed her shyly turn her head from him.

"The village?"

She reached her free hand up to her hair and began to fidget. "Yes, I, or *we*— There's a group—or a whole family—of us who live outside town. In a village not far from here."

"Oh, okay. Sooo, just down the road somewhere?"

"No, it's up. Up in the hills there." She waved her arm quickly over a general area.

"Oh, in the hills? Like a…" George was uncertain if the term *hippie* was offensive. "So, um… you live in this village in the hills? With Granny and other people. Like your family?"

Annabelle sighed. "Yeah, in the hills, in a village called Beelieve." She blushed when she said the name.

"Oh." George sensed her insecurity. "So, you're a… people… that's really…"

"Hippies, you can say it. We're considered hippies, yes. They're not my real family. But, well, they are my real family, I guess. The closest thing I've had."

George stopped walking and looked at her, waiting for her to stop her fidgeting and meet his eyes before he spoke. "I think it sounds really interesting, Annabelle." He smiled. "In fact, I think it sounds incredible. Up in a little village in the hills, free from so much… stuff." He exhaled and looked around the town and across the valley. He took a second, then turned back to her. "I know a lot of people who would love to live that way. Sometimes I've thought about it myself, what it would be like to be… gone." He rocked on his feet and smiled at her. "I'd love to hear more about it."

Her long lashes fluttered, and her smile weakened his knees. This time the smile was pure, with no sense of obligation—Annabelle without the filter. The space between them grew hotter and more magnetic as they looked deep into each other's eyes.

As she relaxed, Annabelle continued telling him everything about herself and her past. And every time she paused, he asked another question, soaking in everything she offered.

With the release of all her inhibitions, her energy became stronger and contagious to everyone around. All who knew her shouted hellos, waved enthusiastically, or brought treats of food and drink to them.

They packed away several pastries, shared a sandwich, and washed it all down with a couple pints of beer. The shadows began to stretch long into the evening as they sat at a patio table.

Annabelle shot to attention.

"Oh my! Oh my, I've been talking about myself for so long now that I forgot all about the show!" She reached for Dennis's reins and stood. "It's friends from the village. They have this magic show they put on every year. It's not far, but I really have to be there or they'll be very disappointed. Do you mind?"

George was already standing. "No, of course not. I'm right behind you."

A couple hard, convincing pulls on the reins failed to get a protesting Dennis to leave the leftovers on the table. Finally, George lured him with a handful of pastry crumbs, and the trio hurried down the street.

They walked into a main intersection that had been barricaded for the shows. In one corner was a small stage for a band, which had modest sound and light systems. They had a good vibe, with a playlist covering forgotten tracks that seemed aimed to remind the crowd of simpler times in their youth. In the middle of the intersection, a cocktail of people from all walks of life danced, some embracing and others of freer spirit moving like no one was watching… or like they didn't care. Across the way, in a forgotten corner beneath the ever-growing darkness, was another small stage where a few figures worked in the shadows. Annabelle pointed there and smiled, then led the way over.

When they arrived, the crew took notice of Annabelle and her company and stopped their preparations.

"Well hello, Annabelle," said a blue-eyed blonde with a smile. "And what admirer do you have following you around this evening, hmm?"

Annabelle gave a bashful grin. "Uh, yes, everyone, this is John. He's a guy I met who needed some, uh, minor medical attention." She looked over at George and giggled. "I took him up to see Granny and she fixed him up as best she could. I think he's going to live, so I decided to show him around."

She introduced him to the two couples: Stella and Griz and Gwyn and Munch. They all welcomed him with pleasant greetings.

Annabelle looked over the stage. "So, what's happening? How's everything going?"

"Not well, I'm afraid." Munch looked disheartened. "We're having some

64

issues with the trap door for the disappearing act. It's the grand finale." He waved his hand over the stage mystically. "I simply can't have it fail. I'll be the laugh of the town."

"Oh, my darling, you are brilliant," Gwyn cut in from the stage, where she was assisting the others at attempting to have the makeshift door fall open. "The most brilliant magician ever. I just know the show will be a success. You have to remain positive about these things, and maybe get over here and help along with the rest of us."

As they watched, Stella stepped on a floor trigger and the section of panelling under Gwyn's feet dropped. Gwyn's eyes bulged quite comically as she fell through the opening, catching herself by her armpits at the last moment.

"Got it!" Griz called out from somewhere below. "I think that did it. We're all ready to go."

Annabelle and George shared a snicker.

Munch smiled and raised his arms. "Oh, it's absolutely wonderful! Everyone, it is finally time!" He threw his cape over his shoulder, clapped his hands, and started toward the stage.

As darkness descended on the small town, the signal was given to the band to cease. Then a thundering boom came from the magic stage as colourful lights flickered to life, racing from one end to the other, and some clever pyrotechnics released quick bursts of sparkles on either corner.

"Lllllladies and gentlemen!" called an anonymous voice over the speaker.

The crowd jumped and simultaneously shifted their attention one hundred and eighty degrees to face the magic stage.

"*Please prepare to be amazed by the mystical wonder of the greatest magic show on earth!*"

Gwyn came out twirling in her dark dress, then stopped in the middle of the stage and held the end of a flaming stick to her mouth and blew, fuelling a massive flame that illuminated the entire square. The audience erupted into applause as Gwyn took a bow, and then she waved her hand toward the side of the stage.

"Put your hands together and welcome the grand master of illusion! The Great and Marvellous Marvin Munchousin!"

The crowd clapped as Munch glided elegantly onto the stage, but he stopped mid-introduction to peek behind a curtain at the back of the stage.

"*The wha?... Oh!*" echoed a muffled voice over the speaker. "*The Great and*

Marvellous Marvin Munchousin… the Sixth!" the voice corrected as Munch put his smile back on and continued with his grand entrance, spinning and jumping while he waved his wand at select points, where more fireworks erupted.

He met Gwyn at centre stage, the spotlight settling on them as they stood side by side with one arm wrapped around each other and their other arm out to the side, raised to the sky, and then they took a bow.

Annabelle, George, and Dennis had joined the others at a special spot right beside the stage. Granny and Cappy had even managed to make it down in time.

Seeing Munch's act was something very special. From conjuring rabbits and birds to cutting boxes and swallowing swords, he had everyone's full attention from start to finish. Then the big moment came for the disappearing trick with the new trap door.

"For this next trick," Munch announced over a microphone, "I will need assistance from a member of the audience!"

"Oh! Oh!" Annabelle waved her hand frantically, then volunteered George when Munch gave her his attention.

"Oh, what is this? This man right here?" Munch motioned to them and the spotlight moved to his target.

Annabelle prodded George, laughing and cheering. George resisted as politely as possible, but the lady won and on he went. His lack of depth perception combined with the intense contrast between light and shadow had him almost on his hands and knees as he navigated the stairs, till Munch reached out a hand and guided him the rest of the way.

"Ladies and gentlemen, put your hands together for this incredibly brave man." Munch placed George beside Gwyn, front and centre stage beneath the spotlight, then made a show of contemplating George's battered state. "It looks like perhaps you have been hanging out with the wrong magician, my friend, hmm?"

The crowd erupted with laughter as George blushed.

The lights flickered and waved as Munch announced the stunt and Gwyn twirled behind the curtain, then emerged again sliding a simple rectangular framed box large enough to accommodate a standing person. She set it on the spot over the secret trap door, then took her time walking in and out of each side of the box and stretching her arms through the open top to reveal there was nothing more to it than what it appeared to be. Then she motioned for George to step inside.

George moved carefully, keeping each hand on secure points in case he tripped. Then a drum began to roll, and some spits of fire appeared as the magic duo draped a silken sheet over the entire box and Gwyn gave it a final spin, then graciously backed into the spot where she could step on the stealthy trigger.

Munch waved his wand. "Moooofumba baroooomba, cosmosis explosis!"

Fire cannons shot sparks to distract the audience while Gwyn placed her foot on the trigger and shifted her weight. But the trigger wouldn't budge.

With Gwyn unable to signal the fault in any way, Munch was oblivious to the malfunction and ripped the sheet from the box, revealing George still standing there, frozen, with one eye swollen shut and the other wide open.

"Well, I…" It was Munch's turn to blush as he walked around the area, doing his best to conceal his examination of the floor.

Small snickers began to grow in the silent crowd, which fuelled panic on stage. Munch gently pushed at George to get out, which suited George just fine. In his panic, he forgot about his visual impairment, and as he turned, he tripped over the frame, which sent him stumbling toward Gwyn, who moved out of the way just in time. With nothing else to support him, George seized the curtain, which ripped from its hanging and sent him tripping across the stage. He stomped on the trigger just as Munch stepped onto the trick floor.

George continued falling into the young kid behind stage, who was in charge of the fire show. The collision knocked a couple buttons, which sent off sparks that lit the tail of Munch's cape on fire right before he fell through the trap door. He yelled as he crashed down, startling Dennis, who then kicked out the stage's corner support leg. The whole platform gave a creak and a groan, then fell flat, revealing Munch standing with a sullen expression as flames began to climb up his cape, until Gwyn arrived a second later and threw a full pail of water in his face.

The crowd paused for a moment, then erupted in cheers and laughter.

"Oh, why?" Munch asked as he walked ahead of the group with Gwyn by his side. "Everything was going so well. It was going to be my greatest performance ever, and now… now…" His head sagged and he sobbed. "I am a failure."

Gwyn rubbed his back. "No, my darling, please. The show was magnificent. You are not a failure."

"I think the show was your best performance ever, Munch," Annabelle said as she and George led Dennis, who was heavily burdened with saddlebags and a wagon in tow. All the villagers were there to help with the cleanup. They still wore smiles from the day, but the sun had set and they were growing tired and knew that the cleanup and journey back to Beelieve would take them into the early-morning hours. "I know it didn't go off the way you planned, but in the end, the audience was standing and cheering for you. There wasn't a face without a smile. And really, isn't that what it's all about? I think it was your best show yet."

Some mumbled agreement came from the others.

The climb to the yard was steep. Steps were laboured, breathing heavy, and conversation minimal. After dropping off the supplies from the stage show, Annabelle connected Dennis to Granny's wagon and hauled it over to the yard, thankful that this distance was shorter and more cross-hill than uphill.

With the equipment all back in place at the compound, George grabbed his pack from the wagon and Annabelle locked up the gate behind them. The others waved to George and began their lumbering stroll down the walk, leaving him with Annabelle and Dennis for their goodbyes.

Though they hadn't had much time for private conversation since arriving at the show, George and Annabelle had stayed right beside each other and a very strong and undeniable bond had continued to grow. But even with that, it was still their first meeting, and neither knew how much further to take it. They stood in silence, smiling and flirting through eye contact, but neither committing.

Noticing that Annabelle's friends were getting farther along, George hoisted his pack snuggly over his shoulder, smiled, and reached out his hand. "Well, it's been just a fabulous evening, Annabelle. I can't believe my good fortune having run into you. Thank you very much for helping me and showing me around. Your friends—or family, rather—are really incredible. So, thank you." He motioned for her to shake his hand again.

Annabelle began reaching for a shake, then bit down on her lip and looked over her shoulder as a cry came from Stella.

"Come, Annabelle our sweetness, we don't want to lose you."

She turned back to George and took his hand. "Where are you staying tonight?"

"Oh, well, I, I really don't have anything planned. All the hotels I checked were booked up. But, I guess, worst-case scenario, I have my trusted tent." He grinned and patted the side of his pack.

"Well…" It was obvious from her body language that she was having an internal debate. "We usually don't like to invite strangers from town back to the village, but… why don't you join us? There's a nice spot for a tent, if you need."

"Um, well, I… I guess it's… yeah, yes." He nodded.

Her hand clenched his as she turned and pulled him along behind her. His heart pounded warmth and excitement through his body, and they rushed to catch up to the others, pulling Dennis behind them.

They headed to the north end of town until the road intersected with a set of train tracks, then continued down the tracks for a short time before cutting a hard right, straight through what was barely a break in the thick brush.

George scrambled through, crouching and ducking, yanking to pull his pack free from clutching branches, till they popped into a clearing. He wiped the debris from himself, then raised his eyes to the beauty. The bright moonlight sparkled off the burbling surface of a healthy-sized stream and caused the bark of the surrounding birch and aspens to glow silver.

He stood motionless, with his jaw hanging, till Annabelle circled back to him.

"What's up, silly?" She giggled.

George snapped to. "It's… it's breathtaking." He turned to her to see how the light enhanced her beauty. It reflected off her natural complexion, lending a shimmering sheen to her hair as her eyes illuminated like those of a woodland fairy in the night.

He then wondered if it enhanced the glow from the swelling around his eye.

She grabbed his hand again and pulled him along.

"So, are there any, um, bears in these parts?" He continually scanned the area.

Annabelle giggled. "Yes, of course there's bears. But we know all of them, they're harmless."

"Right, harmless. So, how far away is this village, Bee-lieve?"

"Right, Beelieve, with two *e*'s, like a buzzing bee. It probably sounds stupid to someone educated like you. It's not far, but if you don't know where to go, you'd never find it. It's kind of like a legend to the people in town. But the people in the hills know where it is. It's a trading post for them."

As they walked along the shore, they came across an uprooted old tree and filed over it one by one. Gwyn grabbed Dennis's reins from Annabelle and led him over in front of them, then Annabelle pulled on George, who resisted.

She looked back. "What?"

"N-nothing. Just, well… I'm not very good at crossing these things."

She giggled again and tugged on him. "C'mon, silly. If you can walk down a street, you can make it across this."

Halfway across, the air around them began to light one by one with fireflies, which George had never seen before. Jumping off the other side of the log, he smiled at Annabelle as they held hands and watched the little lights swirling around them, creating the illusion that they were two stars swirling in a galaxy.

From there, the trip was a blur. Through some more brush, then a tight crevice, and up a staircase that was carved into the rock. A steep climb later they came upon a cliff, with a tall waterfall that appeared to have twinkling moon-dust plunging over it. Right beside it was another path up to the top, and they made their way up it. Reaching the end, George bent over to catch his breath, then looked up at a small lake as still as glass, which was reflecting all the stars in the heavens. To the left stood the village of Beelieve, showered in moonlight.

70

"This is it? This is Beelieve?"

"This is it, our home." Annabelle raised her arms, spun around, and walked toward the village.

They all unloaded their cargo and got Dennis some well-earned food and drink, then gathered themselves together in Gwyn and Munch's yurt. Some light food was passed around, along with some wine and a joint. George had never been much for such indulgence, but as everyone was sharing different stories of mystical happenings and travels, he felt he should take in everything the moment offered.

When the substances hit him, George was content to sit in his silence and watch his new friends laugh and toast in the flickering orange glow of the wood stove. Annabelle sat by his side and a little forward, laughing with the rest. He had lost track of time, engrossed in his own mind as numeric riddles rode streams of drifting smoke.

Annabelle turned back to him and smiled, then grabbed his hand and a blanket and pulled him quietly out into the night.

As soon as they hit the sweet night air, George's lungs sucked in deeply, clearing his mind. "Ahhhhh!" he exhaled and smiled.

Annabelle pulled him across the yard to a grassy knoll. She sat down and tugged on him to follow, then cozied up to him and wrapped the blanket around them. They sat in their state of heightened awareness and watched the full moon shine over the lakes and mountain peaks.

A distant howl carried through the darkness.

"Unbelievable..." George whispered.

She smiled. "What is?"

George was feeling things at that time and place that he had never imagined anyone could ever feel. And he found himself pouring it out in mindless babble. "All of it... Just, I mean, when I started out, when I decided to take this trip, I never imagined... this. I thought it would be great, and I would see a lot of things— I mean, I guess I never really knew what to expect. Get my picture taken at some of the tourist sites. Visit some of the local hot spots. Maybe a go for a swim in the lake. It all seemed so exciting. But this... this is... it's insane. Annabelle... Your name is Annabelle. You're so beautiful—and you live here, in this place up in the forest, in the mountains." He pulled his hands out from beneath the blanket and raised them to the moon, then let them flop back. "This is insane… What the heck happens on night two of this tour?"

He laughed, then she laughed, then it became infectious and they laughed together for a moment before she collapsed to her back, dragging him down with her in the blanket.

They lay side by side, looking up at the twinkling and blinking night sky, so alive with cosmic traffic. It seemed so close and vivid, as though they were passengers on their own interstellar ship.

Annabelle reached her hand toward the stars, then opened her fingers wide and swished them around. "You know, I can move all of the stars with just the flick of my fingers." She giggled. "See…" She swirled her hand through the backdrop. "*Swshhhh*," she breathed.

George slowly slid his hand up along Annabelle's arm—feeling the pressure and friction between them, the particles heating and liquefying, moulding together and soaking into each other—till his fingers tickled hers. "Yes, you can," he whispered.

He was caught in a tornado of emotions, all of them swirling around till he dizzied. Strangely, the one that overpowered the rest was guilt.

As Annabelle parted from him and waited for a reaction, he responded without a blink. "I'm George, George Stanley. I escaped from a secret military think tank in Wyoming."

Annabelle shot upright, her eyes bulging as her hands cupped around her mouth. "You…you…"

George propped himself up and reached for her. "Annabelle, I'm sorry. Please… please let me explain!"

"You're George?" A tear pooled in her eye.

"Annabelle, I'm so sorry."

"You're George?... George! Your name is George?!"

"I… Yes, George."

He was surprised to see an elated smile curling her lips when her hands fell slowly from her mouth—surprised and incredibly confused.

"George!" She pushed to her feet and jumped up and down in a circle, yelling his name repeatedly. "George, he's George! Granny! He's George!"

George was happy that she was happy about him being George, but there were concerns beginning to brew about her being well, mentally. But he vowed to stand beside her and work with her to overcome whatever obstacle it was; it would be theirs to face together.

Finally she quieted and dropped back to her knees before him, smiling like everything in her life was perfect. "Huh." Teary-eyed, she looked at him and nodded. "You're George." She cupped her hands around his cheeks and looked at him, first with love, then lust, then passion, and finally a deep hunger. "My George!" And she pushed him down and threw herself on top of him beneath the moonlight.

***

The need for the universe to have them together could be restrained no longer. Their hearts beat together, she exhaling as he inhaled, and the waves of their passion resonated through the air, perceptible to things on the earth only in the very slightest. But as the waves hit the atmosphere, they grew to cosmic proportions and rattled the satellites, which caused minor disruptions to televisions around the world. Then they grew more and thundered harder, till they slammed into the planets and stars like a mega tsunami.

That night Jupiter tipped 0.974027 degrees on its axis. The daylight hours on Venus extended by 0.771539 seconds. And Mercury's velocity increased by 0.000000045 parsecs.

All of this was imperceptible to even the most studied of astrologists on earth. But whether they could see it or not, change was coming to humankind.

George stirred from what he felt was the deepest sleep he'd ever had. His eyes blinked at an unfamiliar environment, but it took him only a fraction of a second to understand where he was despite it being dark when he had entered the yurt the night before.

Morning light was beginning to filter in through every crack, filling the room with a warm glow. All the furnishings and decorations were handmade to fit the personal taste of the lady Annabelle. All George found himself wanting to do was wrap himself in its warmth and never leave. The large makeshift mattress crunched softly as he shifted his weight, but it was warm and form-fitting. He rolled to where Annabelle should have been to find her missing, though the essence of her hung thick in the air.

He reached up to his eye. It felt a bit better. Then he moved his limbs carefully one by one. He was stiff at first, but everything felt to be on the mend. He lay back and took a deep, relaxing breath, and waited.

But only a few minutes passed before his curiosity got the better of him, along with his want for her to be snuggled in beside him. He could only guess at the time or where she had gotten to. It was a farm of sorts, after all. Maybe she had a field to plow old school. He should go see if she needed a hand.

He slid over the side of the bed, found his clothes on the floor and his glasses on the nightstand, then wrapped a blanket around himself and headed to the door.

Opening it a crack, he squeezed through to a landscape that was equally as captivating in the sunlight as beneath the starlight. The crystal lake held still like glass, and the faint *hussssh* of the falls in the backdrop was calming to the nerves. Colourful flowers popped as birds sang praise to the dawning of another wonderful day in Beelieve. Again, his lungs dug into the air, hauling in deep and full. Filtered through the rich forest, so succulent and nourishing, it almost quenched his hunger.

He scanned the village; not much was moving. He looked around and over to find Annabelle on the grassy knoll they had sat on the previous night, performing a ritual. He stood and watched her beauty. The movement in her body was like silk, and he could swear the flora and fauna were gathering to her, as if her role in all of it carried the same importance as the sun itself.

Then he saw movement, down the hill in the shack he knew to belong to Granny and Cappy. Squinting his good eye, he focused in on a smiling Granny waving to him with a steaming mug. George waved back to her with a smile. He looked to the ground off the stoop he was on and contemplated going to find his shoes, then shrugged and took a barefooted step to the motherland. The coolness of the moist dirt felt welcoming and healing and proper. He scrunched up his toes in it, and his smile heightened, and then he took the next step and then another on his way toward Granny.

"Good morning," she said and welcomed him with a smile and a hug. "I guess it's *George* now, hmm? From what I got out of the yelling and carrying on last night."

George's cheeks grew warm. "Uh, yeah, I'm sorry about all of that. My real name is George. George Stanley."

"Mm-hmm." She touched his swollen eye. "Well, George Stanley, it looks like you're healing up nicely. The question I have now is, was all of this really due to a bear?" Her look turned suspicious. "You see, George, as beautiful as the area is, and as beautiful as the majority of the people are, this area is also a corridor for some not-so-nice activity, which usually includes young men that could fit your description, busted up bits and all." She gave a nod toward Annabelle, who was continuing with her ceremony. "Now, I'm not saying you're the bad type. I definitely don't get that feeling from you, and my instincts are usually spot on. But as I explained before, that young lady's health and happiness are of top priority for Cappy and I and everyone else in the village. So, George Stanley, you're gonna have some explaining to do before we agree to let you stay on here.

If that is your intention?"

George nodded. "I understand, Granny, and thank you for your hospitality. I'll say it again: I can't thank you all enough." He waved his hand toward Annabelle. "She's the most amazing person I've ever met; I can't believe my good fortune. I promise you that I'm not smuggling anything or in any way involved in that type of industry and that all of my injuries are due to a bear encounter. Whether the animal had any ill intention toward me, I don't know. But bears are not something I'm used to coming in contact with. I… I'll explain myself and my story to anyone with concerns, and I'm sure your instinct will find it accurate. Then… I really don't know what to do. I wasn't expecting any of this to happen." He looked over at Annabelle. "She's so beautiful," he whispered.

Granny handed him a steaming cup of tea, following his gaze and sharing his smile. "Yes, she is a very special young woman. As I said, my instincts are quite tuned in my old age, and I sense the universe has something special mapped out for her."

George tried to muster an understanding expression.

She smiled. "It's all right, George. Many people who don't take time to see the world for what it is and how it truly works don't understand—too entranced by the mechanics of humans, burying themselves in their computer screens. As technology grows, nature shrivels. In their quest to become more connected, they disconnect from what really matters in life. I believe very strongly that somewhere in ancient times, humankind had a decision to make about what path to take in regard to the spiritual and mechanical. And because the mechanical was something that could be immediately seen, that path was sold."

George continued to humour her, sipping from his mug whenever the cue came for him to speak. But he knew the front would pass for only so long. He nodded toward Annabelle. "Does she do this every day?"

"Mm-hmm, every morning and every evening, schedule permitting. I think that if we villagers didn't have Annabelle to open and close our days with her tribute, we would be less fortunate. Watching her give herself is one of the times of day I treasure most. I have never missed one since she arrived, not one." George saw her looking at him from the corner of her eye, then she turned to get his attention. "You know, she has been troubled lately, our Annabelle. Sick in her spirit, with voices in her head. They were causing her anxiety and dizzy spells— she actually collapsed one morning, there, during her ritual. She didn't want to talk about it with anyone, but that morning, I got it out of her. I'm the only one she's told. She was concerned others would pass her off as crazy." She smiled with a huff. "One word—a name, actually—calling to her in her mind. People speaking it randomly. It made no sense to her at all and became more insistent over time, screaming at her."

"Oh, a name?" asked George, paying close attention. "Calling to her in her mind?... *Hmph.*"

"She believes in the powers of the universe. You meeting with her yesterday wasn't as by chance as you think. She was drawn to you. She was so certain when she saw you that you could be this someone. She never gave up hope and thought there must be some miscommunication as her intuition was so strong. But then, you had introduced yourself as John..."

The lights went on in George's mind. His eyes widened as he turned back to Annabelle, who was holding a pose on one foot. He remembered her bizarre celebration the night before... "George."

"Mm-hmm, that's right, George. Out of all the names in the world, George. And now, here you are... George."

Cappy brought out some chairs and they all sat silently over tea, waiting for Annabelle to finish. When she finally turned around, a look of pleasant surprise crossed her face. She dabbed at the light sweat on her forehead as she stepped down from her stage and joined them.

As she arrived, Granny held up a cup of tea and welcomed her to have a seat across from George. The two new lovers were full of bashful smiles for each other, not having had time for the morning-after conversation.

Granny broke the silence. "So, I was just bringing George here up to speed on the goings-on with you lately, and the whole George obsession. I think he was quite surprised to hear about it. I'm not certain he believes me."

"Granny!" Annabelle whispered disapprovingly. "That was something I was going to share when I felt the time was right.

"Yes, m'dear, I know, and I would be willing to lend you that time, but you know it is important for us all to understand who this new person is. As sweet as he may seem, there's certain people we don't entertain here." She waited a moment for the silence to settle, then she looked to George. "So, George Stanley, what brings you here?"

"Uh... yeah." He fidgeted with his cup as he thought about what he was going to share and with whom. "I… I'm from Wyoming. At least, that's where I work, and it's my home also. Ah, bluh!… I work for a secret military think tank. My parents passed away a while back. They were the only family I had, and since then, I've had this urge, I guess, to explore life. My mom was always fond of this area, promising to take me someday, but we never managed before… So, I made a plan to escape. I mean, when I say 'escape,' it's not really like that. We can come and go and vacation and everything, I just really wanted to be off the grid for a bit. So, I guess I did cross the border illegally, but I have my identification and passport and everything. I never planned how long I would be gone for. But now… I'm here, I guess."

"Think tank?" Cappy asked.

"Oh, yes. So, we think, I guess. It's a group of scientists and mathematicians working together to create and research different theories. I specialize in quantum theory, the study of the tiniest of particles of matter. I can't really tell you why it's top secret. I don't know of anything we've discovered that is a threat to national security. But I suppose it could happen. We are leading researchers, so many of the things we're working on have never been done before. I guess it sounds strange. If you ask me why here and now, I don't have a solid answer for you."

Granny grinned at Annabelle, then reached and gave her hand a loving shake. Then she turned back to George. "Well, George, we don't need a solid answer, just an honest one. I believe you, and you have our blessing to stay, if that's what you choose. This research you do, it seems very interesting. Believe it or not, I've read a little on this type of science. I'd be very interested to hear more about it—when you're ready, of course." Granny looked back and forth between the two of them as they avoided eye contact with each other. Their smiles had faded. "Well, you two should get along now. I suppose you have some things to discuss." She smiled.

George and Annabelle nodded and stood quickly, then Annabelle led him up the hill to her place. There was no holding of hands and no communication until they stepped in the door.

George could feel her tension. Guilt began to flood him as he considered that maybe things had moved a little too fast between them. He was discovering that he wasn't good with conversation about matters of the heart. He felt she must have many questions but was holding back, and if he didn't step up, she would likely step out.

"I… Annabelle, I can sense there's something wrong. Obviously we need to talk about some things. So, please, can we talk?"

She was busying herself by picking up loose clothing and tidying things that really didn't need it. Then she stopped and blurted, "So, you're leaving? That's it? You came and had your little adventure vacation and now…"

George detected a sniffle. "No, Annabelle." He rushed across the room to her. "I mean, I had intended on going back when I left, I guess. But I didn't know I was going to find this… find you." He touched her waist and she turned to him instantly. He placed his finger beneath her chin and lifted her face to find it streaked with tears. He leaned in and kissed her tenderly, then backed off to see a hint of a smile. "I… you have to understand that… I've never had this before, any of this. You, this oasis! God, I can't believe this place." He smiled and raised his face to the ceiling, fighting back tears of his own. Then he let her go and paced the room as he continued.

"I guess I'm a little embarrassed to say it to you. You're so beautiful, and I never thought in a million years—or ever—that I would meet anyone even close to you. I, I've lived my whole life in this aquarium. I've never known anything else, Annabelle. You were…" He stopped his pacing and bowed his head. "You are my first… everything." He looked back to see her leaning against her dresser, hands crossed over her stomach and holding back a grin.

"I love my work. But I can continue my work anywhere, and honestly, after getting to know you, I think there are a lot of interesting studies I could do here. Spirituality and the quantum world really aren't that different, surprisingly." He turned back to her, then crossed the room and took her hands in his. "I don't want to leave you, Annabelle. I don't want to leave Beelieve. But I do have some concern about how the military is handling my going. I don't feel I'm free to be using any credit cards or speaking my name or flashing my identification around. I mean, it's not like I was a big deal. I wasn't building nuclear weapons or anything. But I was part of a top-secret military program, so…"

She dropped his hands and wrapped her arms around his neck, looking in his eyes. "Don't worry. These hills have a lot of experience in hiding people from the military." She chuckled, then kissed him tenderly. And again, then again.

George smiled and kissed her back, wrapping himself around her. They tripped over each other as they moved across the floor and fell into bed.

That evening, everyone was invited for a family dinner down at Granny and Cappy's, where George was officially introduced to and welcomed by everyone.

"Quantum theory, eh?" Munch looked to George. "The very smallest of particles?"

George glanced around the room; everyone was sprawled out on cushions and mismatched seats lined with small tables, and they all appeared to be taking some level of interest. It was all the encouragement he needed to begin his rant.

He easily maintained their interest as he talked about the basics of the theory and how it relates to life and spiritual theory. He explained how everything in life was connected and everything had a mass; even thoughts and feelings could now be measured, and with mass comes effect. But then—as a scientist usually does—he took it too far.

Candles were lit as the light grew dim, and as the questions rolled by, George began to go into what he referred to as simple calculations. He made his way over to a small blackboard in the corner of the fair-sized room, which Granny said had been donated when one of the local schools upgraded to computers. He began to scribble one calculation, which led to another on top of yet another. Divided by the sum of the degree to the fifth, and that equalled everyone asleep when he finally turned around. Even his beloved Annabelle.

His shoulders slumped as he pulled off his glasses. He rubbed at his eyes; the swollen one was really beginning to feel better. He chuckled to himself, then went over to his lady and gave her a light shake. "Hey," he whispered.

She jumped. Disoriented, with eyes tired and red, she began to clap.

George clasped her hands to stop them, then smiled and kissed her cheek. "It's okay. I get it. It's not the first audience I've overwhelmed."

She blinked and looked around at all the bodies slumped over and cuddled together. Munch was snoring.

He gave her a kiss and helped her to her feet, and they made their way back to their yurt for the night.

The next morning he woke again to her absence. He rolled over a few times to shake off the cobwebs, then grabbed his glasses off the nightstand and pushed them into place, noticing that the pain and awkwardness in his body had diminished and he was actually able to see out of both eyes.

It was a good start to the day. He smiled, then kicked his feet happily over the side of the bed and began searching around the floor for his clothes. As he walked toward the door, he noticed a note on the table where Annabelle kept a wash basin and a few kitchen knick-knacks. The note said *Good morning* (with a little heart dotting the *i*), *Granny brought a pot of tea for you.* And indeed, sitting right beside the note was a teapot and a couple mugs. George poured himself a cup, then headed out the front door to watch Annabelle.

He loved the first breath of mountain air. He closed his eyes and savoured every last crumb. He stretched his arms overhead and his muscles contracted as he let go a massive yawn. He looked down to see Granny looking back up and giving him a wave, which he returned.

There was a small swinging loveseat beside the entrance that he had never paid much attention to. Although it looked rickety enough to only be used for ornamental purposes, he reached down and brushed off a spot, then rested his weight slowly and cautiously at first, till he was convinced it was safe. Then he rested back and gave a couple short swings and smiled.

He lifted the mug to his lips. The steam fogged his glasses, so he took them off and shook them clear as he didn't want to miss Annabelle. Problem resolved, he sat back and sighed a peaceful breath. What a way to greet the day. The sounds, the smells, the view…

He thought about what he had traded them for: waking up in his cement bunker, showering, and…

He realized he couldn't remember the last time he had showered or bathed… and no one had mentioned anything about it.

…Shower and dress, tie his tie, then walk down to the cafeteria to grab a quick coffee and bagel before rushing down to the morning meeting. The only sunshine he got there was via an exterior scene on their screen saver. The only fresh air was sucked down hundreds of feet from the surface and filtered of anything natural. Head down, ass up—thinking in nothing more than emotionless equations all day, every day.

Now, with all the formalities out of the way and some personal time to reflect, he took time to really soak up his new surroundings. No walls, no roof, no computers; nothing familiar to a working day for George Stanley. And as he drank his tea and breathed in the freshness of the life around him—so much life—the numbers and calculations began to dance everywhere he looked. Swirling around Annabelle as she moved through a sea of symbols. Blowing in the wind, bathing in the sun, swimming in ripples on the lake. George felt inspired—true inspiration, not like a technical deadline—to create on his own, beyond boundaries, and to explore his craft the way he wanted, by his rules.

As he continued to relax beneath the sun, he felt his every hair and pore drink it all in. He watched Annabelle till she finished and began the walk home, stopping in with a quick hug and kiss for Granny and Cappy. He disappeared into the yurt and returned just as she arrived, welcoming her with a warm mug.

They sat together on the loveseat, rocking gently, sharing a kiss. Then he suggested she lean back and rest her legs across him so he could rub them.

"So, George Stanley," she said with a smile, "what are your intentions here in Beelieve?"

"Beelieve… *hmph*." He leaned back and grinned. "Believe… Beelieve? What's its origin?"

"What's its origin?" She slapped playfully at his chest and laughed. "I'm not sure of its origin. Please don't fail me, Professor."

They shared a laugh till she continued.

"I don't know, really. It's kind of a play on words, *believe, bee*… something, somehow? We're all spiritual, we believe in… the universe, or in each other, or in love—we just believe. But we also believe in bees."

"Bees? Like *bee* bees? The buzzing insect things?"

"Yes, Doctor, the little buzzing insect things." She grinned, and he flopped his head lazily around. "I guess I haven't given you the grand tour yet, but maybe if you listen carefully?"

They both paused and listened with dorky smiles on their faces. And after a moment, he could hear it. Faint, but it was there: the constant hum of busy bees. "Uh, yeah." He looked around. "Sounds like there's a lot of them, now that I notice." He continued to search for the bees.

"They're over there." She pointed off into the grass and flowers. "You know, how 'bout we get dressed and head out for a walk? I've been neglecting my chores since you arrived, and that won't work much longer—the others will start to complain. And if you're gonna stay in Beelieve, you're gonna have to put out!" She stood and pulled on his hand, toward the doorway.

"Yes!" He pumped a fist in the air.

"Haha, smartass. I mean actual work."

"Oh, right." He got up and followed her through the door. "By the way, where's the shower?"

She seemed entertained by his question but grabbed some linens, then his hand, and led him out the door.

She pulled him along swiftly through the village. Everyone waved to them as they raced by, till they reached the shore of the pond that fed the waterfall.

"C'mon, chicken!" she teased as she began to strip down on the sand.

"Wha… what do you mean, 'chicken'?" He looked around, and though they were a bit of a walk from the village, it was still well within eyesight. "You bathe in the lake? What are you, nuts? That's glacial water."

She continued giggling. "Not all the time. Just in the summer. If you want something warm, you're gonna have to haul water and light the stove. Then the place will be hot as hell tonight. So why don't you just quit being a Georgie-downer." She squealed as she shed the last piece of clothing, ran into the water, and dove headfirst.

He watched her figure glide through water so clear, she could have been flying. Then her head pushed through the surface and her face pressed to the warm sun, and water showered down around her as she flipped her hair back and wiped her face. "Ahhh," she breathed, then looked back to him, standing in his grandpa ginch and crooked glasses with his arms crossed over his skinny frame.

She splashed at him. "C'mon, I know there's some hippie in you."

He looked back at the village. The others were busy with their stuff; none were paying any attention to them. He removed his glasses first and his underwear last, cupping his cuppables while he tiptoed in. "Jeesus! This is goddamn cold!"

But it was too late to turn back, and as soon as he reached waist depth, he took the plunge. He popped to the surface, gasping for air as the cold pressed in around his lungs. "I, I can't believe you do this every day."

"Well"—she reached her hand out, tipping it side to side—"I think 'regular basis' would be more accurate." She giggled, then swam into his arms.

She introduced him to all-natural soap–slash–shampoo–slash–whatever else you needed it to be. And when they came back on shore, she had a couple nice towels to wrap up in and sit on while they dressed and warmed in the sun. She also had a set of comfortable, all-natural garments for George: loose-fitting pants and a robe that tied at the side, underwear optional.

They returned to the hut to finish drying off over another cup of tea. Then Annabelle gave George the full tour.

They once again followed the path that cut between the greenhouse and Granny's place, but instead of continuing to the lake, they took a left up the shallow slope to the houses where Gwyn and Munch and Stella and Griz all lived. They were all out working on chores and waved George and Annabelle over to talk as they passed.

"So, George, look at you, my man." Munch smiled. "You look like you've been reborn!" He fanned his hands out dramatically.

Gwyn sidled up to Munch with an adoring grin. "Aw, look at the young love. You're both absolutely glowing." She closed her eyes and took a long, deep breath before exhaling and looking at them again. She nodded. "Yes… ye-e-e-es, I see only good things for you two. I'm guessing you will be staying on with us for a while, George?"

"Yes." George and Annabelle looked into each other's eyes and laced their hands together. "I'll be staying."

"I'm just giving George the tour, guys, we'll catch up with you a little later."

Just as they turned to walk away, there was a snort from behind the greenhouse, and an attention-starved Dennis came clopping down the slope to see them.

"Yes, Dennis, hello, sir. How are you?"

The mule snorted again and circled around George, sniffing and even taking a nip at his new duds.

"Dennis!" Annabelle scolded, placing a hand to his head and pushing him back. "I'm sorry, I don't know what his problem is."

"I know," George said. He broke hands with Annabelle and let Dennis sniff his hand, then gave him a good scratch behind his ear. "He's jealous of the new man spending time with his lady. And I don't blame him one bit. It's just gonna take some time to adjust, hey, bud?"

Dennis snorted again and shook his head, then relaxed in between them.

As they continued on their tour, they found Stella and Griz smiling in an embrace and stealing a kiss. As they caught sight of the trio passing by, they waved. "Good morning, George, Annabelle. What a beautiful morning to be in love, wouldn't you say?"

George beamed back at them. "Yes, it's an excellent morning for that." He waved as Annabelle blushed and lowered her head.

Up the slope from the greenhouse was a modest garden surrounded by a chicken-wire fence, and between the garden and the greenhouse sat a chicken coupe in a separate fenced-in area, with a couple goats in the mix.

"So, how many chickens and other animals do you lose to predators?" George asked.

"Hmm? Oh, well, I honestly can't say that we've lost any animals to predators. Not to my knowledge."

"That's surprising. I would think that chickens and goats would be an easy target."

"Yes, they would be, if it wasn't for our Dennis. He takes care of all of us." She smiled and scratched his cheeks.

"Dennis?" George gave her a quizzical look.

"Yes, Dennis. Donkeys are very protective of their families."

"Well, I guess they are, but what's he gonna do against something like a grizzly bear?"

"Well, we know the local bears. Grizzlies have big territories, and our resident is Baloo-the-Pooh." She snickered.

"Baloo-the-Pooh? Really? You have a pet name for him? A grizzly bear?"

"Yes, he comes around at certain times of the season. We share some of our crop with him, but there seems to be a compromise on both sides. It's the mountain lions that are the real pests. There's been a couple enter the area at night. Sent the whole place into a frenzy—awful noise to wake up to. But none of those mean old cats get by Dennis."

"Wh— you mean this Dennis?" George looked down at their companion with renewed respect.

"Yes, he takes the term *ride or die* quite literally."

"Hey-ey, buddy." George reached down and gave him another good scratch. "Look at you, taking on the bad guys. I guess I better watch my step with your lady."

As they walked alongside the garden stretching up the slope, George marvelled at all the healthy vegetables and asked questions, especially when it came to the final row of produce, up at the treeline. The plants varied from six feet tall to short and bushy, and they carried a pungent yet floral aroma.

"*Ahem.*" He looked to Annabelle with a side grin. "Now, Miss Annabelle, I admit that I don't get out much, but I have a strong hunch as to what this is."

"Yes, well, we refer to it as our silly-weed crop. Ours is well known as some of the best in the area. We call it 'Honeybuzz' because we credit its high quality to the local bee population. It's honestly the biggest cash crop we have."

"Uh-huh…" He gave her a suspicious look.

They turned and came upon a patch of untouched land covered in a beautiful field of flowers of every possible colour. With acres of pinks, reds, yellows, blues, purples, and greens spreading down to the edge of the bathing pond, it was straight out of a fairy tale.

Annabelle guided him over to the first of many box-like hives. He looked around and noticed all the bees in the immediate area. They were always present throughout the village, but now he realized just how big the population was and how much of a role they must play.

He resisted going farther. "Uh, I don't know if we need to take the tour this far. It's a beautiful field of flowers, I have a pretty good view from here."

She giggled and grabbed his hand with both of hers and pulled harder. "C'mon, if you want to be part of the clan, you'll have to learn to deal with the bees."

"Well, I mean, the bees are really only one part of the operation. Maybe I could trade someone bee duty forrrrr picking extra carrots or something?"

"Oh quit, they're harmless. But you have to get they're trust first. You need to be calm. If you panic, they panic, and you definitely don't want that."

They stepped slowly and softly toward the hive. The buzzing grew louder and George stalled again. "What… Are you just walking up to the hive with nothing but normal clothes? Isn't there some, like, protective gear—net helmets or whatever?"

"C'mon, Dr. Chicken Pants. I'll protect you."

As they stepped up to the hive, the bees grew more active and some landed on them, which made George extremely uncomfortable. But he was scared to move or flinch, so he remained carefully focused on keeping his composure.

He watched Annabelle, seemingly in her glory. Her smile grew as she slid up a panel on the side of the hive and showed him it was full of honeycombs, bleeding with golden-sweet syrup.

The buzzing grew more intense and George closed his eyes, having a hard time breathing or communicating in any way and only opening his good eye a crack when needed. Then he remembered Dennis, and he turned his head around slowly in the swarm to see the jackass standing back on the main path with what looked like a cocky grin.

He looked back to Annabelle and she nodded toward the honey, to which he nodded approvingly. "Mmmm-hm, mmmmm-hm."

She laughed and shook her head at him, then slid the panel down and led him back to the path. As soon as the cloud diminished, he sucked in a gasping breath and leaned on Dennis, catching his breath. "That was crazy! How— Why would you go in there without any protection like that?"

She shrugged. "I love them, and they love me too. I think they do, anyway. They never sting me." She turned back to the field of flowers with hives scattered between the blossoms. Then she looked over the rest of the village. "They're the reason for all of this. It's the reason that Beelieve products are the best. They help take care of us, and I love to take care of them."

George and Dennis shared an *Oh boy* look.

"Don't you two start doing that!" she scolded. "Don't think I didn't see that look."

George straightened and looked around the little piece of paradise. Sure enough, bees were working away in every corner. And though he had never been much of a farmer or gardener, he was sure this patch of land would be in for some big awards.

"Okay." He nodded. "I'll lay off your bee fetish."

On the walk back, she pointed out how they weren't totally free from modern amenities. They had one windmill and a few small solar panels placed sporadically through the village. Some electricity was nice to have in the long nights of winter.

QUANTUM AVIDYA

Everyone had agreed to meet down at Granny's for one of Annabelle's yoga classes, then join in on a hearty meal. It wasn't a daily ritual for everyone to eat at Granny's, but the long, hot summer evenings invited social gatherings.

They decided to have the yoga session out on the knoll beneath the cloudless sky. George had never done yoga before and was self-conscious about showing off his lack of moves in front of everyone, but watching Annabelle over the last few days had piqued his interest. Though he had watched her do her own thing many times, this was the first time he had seen her teach. She spoke very clearly and precisely, having them all start with closing their eyes and focusing on their breathing.

"Draw deep from your belly and up through your chest to the top of your head, now hold… and exhale— ahhhhhhh!" On that note, the resonance of her voice penetrated deep within him. There was a shiver, then a sudden, deep relaxation in his body that instantly focused his mind on nothing. He fell into a calmness that he had never known. Then her voice rang again, and his frontal lobe tingled.

"Focus on the breath, the coolness of every molecule as it passes through your nostrils and into your lungs, then the warm exhaust as you exhale—ahhhhhhh!"

George tried to concentrate as visions of his past spun through his mind, then turned to dreams of the future.

"Ahhhhhhhh!" she punctuated again, like a hammer to his chest that knocked him deeper into the soothing darkness, and everything drifted away again as he found focus. She took them through some stretches and poses that would be amateur to most but were challenging to him. He felt presence in his body, his muscles—the tingles and twitches, the stretching and popping, blood and oxygen circulating. When she finally talked them back to a conscious state, the world looked a lot different to George Stanley.

As the weather was so nice, they decided to bring the furniture outside to eat. There was so much food: fresh-from-the-garden fruits and vegetables and succulent fish and game birds, followed by some homemade wine and silly-weed.

A stuffed George was laid out on a blanket in the evening sun when Annabelle leaned over and gave him a kiss and then snuggled in beside him.

Munch got out some props and put on some tricks he had been working on. Then Griz broke out her acoustic guitar and everyone started to sing along.

Belly full and somewhat inebriated, George fell into a euphoric state of relaxation.

With Annabelle cradled in his arms, he brushed her hair back from her forehead and kissed her softly.

When the songs stopped, the drowsiness could be felt in the air. George listened to everyone's stories of adventure, and then Stella looked to him and asked, "What are your plans here, George? What would you like to do?"

It was the first time George had ever thought past the honeymoon stage of Beelieve. He wiped the fuzziness from his mind. "Hmm, well, I'd actually like to continue with my work. I love my work, really. But now, here, I feel my mind just running free sometimes, and I think I'd like to see what I can discover on my own. Approach my work from a totally different direction. This place and all of you here have really opened my eyes. There's a lot of inspiration. My work is really an art, just like a painting or a song, I guess. Here, I can create without boundaries."

They all applauded George and welcomed him with open arms that night. Granny and Cappy even agreed that the chalkboard would serve a better purpose up at George and Annabelle's place.

George and Annabelle's place... He smiled at the reference and squeezed Annabelle a little tighter as she turned to him with a smile and a kiss. It all had happened so quickly. But he wasn't going to resist, and it appeared neither was she.

As he lay in bed and watched her crawl in, he smiled. "How did you do that?"

She raised an eyebrow. "How'd I do what?"

"That thing tonight, with the yoga. It felt like you were right inside my head—well, not just my head, but, like, inside everything."

She shot him a sly grin as she rolled onto him, resting her chin on his chest and meeting his eyes with hers. He could see the candlelight perfectly mirrored on the glossy surface.

"It's practice. Practice, but also belief—if you don't believe in it, then it doesn't matter how much you practice, you'll never reach anyone. I believe in what I do. I guess it happened over time. People would keep saying things to me like you just did. The more they said it, the more my confidence grew, and my belief." She lifted her chest and crawled up him till their lips were inches apart; they could feel each other's breath.

Still a little lightheaded, George fumbled his words into a whisper as her eyes drew him deeper. "It was just… so… crazy…"

She kissed him with lips sweet and tender, then nibbled lightly at his lip. Their heartbeats began to sync, and the air stirred with passion. "Was it? Was it so crazy, George Stanley?"

He nodded, speechless.

"Yes? Do you want more, George Stanley, hmm?" Her gaze grew more intense, and she pulled herself in tighter to him.

He nodded again.

She pulled in tighter yet, placed her cheek along his, and began to whisper seductively in his ear. "Close your eyes, George."

The voice was back. Like an injection to quench an addiction, he welcomed her direction.

"Breathe in, George. Slow, deep—feel the air drawing in. Smell it, taste it, every drop. Now exhale—ahhhhhhhhh!"

There it was again, like a trigger, and he fell comatose.

She lifted herself for a moment, removed all her clothing, then pressed her naked body back to his, and continued.

As he breathed, his belly and chest inflated and he felt himself carrying her mass. He became very aware of her warmth, of the blood pumping through her veins.

"Breathe in, George, two… three… four. Now out, two… three… four. In, two… three… four. Out…" The pattern continued.

Once he had his breathing tuned, she began to match his rhythm, except that when he inhaled, she exhaled. After each round, they became a little more in sync, till they reached that point where they were complete, feeding off each other. They drew each other in deep with every breath, like vampires in frenzy.

***

The molecules around them became hyper-excited to the point where the air around them began to glow with an intense light that could be seen long beyond the borders of the village.

Their exhales moaned and their lips wandered as they called to each other, bound together, spinning through ecstasy.

Particles joined and morphed, creating their own gravity, pulling and twisting. The earth gave a soft moan, then a gentle tremor, which caused everyone within a fifty-kilometre radius to sit up and wonder, and yet went completely unnoticed by George and Annabelle.

Neither could tell how long it lasted, or even what all had transpired. Every ounce of energy was spent, till they felt as though their bodies had disintegrated from existence. They held tightly to each other, and drifted to the darkness.

A few days later when George woke, he opened his good eye, and then the other, and smiled. Healing was fast in Beelieve. He got up and sat out on the porch swing with a cup of tea to watch Annabelle. He felt good. So good that even a grizzly bear sighting couldn't have wiped the smile from his face.

After her routine, it had become customary for he and Annabelle to visit over a cup of tea, then set out for their daily chores. Sometimes they would work together, sometimes separately. George had learned many new skills, such as weeding and picking vegetables, chasing chickens and gathering eggs. Stella and Gwyn had taught him about harvesting buds and seeds from the silly-weed to sell, as well as how to properly dry and prepare the stalks so they could be turned into fibres that were used to make almost everything in the village, from clothes to yurts. And when the time was right, his Annabelle had taken him to harvest the honey, teaching him how to work on his breathing and focus to an almost meditative state, until a trust was built between him and the bees. There must have been at least a thousand that had landed on him during the process, but not one of them stung him. The couple's connection had become unbreakable—like two particles in quantum entanglement, directly connected, no matter how far apart they are in the universe.

At night, Annabelle would lie in bed with a gentle smile of admiration as he worked on his chalkboard by dim candlelight deep into the night, and at times, early into the morning. Sometimes she would bother him, which he loved. She would point at different numbers and symbols—*"What's this? And this?"*—or rapidly shout out random numbers one after the other, till she mussed his train of thought enough that he would run at her and tackle her into the bed, laughing and loving together. He knew of no calculation to explain the twinkle in her eyes or the sweet scent of her skin. He never felt the need to explain her, only to love her.

Time passed quickly, till the days became noticeably shorter and the nights a little cooler. Change of season in the air.

There had been substantial changes in George. He could feel them. He had never let his facial hair grow past a five o'clock shadow, and now it was long and full. His muscles were toned, his skin tanned, and his mind calm and focused like never before.

Life was easier without the many poisons of society. It shocked him to remember his phone was stashed away in his pack somewhere. He hadn't touched it or thought about it for months. And with it forgotten, so were the concerns of politics, wars, economics, and disaster. He grinned to himself while rolling his morning cup of tea in his hands. *Hmph, it's that easy, just turn it off.* He looked down at Annabelle doing her morning routine, then waved to Granny. The only concerns he had now were the ones right outside his door. How heavy it had been to carry the weight of all the worlds problems on his shoulders. And there were so many people doing it, billions. So many people in small-town America were glued to their phones, thinking they were helping a crisis halfway across the world by sharing a post or liking a tweet.

He broke from his trance as he caught more motion coming from Granny. She was waving for him to join them. He strolled down with a smile and pulled up a chair beside Granny and Cappy to watch Annabelle finish up and make her way over.

"So, George," Cappy said as he leaned back in his chair and held a match to his pipe. He sucked in a couple times till it was lit, then continued. "Everyone is coming in with good reviews of you. They say you've been a big help, quick and eager to learn. Good to hear, son." He ended with a clever wink.

It would seem like a simple compliment to many, but for Cappy to open his mouth about anything took nothing less than an Oscar performance, so George took some hefty pride in it. "Yeah, thanks, Cappy, it just feels easy up here. It really is paradise—for me, anyway."

"Yes, well, we'll see how you survive the winter, eh?" Granny said as she came out the door from behind him with a steaming mug for Annabelle. "Then of course there will be a lot of work in the springtime. You two should get together with Griz soon to start planning the addition."

"The what?" Annabelle cut in. "What addition, Granny? I've never heard anything about any addition. To what, the greenhouse?"

The old lady chuckled. "No, no, I'm talking about the addition to your place."

George raised his brow to Annabelle, who passed the gesture to Granny.

Her chuckle turned to a laugh. "The addition, for the little addition you two are bringing to our family." She pointed slyly back and forth between the two of them.

Clueing in, they both turned nervous eyes to the ground. "Oh, no. No, Granny. We don't have any plans of that anytime in the near future. We're still—"

Granny laughed so hard she leaned over in her chair clenching her gut, then looked back at both of them with a certain intensity. "You… you don't listen too well, do you, girl? You think you plan this? You think the miracle of life is yours to plan?"

George's eyes bulged as his jaw slackened and his breathing ceased.

"This couldn't be avoided, or postponed. There's a very special bond between you. I can't place it yet, though believe me, I've been trying ever since I felt the power between you two the night you first came around." She squinted an eye directly at George. "I'm surprised it took as long as it did."

Her spirit visibly lightened as she eased back in her chair and turned her gaze to the sun. She spoke softly to no one in particular, creating a spooky sort of vibe. "Yes… there is something more to this. Something… this had to happen. None of this is a coincidence. This child will be very special."

19

General Mathis sat back in his office chair, repeatedly depressing the actuator on the end of his pen in a daze as he reminisced about a meeting with George several years earlier.

"George, good morning. I didn't even have time to enjoy a morning coffee before I was called down to see you," he had said with a smirk. He had worked with George for many years and admired the young man's intelligence and dedication to his work.

George turned around. "Good morning, General," he said with a smile. "Yes, sorry, I, I really… I just was so excited. I finally solved—"

"George!" he exclaimed, noticing George's bloodshot eyes and crinkled attire, which were totally out of character. "My god, man, when was the last time you slept?"

"Uh, yes." George looked down and brushed some crumbs from his tie. "I'm very sorry again, Your Honour—uh, General. I just… I got on a roll yesterday and, well, it took me all night, but…" He pointed to the blackboard behind him, on which he had puked out equations.

The general raised an eyebrow. He was schooled to some degree, but he was no scientist. His job was to keep everything and everyone in order and make sure that the information was delivered to the proper sources, and only them. "Uh-huh…" He took a seat, then a sip of his coffee. "Okay, George, explain."

"Well, remember a couple weeks back when you brought me to meet with those lab guys who were running the experiment to measure mass in human thought?"

The general raised his cup to his lips and took another sip, his curiosity growing with George's mention of the experiment. "Mm-hmm, yes."

"Well…" George waved his hand at the blackboard again with a toothy smile.

"Yes, George, please. Explain it to me as if I were stupid."

George's cockiness faded as he corrected his posture. "Well, General, sir, this calculation proves why. Why they were able to get the results that they did."

"Uh-huh… which calculation, George?"

"Well"—George grew awkward as he looked back to the board—"all of it, sir." He stood straight and fidgeted with his tie.

The general kept his eyebrow raised. "Yes, well, this is big, George. Very big."

George's confidence returned as he walked through the ridiculously complicated equation, turning back to the general occasionally to sometimes find him nodding off. "Don't you see, General? This… this proves the whole concept! With this, we could— I mean, humankind could! It would be a totally different direction for everything! Life as we know it would change. The way we do… everything!"

The general feigned enthusiasm, scanning the board as if he knew something about something. The trick to the think tank was to develop different departments, with people in each department sworn to the highest level of confidentiality, even between departments and with their spouses, parents, children… they couldn't even breathe a word of it to their dog.

The departments worked in their fields and the findings were shared with only the very highest of echelon. It wasn't always a quest to develop new technology. It was also a mission to figure out how the world and everything in it works so they could control it. With the departments kept separate and sworn to secrecy, no one from any single department could fit all the pieces together to see the big picture.

George was the closest thing to a friend that the general had in the bunker. A trusted friend, whose intelligence was well-documented by the top brass. And they needed him to cross the line between departments that one time to help sort it out— exactly the way he had done. Crossing boundaries was rare but not unheard of.

"Yes, George, well done." The general walked over to George and shook his hand, then placed his other hand on his shoulder and looked him in the eyes. "This is good work. I want you to know it won't go unnoticed. So, why don't you type this out legibly and get it to me on a pen drive. I'm going to pass it on to the people who've been waiting for it. I told them you were the man for the job, and you didn't let me down. Thank you, George."

That was it. George had done as instructed, the general had passed it on to the upper ranks, and that was the last they had heard of it. He had avoided George the best he could for a while after. When George did manage to corner him, he would put a disgusted look on his face so George wouldn't have the balls to ask. After time, like every other time, it had passed.

Now, months had gone by without a word of any kind from George. General Mathis wasn't someone to take a breach of his personal trust lightly. But he had also put himself in a very delicate position by not immediately notifying the people he answered to. They would not overlook this, knowing George and what George knew. He was one of the few people with enough intelligence to link things together, if given time and motivation.

He could be down partying it up on a tropical beach, backpacking through Europe, or handing secret information over to Russian intelligence.

If that were the case, he should pray they killed him when they were done because General Mathis would not be as merciful.

The general clenched his jaw, and a strong knock hit the door just as he snapped the pen he was holding in two.

"Yes, come in."

His assistant entered the room. "Sir, you wanted to see me, sir?"

"Yes, Tardy. It seems I've been a bit too lenient with our missing thinker, Mr. Stanley."

"Yes, yes sir. I understand."

"There's still no indication he's been up to anything treasonous at this point, so I don't feel a need to sound the alarm yet. Please explain to his coworkers that he has been temporarily reassigned. Then, call in a favour to law enforcement. Tell them we have a missing person of interest and I want to know if he flashes his ID, uses a credit card, crosses a border—anything. When he moves, I want to know immediately. Me and no one else, for the time being. Is that understood, Tardy?"

"Yes, yes sir, General Mathis."

Back at their hut, George paced the room.

"Is she… do you think this is right? Are you… you think you're pregnant?" George felt nauseous, having to pause on occasion to support himself.

"I… I don't know. I've never been pregnant before, George."

"Yes, right, right." He looked to her concerned face as she sat on the side of the bed leaning forward. "I'm sorry," he said and smiled.

"Are you okay?" she asked him. "I mean, I really don't know if I'm pregnant. But I've never known Granny to be wrong about anything, and she seems pretty convinced of this. So, what if I am?"

George leaned against the table, stroking his beard so vigorously it might start to smoke at any time. So many things were passing through his mind as he tried to douse the panic with rationality. He took a deep breath and closed his eyes, focusing the way she had taught him. Minutes later when his heart rate had steadied, he opened his eyes and looked at her.

"Well, if you are, then… then we're going to have a baby." He smiled and walked to her, covering the distance in a couple strides.

She stood and they wrapped their arms around each other and let their emotions flow freely, kissing and caressing as tears streamed down their faces, and they fell back into bed.

Later, she lay in his arms snuggled beneath the covers, tracing a finger around his stomach while he stared at the ceiling.

"When will we know for sure?" he asked.

"I don't know."

"Don't you know about your… stuff—cycles and…"

"Yes, George, I know about my cycles." He could feel her smile as she turned and kissed his tummy. "There's reason to be suspicious; there's been reason for a couple weeks now."

"…Oh… okay."

"You're not mad at me?"

"Mad… For what?"

"For not telling you."

"Well, would telling me affect the outcome at all?"

"No."

"Then no, I'm not mad." He kissed the top of her head and weaved his fingers through her hair. "I love you, Annabelle. I love you completely. I'm dedicated to you for the rest of our lives, without question."

She wrapped her arms tightly around him and they shared a tender kiss. "I love you too George Stanley." She returned to her rested position.

"So… what do you think Granny was talking about with all of this *powerful bond*, or whatever between us, and all of this is from a higher power and whatever?"

"I don't know. She has connections in this world that none of us could ever understand. She's not a god, but when she talks, you best listen. That's been proven, repeatedly."

George began to think about how this would change a lot of things for him, for them. If he was about to become a father and raise a proper family, the time would come soon when he would have to face his past. Hiding in the hills wasn't a responsible choice for him anymore.

It didn't take long for everyone to know Annabelle was pregnant. The next morning they all saw it during her morning salute. She was a little more tipsy than usual, and then finally she ended up having to cut it short due to morning sickness. It was official.

Granny smiled as she helped Annabelle home, where she gave George a smiling nod and left them alone.

George sat beside Annabelle, holding a bucket in front of her and rubbing her back. "So, we're having a baby." He smiled.

Annabelle grinned. "We're having a baby."

They laughed and cried while holding each other. And when the excitement dwindled, George stood and began pacing the floor as he ran his plan by Annabelle.

"Okay, so, I mean, I broke a few rules when I left work, and likely have upset a couple higher-ups. But I think they'll be happy to have me back. I've been thinking about how to approach it all, and I think maybe a phone call is best to—"

"Wait." She looked puzzled. "You what? You're going back to work? You want to tell what to who?"

George returned her puzzled look. "I… well, I mean, we… I have to go back to work, Annabelle. We have to get back into society. We're having a baby; it's going to need food and clothing and an education. I have some money with me, and it's a considerable amount, but it won't last long. I have more in a savings account, but I've been afraid to try to access it as there may be people watching. So, I mean, we have to integrate back into—"

"No, George, no." Annabelle sheltered her belly and stepped back from him, shaking her head. "This baby will be born here. It will be born and raised here, educated here. This is our home, our family's home. We're not leaving here. I won't raise our child in that… that garbage world."

George's jaw fell open. "Wh-what do you mean, sweetie? This is real, we're having a baby, a child that we're responsible for. We need—"

"We need to raise this child here, with its family."

"But… what… What? We have to get you to a doctor, Annabelle."

Annabelle continued to shake her head. "No, Granny will take care of me and deliver this baby. This baby will be born and raised here in Beelieve."

"But… but… What about school, university… little league?"

Annabelle stood, looked George square in the eyes, and put her foot down very hard. "Beelieve has everything needed to raise a healthy and happy child. This child will be born and raised here, and that is that, George Stanley!"

George blinked a couple times, then took a seat, removed his glasses, and rubbed at his face with both hands. His father's voice rang in his mind: *Happy wife, happy life, son. Remember that.*

George found a chuckle with the memory. He sniffled and rubbed at his eyes one more time, then set his glasses back in place and stood. He lifted his gaze to the ceiling and took a breath, then placed his hands on his hips and looked at Annabelle. A smile curled on his lips and he began to nod slowly, then more confidently.

Annabelle's eyes brightened. "Yes?" She wiped at a tear. "You agree, we can stay here, our family?"

"Hah!" He continued to nod. "Do I really have a choice?"

She laughed. "No, you really don't." She raced across the room, right into his arms.

They didn't waste time announcing the news to everyone. They walked around the village to let them know about the baby and that they would be staying in Beelieve. The ladies gushed over Annabelle and everyone congratulated George with hugs and handshakes, and then Cappy and Granny called it a day for everyone and their chores so they could celebrate. Cappy even broke out his stash of fine cigars that he had been saving for just such an occasion.

As the sun began to set, Gwyn grabbed some of her cards, pulled Annabelle inside Granny's place, and sat her down at a table. Granny poked her head in with a smile, then stepped in to join them.

Gwyn pulled card number one. "Oooohhhh, yes, yes." She looked up at Annabelle. "It looks good, yes, good." She tilted her head. "Everyone is happy and healthy, but there is a suggestion of confusion at first. I suspect this will be related to trying to guess the sex of the baby before the birth."

Annabelle brightened. "Does it say the sex? Oh no, wait! Don't tell me, I don't want to know, if that's what it says. ...Is that what it says?"

The three ladies shared a laugh.

Gwyn flipped over card two. "Oh, yes, uh-huh. Everything is very good, Annabelle." She flipped the next card. "Yes, good, good. The child is strong, very healthy and so much love." The next card was flipped. "And you and George..." She blushed. "Oh my, you two are very lucky to have found each other. There are very big things for you to accomplish together." Then the next. "Oh my, yes, many accomplishments with the child also. It suggests that this could be a very big change for life—the life of everyone. It's showing everyone as big, so many people are affected." Gwyn held Annabelle's hand and patted it softly. "Now, the next card is yours to pick. Go ahead." She nodded to Annabelle.

Annabelle smiled and held one hand over her belly as she pulled a card from the pile with the other, then flipped it over.

Gwyn's brow scrunched. "Oh, well."

"What? What is it, Gwyn?" Annabelle leaned over the table. "What do you see?"

"Um, well, it is unexpected, especially for this type of situation. It is just a suggestion, and it's likely a long way into the future, so I wouldn't put too much thought into this card."

"But what is it, Gwyn? It's bad, isn't it?"

"Now, now." Gwyn patted her hand again. "It's likely nothing big, sweetie, don't worry about it. We'll do another reading again sometime later. For now, what I'm confident of is that this baby is going to be born a beautiful miracle, and everyone is going to be happy and healthy. Honest, Annabelle, everything will be fine. Go"—she pointed to the pile—"pick another."

Annabelle chewed her lip for a second, looking at the cards, then reached in and flipped over another.

Gwyn's hands clapped together when she saw the card, her eyes bulging and her cheeks inflating till she let the breath out slowly, causing the hair above her forehead to flutter. "I, oh, ummm, well…" She looked up at Annabelle with a forced smile. "I-I-I-I-I—"

"Okay, my ladies," Granny cut in, "I think it's time to put away the cards for now. No sense stressing Mom over uncertainties." She looked right at Annabelle and held her hand tightly. "Your only concern right now, m'dear, is that little life you carry. You need to stay focused on health and happiness, and avoid all stress when possible."

Annabelle nodded. "Thank you, Granny," A tear streaked down her cheek.

"Oh, now, honey, you've got to get control of your hormones." She smiled sweetly and held Annabelle's hands. "Everything is going to be just fine, my Anna. I know this, trust in me, yes?"

"Yes." Annabelle smiled as she burst into tears.

Gwyn and Granny came around the table to comfort their friend.

"We're all going to be here with you every step of the way, Annabelle," Granny whispered to her while hugging her tightly to her breast. She kissed her on the head.

***

Feeling the warmth and the love, the miracle in Annabelle's belly sent waves out into the universe for the first time. And at that very second, all pilots flying their planes in the air saw a momentary flicker of the lights and felt a quick stutter in the engines as the compasses turned wild before settling back into normal function. And every passenger on each one of those thousands of planes sat up and took notice, if only for a second.

A few weeks later, George woke before Annabelle and took his tea out to the morning darkness to find the moonlight sparkling off the pristine blanket of the season's first snow.

Must be at least a foot. He smiled at the beauty and let his warm breath cloud the air.

Despite George's cautionary warning that maybe Annabelle should take things a little easier than normal now that she was pregnant, she insisted on continuing her morning routine, though she did agree to make adjustments as her body changed. So before she stirred from bed, George grabbed the shovel from beside the door and began blazing first trails through the snow, the first leading to her spot of worship and then another shorter path to Granny and Cappy's.

Ecstatic about becoming a new father, George was overprotective and madly in love. His mind was constantly clouded with thoughts of Annabelle and how he couldn't believe it possible for her to get anymore beautiful—but she did, as every day she grew into motherhood, always smiling and radiating with a warm, angelic glow. Like a bee to a flower, his passion for her only grew, unable to resist her to the point where he feared he was smothering.

As the days grew shorter, the chores and celebrations grew fewer. He and Annabelle spent a lot of time staying warm inside their hut. It gave him more time to dedicate to his work, and to pampering Mommy. It was the happiest winter George had ever spent, with pleasant thought of future winters to come with his little family.

By the time winter solstice had passed, Annabelle's tummy had grown big and she loved it. Every evening she would rest in bed, smiling and stroking her tummy while she watched Daddy work on his numbers in the flickering warm light of the wood stove.

One night she snuck up behind him as he sat in his chair, giving him a bit of a start when she placed her hands gently on his shoulders and began to rub. She bent over her tummy and laid a tender kiss on his neck. "What are you doing, Daddy?" She grinned at him upside down as he tilted his head up to her. "What is all this… stuff?" She walked over to the chalkboard covered in mathematical riddles. "How does any of this work?"

He took off his glasses and rubbed at his eyes, then looked back at her silhouette in the flickering orange glow as she gently caressed her stomach. "Well, it's a bit complicated, honestly. Right now I'm replicating a formula that I figured out several years ago. I presented it to my superior, and he said took it up higher but then I never heard anything about it again."

"What was it?" She paced slowly in front of the board, looking curiously at every numeral and symbol. "What did it do?"

"Well, it was the proof that we could manipulate matter with our minds, like our emotions and thoughts and, I guess, our will."

"So, all of this is proof that we can manipulate matter? Change things with our will?"

"Well, it's mathematical proof, and it actually can be measured to some extent. They've actually measured the mass of thoughts."

"Mass? They've measured the mass… of our thoughts?"

"Yes, the mass. So, then, if something has mass, even if it's microscopic, it has the ability to make changes. We've known for years now that everything in the universe is made up of the same matter. You, the desk, a tree, even a rock—all the same. So, to take it to a deeper level, there's a theory that everything in life can be manipulated by will. And everything in the universe exists in its current form simply because that's the way we know it to be. We're taught that the sky is blue, so it is, and the grass is green, the earth is round, and so on… talk on phones, drive with cars. But, because everything consists of the same matter, we should be able to manipulate things by will. To put it simply, if you wanted to walk through that wall, by these laws, there's no reason you can't. If you wanted to walk on water, or even if you wanted to walk on air, or communicate telepathically across the universe, by everything we know, you should be able to do it."

He watched her reach her hand up to the board, slowly and softly, her eyes reflecting the dancing firelight. Her finger lightly traced the surface along the edge of one of the symbols, then she lifted it and rubbed the chalk dust gently between her fingers as if she'd never known it before, releasing a cloud of small particles into the flickering light. "So… why can't we?"

"Why can't we what?"

"Why can't I press my finger through this board? Why can't I change the world with my will?"

"Well"—he leaned back in his chair and cupped his hands behind his head—"according to our experiments, you can't just explain it to someone and then it works. It's a lot like the struggles people have with spirituality, honestly. Everything says that you can do it. But you weren't raised to know it to work that way, and so it doesn't. You can't."

He leaned forward and rested his elbows on his knees as he looked at her. "It has to be more than just belief. It has to be known, right to your core. You can't believe it to be, you have to know it. So, you would need to literally erase someone's mind completely, and then somehow train them that the world works in this other way, which wouldn't be easy. But with all the new tech, some of us think it could be done. But erasing someone's mind? I mean, the human rights issues, *pfft*." He waved it off as he leaned back. "Don't even get me started."

His eyebrows drew together. "The higher-ups I worked for—it's kind of a weird situation. It's as if they want to know, but they don't. Like, remember how I said I'd figured it all out mathematically and passed it to them, but it just somehow was forgotten? It's as though they want to know that it's possible, but they don't want any of it physically proven. None of us can figure out why. Damn politics."

He snuffed.

The days grew longer and the sun gained strength. Stepping out of the hut in the morning, George was greeted with rays of warmth on his skin and the smell of melting snow and life reviving from beneath. Spring was heavy in the air: time for new beginnings. Their new beginning would be opening its eyes to the world in the coming months. The closer the due date came, the more something was eating at him. Though George knew it wasn't the way of the world in Beelieve, it was the way of his world.

He told himself repeatedly that he was stupid for being nervous. She was having his child, after all. Although he had never carved anything before, on a few of their journeys to town, he had picked up a couple key tools to carve her what he felt to be a pretty spectacular wooden ring. He admired it as he rolled it around in his hand.

He had been struggling to map out the appropriate place and time, but time was running short. He knew she loved him, but there were certain things in civilization she was dead set against, and they had never discussed marriage before.

That evening he paced the floor as she lay in bed, reading to baby.

"Really, George," she said and looked over, "I can't understand what's gotten into you. Your restlessness is almost unbearable. Oh!" She startled. "George, come, the baby's kicking." She rolled her legs off the side of the bed as George raced to her.

He knelt beside her and placed a hand on her tummy, then jumped with excitement. "There! I felt it! Oh, it's so incredible, Annabelle." He rubbed his hand over her belly some more, then leaned down and kissed their child. "Daddy's waiting here for you, baby."

George felt her loving hand on his head, combing through his hair. He looked up to her, and, at that moment, decided it was time. He clasped her hand and drew it toward him as he reached in his pocket and pulled out the ring. "A-Annabelle…" He looked up to see her jaw slacken as she raised a hand to her lips. Her expression was so hard for him to read, but he was sure he had crossed the line.

"I… I know it's not the way things are done here. I mean, we don't have to do anything in court or anything, just some ritual up here, but I really…" He exhaled and sucked in some courage, then looked her in the eye. "Annabelle, will you marry me? Please say—"

Tears burst from her eyes and she pulled him to her. "Yes, George… Yes!" she squealed. "I will marry you, George Stanley, a thousand times, yes!"

He stood and wrapped his arms around her, then they fell back into the bed and rolled around kissing with baby smooshed in between, kicking happily.

They announced the wedding to the others, who shared in their excitement and joined Annabelle in putting together plans for the ceremony. It would take place there in Beelieve as soon as the snow cleared, and Granny would marry them.

***

Spring was in full bloom, with the bees busy at work to bring all the colours alive in the village for another season.

The day was warm and the vegetation lush. The scene couldn't be anymore picturesque, with Annabelle in a beautiful white dress specially tailored by Stella to fit her round belly and a freshly weaved wreath of flowers for her head. The ladies all wore matching dresses and stood with Granny at a beautifully decorated altar. Cappy led the bride down the path to a very nervous George, who was waiting with Munch standing in as best man in his very best magician wear.

Standing on the side next to a very handsomely dressed Dennis, Griz began to strum a love ballad on her guitar until George and Annabelle stood before each other, hand in hand.

George began his speech. "Annabelle…" He choked up, wiping quickly at a tear and sharing a nervous smile with his bride, who nodded encouragement.

"Annabelle, before we met I used to spend my days calculating possibilities. I look back over the almost a year that has passed, and I realize how quickly this all happened. So many believe that things happen for a reason, and I think there's no better example of a greater, all-universal power at work than you and I finding each other." He dropped his head and shook it with disbelief, then raised it and looked to her, then to everyone else. "I don't know why I came here—maybe a distant childhood memory?—but I knew I had to, there was urgency in my gut. And I had to do it in a certain way. I was so close to leaving and giving up until…" He looked into her eyes. "Until you found me."

Annabelle sputtered with happy tears.

"You saved me, Annabelle. My life has changed in every possible way a life could, and it's all for the better. I love Beelieve and I love our family!" Shouts of appreciation came from the small crowd. "And I love you, Annabelle. I love you with a love so complete, it will never be broken and I will gladly spend the rest of my life proving it."

"I love you, George Stanley!" Annabelle cried out.

They burst into each other's arms as Granny pronounced the union, and they sealed it with a kiss.

The celebration began, and people from all over the area came to congratulate them and give wishes of happiness and health for their marriage and soon-to-be family.

The hours flew by. As the afternoon grew late and the heat of the sun began to wear on some, George couldn't find Annabelle in the crowd. He took a walk around the village and up the hill, where he found Dennis standing on the path by the field of flowers, still dressed in his vest and bowtie.

George turned toward some movement in the flowers, and there his wife wandered. She was smiling so brilliantly, her arms wrapped tenderly around her belly.

He had his concerns, of course, for her and their child in a field so heavily bee infested, but how could he ever interrupt such a vision?

He smiled and placed a hand on Dennis, scratching behind his ears. Then he knelt beside him. "What d'ya think about all this fella, hmm? You know what's about to happen, don't ya? You're a good man, Dennis old buddy. You look after her well. I know we're gonna need your help once this all goes down. It's good to know you're there for us; you have no idea how nervous I am."

George and Dennis watched as Annabelle laughed and raised her head to the warmth of the sun, just like the millions of flowers surrounding her. Then she turned away from them and took one casual step after another, letting her hands drop from her belly and fingertips tickle the tips of the petals, causing a steady swarm of bees to rise into the air. Golden flecks swirled and undulated around her as she raised her arms to them, laughing and welcoming.

That night, George tended to some thoughts he had on the chalkboard as he waited for his love to return.

Annabelle walked through the door with an extra bounce to her step. "Okay, let's do it." She giggled as she made her way over and flopped out on the bed.

"Uhhh…" George looked curiously at her. "Do what, honey?"

"Like you said, let's train our child to… you know"—she waved sloppily toward the board—"manipulate matter."

"Uh, what now?"

She rolled on her side and looked at him as if he were a little slow. "You said that you would need a new mind, one that's never seen anything before, like a blank slate. Well, we can't erase anyone's mind, but our baby—it has a brand-new mind."

George paused everything, including breathing, while he dissected what his wife was suggesting. Visions of his newborn child being thrust into a lab experiment plagued him as much as the idea of his wife wanting such a thing.

"Well… honey, it's all just… I mean, it's just theory."

"Yes, I know, I was listening to you George. It's theory that needs to be proven. They wouldn't let you do it at your work, but I've been thinking about it ever since that night, and honestly, we have everything we need here to try this. Well, were still waiting for one." She smiled and rubbed her tummy.

"I…" George was dumbstruck, waiting for her to jump up and say *Gotcha!* or something, but as the seconds ticked by, he realized it wasn't coming. "I… are you serious? You want to use our child as some type of lab rat?!"

She chuckled. "George dear, we're not on the same page." She gave him a sweet smile, then propped some pillows up, leaned back and patted a spot on the bed beside her. "Come here."

He went over, though he was hesitant. He knew she would never do anything like drink alcohol or consume silly-weed while with baby… but he was beginning to wonder.

"Of course I don't want our child to be treated like a lab rat. I've actually put a lot of thought into this, and I think we can try it as an innocent experiment. And if it works, then wow! And if it doesn't, our child will be, well… well-educated."

George gave his head a tiny shake. "Okay, I'm listening."

She smiled and relaxed into her idea. "I think we have everything we need here to try and do this. You said that it has to be known, not a belief. And we have a chance to make some things look a certain way out here. Of course we can't change the colour of the sky or the shape of the earth, but we can create some illusions." She must have noticed that George was still leery because she went on. "Listen, you're like a super-genius with all this quantum theory stuff, and it works, right?"

"Well, yes, in theory."

"Right, so you'll teach baby from day one. His—*its*—very first day, you start to teach baby about all the quantum stuff, it's like subliminal… I've read about it, and it's supposed to really work. You could even make some recordings and stuff to play when baby sleeps and maybe get some video screens or something—we can make it work. So, then, we set up our place and as much of the village as possible with a little magic. You know, get everyone onboard. They would love it! Munch could use his magic knowhow, and Griz and Stella and the rest of us could help build everything and strategize how it'll all work. Like, having things magically float through the air by just moving our hand, and making it seem like we're communicating telepathically, and somehow get some walls made up that we can walk through—and whatever else anyone can think of. So, if nothing else, it'll be a lot of fun. And George, imagine if it works!"

George attempted a chuckle, but with having the idea just dropped on him so suddenly, he wasn't anywhere near the boarding ramp for this cruise.

Annabelle didn't let up. "George!" She looked at him seriously and then pointed to his blackboard. "You told me that all of this would be possible if you could have a clean slate, right?"

George stood, took his glasses off, and rubbed at the bridge of his nose as he walked slowly back to his scripture. Placing his glasses back, he crossed his arms and looked over his work while Annabelle continued.

"You believe it, don't you, George? Your work? It's what keeps you scribbling all that stuff all the time. If you don't believe in it, then why do you do it?"

As he listened, he heard her moving toward him. Then he felt her gentle, loving touch on his back and her hands slid up to massage his shoulders. Then she pulled herself closer, till he could feel their baby between them.

As the minutes ticked and he calmed down and absorbed everything she was suggesting, it still seemed crazy, but maybe it wasn't *so* crazy.

"Think about it, George. You put your whole life into this. Are you ever going to let it amount to something?" She hugged him closer. "I believe in you, and I believe in the work that you do. I love it. To have a breakthrough like the one you're talking about, it would be huge—for science and spirituality. It seems like both sides have hit this wall that no one can get over. Someone has to take the initiative. We have this chance, this opportunity to do this. Without having to violate anyone."

He sighed.

She turned him to face her, then placed her hands on either side of his cheeks. "It's harmless, George. It'll be like living in a circus—think about it. And on your end, you'll be educating our baby. They'll grow up to be a super-genius. No harm in that. There's no electric shock treatment, or genetic mutation. I'd never let that happen to our baby. I have no interest in harming our child in any way. But think… this is possible. You said it in your vows—you don't know why or how you ever ended up here, with me, and now we're married and we're going to have a child. I understand how incredible it is that we've found each other. Now it's time for you to put down your chalk and listen to me for a minute. Believe in this. Believe in us, George."

"Well… it does kind of sound like fun." He grinned.

She smiled sweetly, then plucked his glasses off and pulled him in for a kiss…

***

They lay in darkness under the covers, giggling and planning how to create their master illusion. The baby seemed to approve of the plan, kicking and squirming about in Mommy's tummy. There would be no time to waste as baby was due in a month's time, give or take.

As the three lay together in happy anticipation of when they could all be together, the love energized the molecules around them and that energy quickly passed to others, till small bolts pulsed through the air in the dead of night. One particle excited the next and the magnetism grew, right out to the atmosphere and into space, where it pulled and pulled all the way to the sun till it excited a massive solar flare that exploded and reached far out into space and down to earth with finger-like tentacles.

Granny stirred in her bed, suddenly unable to sleep. She got up and poured a cool cup of what was left in the teapot, then stepped outside to have a seat.

As she rested, she looked up to the sky and sighed.

Not long after, Cappy followed her out. He immediately looked at the sky, then fell into his usual seat, picked up his pipe, and lit it up. Taking a couple healthy puffs, he blew a thick cloud into the air. The night sky was ablaze with beautiful northern lights flickering across its entirety, every colour one could think of. The lights had never before been seen this far south of the pole with such intensity… maybe nowhere ever? Not like this…

"What do you make of it, Granny?"

"Ah, Cappy." She grinned. "I get the feeling something very big is coming to our little village. I get very good feelings about it… and not so good."

The next morning, George and Annabelle stepped out of the hut to greet Dennis, who was standing right at the door, as he always was now that Annabelle was growing close to her due date. The mule had become overly attentive to her, following her everywhere, which suited George just fine. The newlyweds found it interesting how in tune he was with Annabelle and their child. It was as if he could hear it kick because whenever any kind of movement started when he was around, he would step carefully over to Annabelle's belly and brush his nose against her.

Dennis escorted Annabelle down to Granny's while George went around the village, gathering the others for their latest announcement.

It took the drawing of a few pictures and the drinking of a couple stiff cups of coffee for some to get through George's explanation of the scientific side of the experiment. But when all was said and done, everyone was excited to participate.

Munch paced the room, stroking his long beard and shouting out ideas as they came to him. "Yes, yes… This will be my greatest creation!" He raised a triumphant finger in the air.

The rest of them all joined in, rattling off ideas and placing plans.

But in all the excitement, George noticed that Granny and Cappy were sitting calmly off to the side, Cappy patting Granny's hand as it lay softly in his lap. They were smiling, but they were modest smiles. They just seemed a little distant. George wasn't sure why he took such special notice of them. But then Annabelle tapped him on the shoulder, and the collaboration continued.

Work started that very day. They first went up to George and Annabelle's place and decided where the key places would be for the baby to eat and play and sleep in order for the illusions to work best. They made plans to gut the yurt and dig out a pit beneath it so they could install some secret passes. Secret doors and curtains would also be placed throughout the village, and Gwyn had some genius ideas for inside the greenhouse. Much would have to be done down at Cappy and Granny's as well.

Completing the mass village renovation in addition to all the spring chores took complete cooperation from everyone, working long days from the crack of dawn into the moonlight. George also had the duty of putting together some visual and audio material for when baby was sleeping and for daily teachings. He wrote all the material but got Mommy to do all the narration with her strong, hypnotic voice.

The time flew by. When the last prop was installed—almost as if the baby had been waiting patiently—Annabelle went into labour.

George was a controlled disaster. He ran around screaming and calling out nonsense to everyone while Granny calmly helped Annabelle into position.

The routine had been rehearsed several times, but nothing can properly prepare for a natural childbirth. Gwyn, Stella, and Griz were all there to help as George bounced around in the background, barely keeping himself together during all of Annabelle's screaming and pleading.

Then finally came the tiny voice of a newborn delivered to the world. Granny took the little one to clean and assess for health.

George rushed to his wife's side and ran his hand over her head. "It's done, sweetie, you're such an amazing woman." He kissed her forehead. "It's all over."

Annabelle failed to relax, continuing to huff and puff as she shook her head. "No, not over." She leaned her head back and let out another scream.

George turned to Granny, who at the same time turned to Annabelle. She left the baby with the others and hurried back.

Taking George's place as the new mother continued her laboured breathing, Granny looked Annabelle over, then pressed her hands against her tummy. A look of shock came to her face. "We're not done here yet, ladies!"

George watched as Gwyn broke from the others and rushed back to Granny's side. And they began again.

"Wha...? George began to feel queasy. "What, is she...?"

"There's another!" Granny announced, getting back into position. "I can't believe it, but it's twins."

"Oh, yeah…" A drunken smile laced George's face as he began to teeter. Then everything went black.

Alone for the first time as a complete family—an even more complete family than first thought—George could be found pacing the floor yet again while beautiful Annabelle rested peacefully in bed holding her two very healthy newborn twins: one boy and one girl.

Granny had been baffled by the arrival of the second child, especially because the two babies were of healthy weight and size. Annabelle had not grown large enough to suggest twins. After everything was settled, Granny had announced that she had to go lie down and ordered everyone to leave the family to rest.

"Quark!" George shouted.

Annabelle crinkled her nose with a smile for the baby boy. "No, George, not Quark."

George had been awarded the task of picking out a name for their boy. Annabelle already had one ready for the little girl: Asana. It was one of the steps toward enlightenment in the world of the yogi. And it also had the word *Ana* in it, to link mother and child.

"Magnet."

"No, George."

"O."

"Nope."

"Sphere."

"Not feeling it."

"Particle."

"You have to be a bit more creative."

"Hei-sen-berg…"

"Heisenberg?" Annabelle lifted her head and frowned at him. "You want to name our child Heisenberg?"

"You said to get more creative."

"Isn't that just someone's name? How is that more creative? Who's Heisenberg anyway?"

"He created the uncertainty principle."

"The what?"

"The uncertainty principle. It states that there is always a certain level of uncertainty with everything in the universe. I've also heard it referred to as the free-will principle."

That made Annabelle pause. "The free-will principle? Hmm, I like that."

George watched her in thought, pacing, then pausing, then pacing.

"Eisen!"

"Eisen?" George's face scrunched. "That's very… original, I guess." He tilted his head, then returned to his pacing while repeating the name.

"Yeah," she said and smiled. "Eisen, but we'll play with the pronunciation a bit, so like Ethan, except Eisen. What do you think?"

George paused, then continued pacing and repeating the name, hoping it would grow on him. It was definitely original. But so was everything else about them. He stopped and looked at her. "Well, okay, but then you have As-*ana*, right? A little reference to yourself? So, how about we play on words a bit and make it, Geeeoooreisen… berg?"

Annabelle pursed her lips, then gave her head a firm shake. "Nope, not that. Eisen, that's it."

She looked down at her little gurgling and chirping bundles in their blankets, taking turns rubbing the tip of her nose on each of theirs. "Little Asana and Eisen, to represent enlightenment and free will. Asana, Eisen, George and Annabelle— the Stanleys." She smiled at him.

George's eyes brightened, and he took a couple quick steps to fall into bed and snuggle into the pile.

With the names decided, Annabelle wasted no time implementing their plan. She fed the babies, then played with them on the bed till little eyes grew heavy. She placed them in the crib Griz had built for one baby, but as she had left room for growth, they both fit for now. Then she placed a small television screen above them, loaded with content on particles and equations, waves and planets. The accompanying two-hour-long audio recording repeated mantras about the workings of the universe from both a spiritual and scientific perspective.

The babies happily accepted the pacifiers Granny had supplied. Annabelle did not want anything store-bought for the children, but Granny had just smiled and said she would make this one exception at some point.

George and Annabelle stood silently off to the side and watched, and watched, and watched some more. The babies gazed at the screen and listened to the audio and didn't fuss a bit, for hours. When they finally closed their little eyes, Annabelle turned off the screen and left them to sleep with the audio. She and George returned to bed, exhausted, and the newborns slept through the night, though Annabelle got up to check on them every fifteen minutes.

The next morning, the magic began.

It took some habitual retraining for George and Annabelle to remember to do everything the new way. With strategically placed strings, cables, and magnets, things floated through the air or slid to them through quick, sleight-of-hand parlour tricks that Munch had taught them. There was even a wall erected in their yurt, dividing the sleeping and dressing room from the kitchen and eating area, for no other reason than to play a role in the illusion of people being able to pass through solid objects with the help of some clever screens and lighting.

Adults would be able to discover the tricks immediately, but they didn't need to convince adults, only the virgin, sponge-like minds of their children, who eagerly soaked up any information offered. And from the strategically placed crib, the world and how it worked seemed completely legit to ones who had no reason to question otherwise.

Annabelle got the children bundled warmly and had George take them down to her yoga knoll to watch as Mommy welcomed the sun. Then they returned to the yurt and got ready to meet everyone down at Granny's for brunch.

Everyone was waiting anxiously when they arrived, anticipating the announcement of the names.

Annabelle beamed when she finally introduced Asana and Eisen to their entire family. Everyone loved the names but seemed to care little when George began to explain the origin of Eisen. They all walked right past him to get their baby fix.

What a fun morning it was for everyone as they figured out how best to execute all the trickery built into Granny's place. It was very similar to George and Annabelle's, but on a bigger scale and a lot more hectic with everyone taking turns, waiting for the proper prop to accomplish what they needed. Several dishes were spilled and heads bumped, but it was also very interesting to see how much more efficient everyone had become by the time brunch was served.

After all were fed, everyone revealed some gifts that they had made together. The first was a safety seat for little baby to be buckled in securely. It had been ready months ago, but then a second baby came, so Stella, Griz, Gwyn, and Munch stayed up all night building another. Then they took the new family outside, where a very proud Uncle Dennis sat with his new rig: a now double-seated saddle set up for both babies—again, converted to fit two overnight. It strapped securely around the mule's belly and had two seating baskets for the babies, one behind the other. Annabelle was hesitant about using it at first, but both seats were stuffed full with soft blankets and Dennis was insistent with his nudging, so she set the twins in. The darlings gave a little smile, and Uncle Dennis stood tall and proud, and when he stepped it was with the utmost care.

For the trial run, George and Annabelle flanked either side of Dennis as they toured the magical village. The rest of the gang took off ahead to be ready for the show. Most of the props wouldn't be used this early in the children's life, but there was one special illusion where thin zip lines had been set up between buildings and special harnesses had been fabricated to fit seamlessly beneath clothes so people could appear to hover.

Of course it required someone hidden away in a building to pull on ropes attached to pulleys that were attached to more cables. And, with limited time for testing, there were still some kinks to be worked out. But out of all the tricks, this was the one Munch was most proud of.

As the children came around the corner, Munch sprang through the wall, very convincingly, dressed in his full magic attire, waving his wand and calling to the babies.

"Helllooooo, babies! Look at Uncle Munch… I, I mean"—his voice deepened and his expression changed to one of mystical wonderment—"the Great and Marvellous Marvin Munchousin the Sixth!"

Sensational was what Munch had been aiming for. Less than spectacular was a more accurate description.

One may picture levitation as a smooth glide. This was herky-jerky. Griz and Gwyn were stationed in the greenhouse where the lines ended. They had two sets of lines to pull: one that propelled Munch from his place, and the other to move Stella from her place. Due to the difference in weight, it would have made more sense for Gwyn to do the maiden flyover, but Munch's love for the theatrical made him insist he go first.

He jerked forward dramatically for a couple inches, then stopped, rolled back half the distance, then jerked forward again.

"Whoa! Haha." He continued to look at the twins as his smile grew more uncertain. He jerked again. "Oh, wow, yes… Look at me, little babies— whoa!" He lost his balance and twisted one way and the other, which grew worse as his arms began to flail for control. The next pull tilted his body parallel to the ground, and another quick tug turned him straight upside down.

But Munch never broke character. Even as he hung upside down, he simply brushed the cape from his face and continued to smile, waving his wand as he bumped and ground all the way up and through the wall into the greenhouse.

There was an extended pause and a couple shouts of inspiration before Stella exited the building. Her go went much more smoothly. But it still wasn't as convincing as they wanted it to be.

Everything else went as such. It turned out that none of it was easy. And after the full tour, there was a feeling in the crowd that maybe this would turn to a half-hearted effort and end up as nothing. And it wasn't hard for one to roll over to the side of the whole thing being ridiculous.

But it was Annabelle who continued to inspire. They had already gone through so much work, she said, and they wouldn't be doing it forever. There would come an age when the children would be able to see through the charades and then it would be time to accept it for what it was… charades.

But now was the time to try. She explained repeatedly how life could change if it worked. And in dire times, she recruited George to sit them down and explain the actual logic as best he could, in terms they could grasp. It turned out that it required as much work to convince their family as it would to convince the twins. But for the life of her, Annabelle would never let up.

As she drew them together, the illusions became more fluid and convincing with less effort. With one success equalling another, they found a knack, and expanded it further, till the little village of Beelieve became a truly magical wonder.

The one-year anniversary of George Stanley's disappearance had arrived. General Mathis had done what he could to bide his time and keep it from the attention of his superiors, but when George remained absent, the general had no other option but to come clean. And he was disciplined for his lack of judgment.

They had threatened to demote him. But due to his knowledge and relationship with George, they instead tasked him with finding George and bringing him back. But not before taking away his grand office and shoving him into a small closet in a forgotten corner of the tank.

The general wasted no time putting out every feeler he could to sniff a trail to George. But he continually came up empty-handed. The last paper transaction of any type was a sizable cash withdrawal from his personal account. But as interesting as the amount of the withdrawal was, there was still a much larger portion left in place, suggesting strongly that wherever George Stanley had run away to, he had intentions of returning. Or at least not completely disappearing. Yet that was exactly what appeared to have happened.

There was nothing: no plane tickets, hotel rooms, border crossings, truck-stop breakfasts… nothing.

He sat in his tipsy old office chair with the pleather peeling from its armrests and lifted a stale cup of coffee to his lips.

The top brass wanted weekly updates. But although the general had informed his people all over the world of the missing George, there was nothing he could do until George stepped back into civilization—nothing but sit in his chair, and stew. And if George Stanley was dead, the general would be stewing for the rest of his life.

But the minute George Stanley stepped a toe over that line, the general would be waiting.

A new day dawned, and when the babies' little blinking eyes opened, the world was alive with a family who could move anything at will. Objects and people floated everywhere. Things that seemed solid could be penetrated as if they were air. Their family even worked on appearing as if they were communicating telepathically. Father would close his eyes and smile at Mother, then Mother would laugh and smile back at him. At times she would pass him things that made absolutely no sense, and it became a comical game on more occasions than not.

The babies observed the world with their eyes when awake and listened to the science spoken by Mommy's spiritual voice as they slept. No exceptions. The children were always exposed to the teachings, one way or another.

It took Granny to point out how rare it was to see two babies sleep so soundly through the night.

As they grew and became more aware, so did the act grow. Now sitting upright and stable in their uncle Dennis's seats, they would walk with Mommy through the greenhouse and watch as she hovered her hand over the soil in the planters with eyes closed until, sure enough, little green sprouts would begin to stretch from the dirt.

And although there were no schemes to play in the fields of bees, Mommy would take the twins there to watch her dance among them and to show them the love and respect they had for each other.

As a scientist, George liked to measure results, so every week he and Annabelle would sit with the children and observe. But science experiments need to be carried out in a controlled environment so the results can be properly measured. To keep better track of how things were progressing, they would use George's camera to record them during the day, but with the batteries constantly having to be kept up and with the footage so uneventful, they found themselves neglecting it after some time.

The children began to crawl, then the transition to walking came. But nothing suggested that they were anywhere close to manipulating matter or transforming the universe. As the clock ticked on, the window in which the children could be so easily convinced grew smaller. With not even the slightest of results, Annabelle was struggling to keep the rest of the village engaged. But she made them all promise to give it their all till the twins turned one year old.

"Honey! Have you seen my glasses?"

Searching for missing things had become a common morning routine. George had worn glasses for the better part of his life, and as he was all but useless without them, he'd always had a system for keeping track of them. In the last few months, however, it seemed he was setting his glasses down in the strangest of spots, and always within reach of the children. He would have to hold back a curse word every time he finally located them and put them on, only to find them heavily smudged with tiny fingerprints.

"George, sweetie, have you seen my brush?"

Hairbrushes, utensils, glasses, toiletries—all misplaced and then located in places beyond the usual. Happenings that were out of the ordinary but went undocumented in the hustle of everyday life.

It wasn't until a little over a month from the one-year deadline that George and Annabelle finally clued in.

"George! Honestly! How could you be so careless?"

George wasn't careless. He was very organized and methodical. So when he ran into the room to see Annabelle holding his pipe, which she had found in the children's enclosed play area, his expression relayed his bafflement.

"I, I…" He scratched his head and then looked back at the high shelf where he usually kept the pipe for use in times of creative block. During his time in Beelieve, he had developed a fondness for silly-weed. He found it had a positive effect on his studies, helping him see outside the box. Although he had never used it around the children, it was possible they had watched him pack it on occasion, from their play area.

"Let me see that." He stepped toward her as she passed it to him, her arms crossing beneath a disapproving look.

He turned it around slowly in his fingers, and sure enough, there were little smudged fingerprints on it. He looked back to its shelf, then to the twins, then back to the shelf. Cappy had carved it from a special hardwood. It was curvy and held a sheen in the light. Something that would surely draw the curiosity of children.

He cradled it in both hands, holding it between himself and Annabelle. "I would never do this. You know me. I would never do this. Nor would I ever leave my glasses within the children's reach. I need those glasses." A light bulb went off in his head and he lowered the pipe and looked at her. He could see thought in her eyes, till she reached his same conclusion.

Wide-eyed, they both turned instantly to the twins.

They took a seat on either side of the play area and sat silently, watching and recalling recent events of missing or misplaced items. So many strange occurrences, they realized, before they finally stopped long enough to put it all together. There was only one conclusion.

"Th-they're doing it," Annabelle gasped.

George stroked at his beard. "I really don't see any other explanation. There's too much evidence. Overwhelming, really."

Their eyes connected, and slowly, as they both let the reality seep in, a smile curled on their lips.

Annabelle righted in her chair and clapped her hands in front of her. "Okay… Okay, so… what? How do we do it? How do we do the proving thing?" Her eyes were trained on the children as she bit her bottom lip.

George sat in concentration, almost pulling his whiskers out by the roots. "Well, I guess what we do is take all the things that we think they've been… attracting?... how ever they're doing it. I mean, I don't know if they're levitating it across the room. I can't believe that we haven't caught it yet, if that's how they're doing it. But, I mean, that's what they've been seeing, so." He raised his hands to the side and looked at her. "We have to take all that stuff out of here. Then we both have to witness it and record it and then… see what happens, I guess."

They nodded to each other and then got to work taking every odd item from the children's fenced-in play area and putting it elsewhere in the yurt.

"Keep it within their eyesight!" George said. "I think maybe they'll have to be able to see it?"

George and Annabelle took the first round of objects away, and waited. The two toddlers continued about their business, looking to Mommy and Daddy as if questioning their well-being. Eisen was walking around the perimeter of the play space, using what he could to balance himself, while Asana sat in the middle playing with some wooden shapes Griz had made for them.

The parents waited and waited, then they went in and took another round of items. They waited again and then took more, until the twins had nothing but quizzical looks.

George and Annabelle sat down close together and hunched over the children with looks of anticipation.

"C'mon, Asana, Eisen, don't you want your blocks? Huh?" Annabelle turned and pointed to them, sitting on the table.

Getting no reaction, she walked around the room, holding up or pointing to different items. "Look, Asana, Mommy's hairbrush, hmm?" She passed it through her hair a couple times. "Brush your hair just like Mommy." With no immediate reaction, she moved on. "Oh, look, Mommy's beaded necklace, you love this." She held it up and danced it around. "So shiny and pretty."

She continued through the room, item to item, while George remained in his seat, intensely focused on both children. As each temptation drew no response, Annabelle's tone grew tired and her enthusiasm lagged. She looked up at the high shelf. "What about Daddy's pipe, huh? You want that?"

George turned to her and frowned at her last-ditch effort, then turned back to see Asana tapping the floor with one of the wooden shapes.

"H-honey!" he whispered, barely able to speak. He waved and pointed frantically.

Annabelle looked to the table where they had set the blocks, then back to the children. She stepped quietly and carefully back to her chair, not wanting to disturb their momentum.

"How?" She sat down slowly, never flinching her eyes from the twins. "How did she?… I didn't see a thing."

"No, I didn't see anything either. I, I don't know."

"Good girl, Asana," Annabelle said encouragingly.

Then a flash of colour drew their attention to Annabelle's necklace, now hanging from Eisen's hand.

"Huh!" Annabelle's hands shot to her mouth and elated tears pooled in her eyes as she looked to her husband. "They… they're doing it," she whispered. "Oh my god, George, they're doing it!" She shuddered and the tears began to run.

George smiled, and they embraced. Then they turned their attention back to the children, who had by then acquired a couple more items.

"But how, George?"

"I don't know. It may be some sort of—"

Then they caught it. Asana raised her little hand, only for the most split of seconds, and Mommy's hairbrush seemed to magically appear in her little hand. Then she immediately dropped it.

They both looked back to the counter where the brush previously sat, then slowly back to the children.

"Are they teleporting them?"

George took a slow, concentrated breath. Then he let it go. He shook his head softly. "No, I don't think so. They have to be acting in the way that they've been taught, so they should somehow be levitating or drawing them, physically, toward them. Just like we've been mimicking." He got up and walked around the room, watching both the children and the items. He decided that because the table of blocks had the most items, he would focus his attention there, and that's when he caught it.

"There!" His finger shot across the room. "I caught it! I, I think." Then it happened again. "There! Yes, yes, there it went. It's really, really fast. Which makes sense." He began to pace the room with a smile of revelation. "We have to stop thinking in terms of, like, a sci-fi movie. They know they can get it, they know how to get it, so they just get it. There's no need to have it hover through the air slowly, like some demonstration, so it's fast! They want it…" Another block shot from the table. "They got it."

Annabelle looked at the twins. "They want it… they got it. They want it, they got it. They got it!" She turned to George. "They got it!" Ecstatic, she waved her hands high over her head. "They got it, George! My goodness, they got it! We did it! We did it!" She ran across the room and jumped into his arms.

"We have to go and tell everyone!" Annabelle shouted.

George held his hands up, signalling for calm. "Yeah, uh, wait."

"What? What, George? We did it! We did it!" She bounced excitedly.

"Yeah, we did it." He looked back to the children.

"What is it? We have to tell the others; we have to share it with them. All the hard work they put in—this needs to be shared, and celebrated."

George eased himself back into the chair, his eyes trained on the twins the whole way down. "We need to stop for a minute, honey. I think we need to let this all sink in first. This is bigger than you realize. Bigger than either of us realize. This opens so many doors… for… everyone."

"Yes, George, dear! It's incredible! I don't understand…"

"Neither do I, honestly." He turned to her with a stern look. "This is a big deal. This isn't something we should be taking lightly, Annabelle. These are our children. I think we need to understand the weight of all this, now that it…" He sighed heavily, his face in his hands. "I can't believe it. I just really can't believe we're sitting here right now, actually facing this." He held his hands out to the side. It was amazing. He knew it was nothing short of a modern-day miracle. But as the reality sank in, he realized how great of a power they had just unleashed. The children—their children—had learned to manipulate matter. And with the seal broken, flying objects across the room was only the beginning. He thought about everything they'd been teaching them, and he shook his head slowly.

Annabelle placed her hands gently on his shoulders. "George, dear, I don't understand. What's wrong?" She cupped his cheeks and turned his face to hers, looking caringly into his eyes. "Sweetie, we did it."

He grabbed her hands and stood slowly, maintaining eye contact. He wiped at a stray tear on her cheek. "Yes, we did it. Annabelle, this power—it might all seem innocent right now. But to my knowledge, this has never been done before, and there will be many people—many organizations—that'll be very interested in getting their hands on this. On *them*." They both turned to little Asana and Eisen, who were blinking up at them innocently with their Mommy's beautiful jade eyes. Asana lifted Daddy's chalk brush to her light-brown hair and began to stroke.

"Asana, no." Annabelle jumped the little wooden trellis fence that enclosed the play area and snatched the brush from Asana, who now had what looked like icing sugar dusted through her precious curls. "Silly little princess." Annabelle touched her finger to her little girl's nose, which lit her chubby cheeks with the cutest little smile. "How did you get… Oh, never mind."

Annabelle giggled and returned to George.

"Okay, sweetie," he said, "we'll share this with the others. With all their hard work, they deserve to celebrate with us. But beyond that, no one can know about this." He squeezed her hands. "We have to keep this a secret from everyone outside this village."

"But, George, I— We did it! We did this to change the world."

"I know, I know, and I still want to change the world. I want to show this to the world, but I think it's best to give it some time. Maybe until the twins are adults. By then, their skills will be a hundred times what they are now, and we'll have that much more to show. But I think if we show this too soon, we'll risk losing our children. I love you, and I love our babies. We have to keep them safe. Please." He stared at her, waiting.

Annabelle chewed on her lip and looked at the children, then back to George. "Okay. Okay, sweetie, I understand."

They smiled and embraced.

"I promise we'll show the world one day. But for now, it's about keeping them safe. I think till they're old enough to fend for themselves."

Annabelle nodded, then slipped him a tender kiss. "Now?" She clapped her hands and bounced on her toes with a pleading look.

George smiled. "Haha, yes, dear, show the rest of them."

He watched the twins closely while she ran to gather the others. He chuckled at their cute, pudgy faces that seemed to be asking what the big deal was. Now that they had the knack of moving objects around, he started to wonder what kind of trouble they would find next.

It was only a few moments before Annabelle returned and all their friends began to file in, one after the other.

Anxious, Annabelle looked at the children. "Uh, okay, help me George."

Once again the twins sat in the play area, empty of any toys. They looked to all the people—Granny, Cappy, Griz, Stella, Gwyn, and Uncle Munch—leaning over the fence, making goo-goo faces at them, unsure why Annabelle had gathered them together to watch the babies.

"Well"—Stella shrugged and looked to the others—"the babies look absolutely adorable, just as always."

"No, wait!" Annabelle held up her hands to everyone to ask for their patience. "Just wait."

Eisen held his tiny hand toward Uncle Munch and made a squeak.

"Oh!" Munch looked boastfully at the rest, then back at Eisen. "Yes, little Eisen, what a fine young man you are growing into. You like your uncle Munch? Is he your favourite?" His voice grew more childish as he stood and leaned over the fence toward Eisen, making silly faces. "Yes? Yes, you like Uncle Munch, little Eisen, you'll be a great magician some—"

Whack!

"Ohhhhhhh!" Munch wailed as he fell over the fence and onto the floor, along with one of the children's blocks from the table.

Munch sat up, flipping his cape back from over his head. He glared at the others with a snarl. "Who did that?!"

Everyone looked to each other and then to the block, which had made a hard impact into the Great and Marvellous Marvin Munchousin's derriere, sending him screaming and falling over the fence.

"Munch! Munch!" Annabelle waved at him to get out of the way.

Looking confused and annoyed, he scooched aside just as he felt a breeze across the tip of his nose, and a hairbrush magically appeared in Asana's hand, right before the eyes of all watching.

The room held its breath.

Gwyn took a step forward, then raised one of her crossed arms, twirling a finger. "She…" She looked back at the table where she had watched Annabelle place the brush after everyone walked in the door. "H-how? That—"

Another block flew to Eisen, and then Mommy's necklace, and then Asana reached toward Stella. Everyone watched in shock as Stella's beaded necklace rose in the air and pulled against the back of her neck.

"Oh, oh my." Stella resisted, but she was forced to take a step closer as Asana grabbed onto the fence and pulled herself to a stand, reaching more insistently toward her.

"No. No, Asana." Annabelle stepped past the onlookers to grab hold of her daughter's hand and break her focus. "It's not nice to take other people's things."

Asana looked at her mother as if she had no care for the rules.

Annabelle bounced her daughter gently in her arms and watched everyone as it all settled in. Munch sat on the ground, rubbing his butt in confusion.

Granny broke the silence. "We did it."

Annabelle nodded from the play area, looking to everyone as tears began to flow again. She smiled. "Yes, we did, all of us. We all did it."

Stella huffed as she to began to shed tears, her hand held to her breast. "This is going to change—"

"It's going to change the world," George interrupted, stepping out from the background. He clasped his hands before him and looked at everyone with sincerity. "I can't say thank you enough to all of you. And I can't say enough what an incredible, just amazing accomplishment this is. Each and every single one of you contributed to this, fully. Without all of you here, without all of your support, this never would've happened. Now, we have this power, and with power comes responsibility." He paused as he noticed Granny taking an extra-special interest in his speech. "Celebrate, everyone, please—we've all earned it. But Annabelle and I have had a serious conversation, and we feel strongly that for the time being, until the twins are considerably older, we need to keep this a secret. Only the ones in this room can know of this, for now. None of the traders passing through, none of the people in town, even ones you consider your best friends cannot know, not now. I promise there will be a proper time to release this miracle onto the world, but it's not right now. I feel very strongly that what we have seen today is only a small glimpse into what will come. These children have learned to manipulate matter; the only thing that limits them now is their own imagination. Soon, we won't be able to fool them with our tricks, and they'll be on their own to grow and develop. So, watch and enjoy. These children are going to teach us what life will be someday in the future. I'm very excited, and so should we all be. Thank you again, to all of our family." He smiled and stepped aside as everyone cheered and rushed to the twins.

George returned his eye back to Granny in the corner, who, he could feel, shared his concern.

She saw she had his attention and nodded toward the door, and then they both made their way outside while everyone was distracted.

"So," she said with a grin, "we did it."

George nodded back, but he didn't get the feeling this was about celebration. "We did it."

"Now what? How do you see this all unfolding?" She sat down in the loveseat and patted the spot next to her.

George sat down and rubbed his face in his hands. "I don't know, Granny. I can't believe we did it. It seemed like such a long shot. We did the impossible, really."

"Yes, the impossible. So now what, George? What have we opened?"

He nodded. "The twins have to be kept safe. I really haven't put much thought into it as… who in the hell would?" He sighed again. "I guess they have to remain here, especially at this young age when they can't be reasoned with. If they go into town and start pulling things from across the street, the gig will be up."

"And what happens when or if they find out? I say *they*, as in the type of people you used to work for. You're putting a lot of stress on keeping the children safe. You think they'll want to take the twins for experiments? Take them away from us and try to learn what they can do?"

"Well…" George leaned over and rubbed his hands nervously. "The children don't see life the way we do. They have the skills to transform anything into what they want it to be. It really is just a matter of them learning and strengthening. They could live in a world where they need nothing—no phone, power, transportation, heat, house, or even money. It would change everything. All life as we know it. It would eliminate the need for economy, materials… everything. Now, I'm less concerned about someone wanting to take the children for research and to try to learn their skills. I'm more worried about them wanting to…" He placed his face in his hands with another heavy sigh that bordered on a sob. A tremble coursed through his body.

Granny placed a hand to his back. "Shhh, George. I know, it was also my fear when we started this." She tucked a finger under his chin and lifted his face to look at her. "This thing that we've done here, it needs to be done, George. No matter what, this needs to happen. Who else in this world could have made this possible but you and Annabelle? Be strong—for you, for your wife, and for your children. We're all in this together, and we'll be beside you no matter what happens." She cupped his cheeks. "This has to happen George. Don't stop for anything. The world needs this change. You can't let your concern for safety hold this back. Promise me!"

Tears of an uncertain future streamed down George's face as he looked into her eyes. Her insistence made him feel that she knew more than she was letting on. George nodded, and she pulled him to her.

The toddler stage can be one of the most challenging, with baby walking around on its own, grabbing at this and pulling at that. Everything of concern must have its place and be in that place, away from the child's reach.

Now, make that toddler a set of twins with the ability to transport items from anywhere within sight. That was a trick George and Annabelle learned quickly: out of sight, out of mind. But even then, keeping an eye on them was exhausting. They could not be left alone, even for a second.

For the most part, they could leave the children saddled up in their Uncle Dennis seats during chore time. But that too could be tricky, as Uncle Dennis was equally as mischievous as the twins. He liked to meander through the village when Mom and Dad weren't looking, and as he did, the children grabbed at things. They loved anything shiny: glasses, jewellery, glossy cups. Anything hot had to be kept out of sight, village wide.

It was a fun tug of war at first. As the villagers went about their daily business and felt the gentle pull on a necklace or tea mug, they would smile and look around for the twins, then say, *"No-no, little one."*

But as Asana and Eisen grew, so did their strength. One day Munch got caught outside in a flashy cape with his back turned to the children, and he ended up being choked as he was drug halfway across the yard. After that, everyone looked both ways before leaving their dwellings and refrained from wearing or carrying anything attractive to the twins.

Despite the challenges, the village continued in their charade: passing through walls, communicating telepathically, growing vegetables overnight. But they put less effort into the moving of objects, feeling the twins had that skill down pat.

By the time summer arrived, the children's skills had expanded.

It was the middle of the night when George stirred from slumber for no reason other than he had become an extra-light sleeper since the children's first breakthrough. He wiped at his eyes and then put on his glasses—and found both twins to be missing from their beds in the play area.

"Annabelle!" He reached over and shook his wife. "The twins, they're gone!"

They sprang from bed and searched the entire place, only to find nothing. They checked the latch on the door and found it secure, but they knew better than to trust their common sense when it came to their children.

The fresh night air was welcoming to the skin. Night sounds beneath the bright moonlight set a peaceful scene.

Tiny giggles made the parents snap their heads in the direction of Granny and Cappy's. Annabelle gasped when she saw them, but, thankfully, Uncle Dennis was right beside them, keeping them herded together, like his little sheep.

The scene was transfixing. Light shimmered off the valley lake, glistened from the leaves of the lush forest, and glowed from pudgy cheeks as the twins giggled and explored in the wonderful night.

After a brief pause, George and Annabelle continued down the path toward the children.

Mommy whispered a scolding. "Asana! Eisen! How did you two get out of the house?"

"*Good* man, Uncle Dennis." George picked up Eisen, then gave their furry security guard a well-deserved scratch. "You have no idea how thankful we are, big guy. I'll be getting you some special treats in the morning."

With Asana in Annabelle's arms, the two parents looked at the children, then at each other.

"Well, you thinking what I'm thinking?" Annabelle asked and sighed, looking back to their home.

"Yeah, well, we knew it was only a matter of time."

"Right." She yawned as they made their way back. "So, you want to take the first shift?"

"Yeah, sure, sweetie." He sidled up beside her and they slid their hands together and shared a kiss.

"How do we deal with this, George? How are we ever going to keep up with them?"

"*Buh*!" He raised his head and took a deep breath. "We're going to have to try to figure out a way to teach them, I guess? We really should've taught them speech before matter manipulation."

"Yeah, right. Well, we'll know better for next time." She looked at him with a sly grin.

He smiled back. Dropping her hand, he wrapped his arm around her and pulled her in for another kiss. "I guess we will."

They reached the yurt and Dennis assumed his position, standing guard out front. Inside, George and Annabelle tucked the happy tykes into bed with a shower of kisses. Then they plopped in their chairs, watching the children watching them. It was a battle between young adventurous souls, who only wanted to explore the whole world and didn't look in the slightest bit sleepy, versus the old, who wanted only sleepy—very, very muchy.

Mom's and Dad's eyes closed and their heads nodded them back awake. George patted Annabelle on the leg and told her to go to bed. He tried hard to stay up, but he nodded in and out of consciousness. He was never able to catch the twins in the act, and they never ventured back outside, but they did prove the fencing around the play area to be completely ineffective when Daddy woke to find smiling faces and little hands tapping his legs and petting his eyebrows.

George smiled. "Oh, my little troubles." He yawned and stretched, then picked them both up and set each on a knee. They giggled, and when they looked up to him, he could see a bit of sleep in their eyes. "What are we going to do with you two, hmm?" Their eyelids began to sag, and they rested against the warmth of his body, each one reaching a little hand up to scrunch Daddy's beard. "You have no idea how big a deal you are… to the whole world." Sleepy eyes grew heavier and he lifted them up gently and walked over to his and Annabelle's bed. He set them down softly and shooed them both over to snuggle in with Mom, who opened a heavy eye only long enough to see them coming and lift the blankets for them to snuggle in tight. Daddy followed right behind.

The next morning, Mommy loaded the children on Dennis and took them to watch her ritual, letting them down to wander about while she worked. They never wandered far and paid very close attention to their mom through the entirety of her routine.

Then they met the rest of the family for breakfast down at Granny's and told everyone the news. The reviews were… mixed. Of course everyone was excited for the progress, but there was also some anxiety.

Munch crouched down to look curiously at the twins, till Eisen tugged at one of the elastics in his beard. "So, they can walk through walls? Any walls?"

"Well," George answered, "we haven't actually witnessed it yet. But there is strong evidence that would suggest…"

Everyone in the room gave him the look that told him to drop the scientific mumbo-jumbo.

"Yes, they can walk through walls."

"Any walls? Do we know if there are any limits, say like lead?"

"Lead?" George raised an eyebrow. "As in, Superman can't see through lead? Maybe kryptonite?"

Munch took the cue to raise an eyebrow of his own. "Is this your attempt at humour?"

George smiled, dropped his head, and waved it off. "No, no everyone, I apologize. Until we start monitoring them with the video camera again, we have to assume there's no limits to what they can walk through. We also have to stop thinking of this as a superhero phenomenon. As fictional as this may seem, this is a skill, not a power. Remember that these children weren't born on another planet, or bitten by radioactive insects, or hit by lightning. This is a skill that they were taught, by all of us here. And just as they have learned, so can every other human on this planet. In fact, we here in Beelieve are that much closer to learning these skills ourselves because now we see it to be fact." He paced before them. "So, no—as of right now there is no limit, and I don't expect we'll find one."

Stella stood and glanced over at the twins, who were paying close attention to her. She clutched her necklace. "So, we could expect them to show up really anywhere, anytime?"

Gwyn jumped from her seat. "How do we control these children? How can we know where they are, and how can we keep them safe?"

George held up his hands as the others began to mumble. "We brought that up last night and we're going to get to work on a strategy right away. Really, it's only until they get old enough to understand…" He took a deep breath. "Well, understand everything else in life." He could see that his speech had failed to instill confidence. "I, I don't think it's going to be as big of an issue as you all fear. I mean, Dennis is really on top of things. Last night—"

"Dennis?!" Munch exclaimed. "Dennis the donkey? He's really on top of things?"

"I know, Munch, I know. I'm not saying to leave everything in Dennis's hands."

"Well I should hope not. Because he doesn't have any, does he?"

"All I'm saying is that Dennis doesn't move without those children. So, worst-case scenario, say Annabelle and I have fallen asleep and the twins get out. Dennis— Oh! What if we get a signal? Like a… a bell. A bell for his neck?"

The looks were skeptical.

"It's something, right? Something that would say, 'Here come the children.'"

"Or 'Here comes Dennis,'" Munch added sarcastically.

The discussion continued among everyone until they agreed on what measures to take to ensure the children's safety.

Dennis looked less than impressed with his new collar, but the clumsy cowbell Cappy dug out worked perfectly. Every time Dennis flinched, it rang a note. Which resulted in Dennis moving even less.

"Oh, Uncle Dennis." Annabelle couldn't help but chuckle as George loaded the twins up in their baskets. "It won't be forever. Just until they develop some responsibility. You're such a good sport. We wouldn't be able to do any of this without you." She fed him an apple.

Annabelle and George went to work setting up a daily tutorial session for the children, who were quick to grasp the societal boundaries of right and wrong.

During the day they were allowed to wander and play as long as they were within eyesight of Mom or Dad. On the rare occasion that they wandered too far, it was easy to locate them with Uncle Dennis and his bell always on their tail.

Their skills progressed naturally. It was strange at first for Mom and Dad to see their children passing through the fencing around the play area, but it eventually became commonplace for them to simply pass through doors rather than open them. Hide-and-seek had the odds stacked highly in the favour of the giggling, curly-haired twins.

As the summer passed, they became quite handy around the village, helping people hang things and even helping Griz erect some simple structures in half the time it would normally take.

Annabelle and George suspected that the children were communicating telepathically because they often observed one rushing to the other or passing something without a word spent. But proof of it would only come when the twins could actually talk.

They also began to wonder if the children were somehow able to communicate with animals. Every time they went outside and ventured anywhere near the edge of the woods or away from adults, forest creatures came to visit them. Deer, rabbits, squirrels, and birds would always flock around and had no qualms about eating from their hands when food was offered. And like Mommy, they could wander free around the bees, with never an issue. It became a concern when small predators ventured out from the shadows of the forest to come within a few feet of the children, putting Uncle Dennis on full defence. But the animals never gave indication that they ever meant harm. They seemed very curious about the twins and braved exposure that most animals would never risk in order to be in their presence. Sometimes one of the twins would hold a hand to them, but Dennis never let anything of possible threat come near.

Real evidence of some form of communication came when George and Annabelle were out working in the garden with the others while the children and Dennis wandered through the flower field. They were over the crest of the hill when an awful commotion came from Dennis, his bell banging and clanging alongside his harsh braying. Everyone shot to attention to catch a glimpse of Dennis's hind legs kicking in the air. Annabelle took off at a swift run, followed right behind by George.

As they came over the crest, they saw the heads of the twins poking through the flowers while Dennis swirled around them madly. Annabelle looked toward the treeline and the colour drained from her face.

An enormous grizzly.

"Baloo," she breathed.

She and George raced toward their children.

Baloo-the-Pooh was the local resident bear, who usually made a visit to Beelieve toward the end of the summer. The old male had developed a palate for the village silly-weed, and after eating his share he would raid some of the hives. He was never a bother to any of them past that, and so they just accepted it as a loss they would have to take for the greater good.

But Baloo was creeping very close despite Dennis's protests. The time was coming any second when a clash was going to happen, between someone.

"Baloo! No! Noooo!" Annabelle screamed from deep in her gut. "Don't you touch them! Don't you touch my babies!"

Life moved in slow motion, and Annabelle and George couldn't run fast enough.

Baloo took another step toward the children and Dennis cut right between them, braying and kicking madly at the massive hulk. The giant reared on his haunches and reached back with his brick of a paw. Just at that point, both Eisen and Asana took a couple purposeful steps toward the frothing Baloo-the-Pooh.

"No! Noooo!" Annabelle's shrill cry echoed through the valley.

The twins never flinched. They each held a palm up to the bear, and instantly, his body relaxed, as did Dennis's. A sudden peace fell on all—even George and Annabelle, somehow, felt everything was just fine. They stopped running.

They drew closer to each other and continued at a walk toward the children. They even found a loving smile for each other and joined hands. Uncle Dennis stood calmly beside the twins, and Baloo. Everything was just a little numb, as if it were cloaked in sedative. George and Annabelle watched as Baloo crept ever so close to the kids, with not a protest from anyone, and stretched his nose out to the tiny hands. He sniffed a few times, then huffed. George and Annabelle finally arrived, leaned down, and picked up their children. George hugged Dennis around his neck while Annabelle stepped right up to Baloo-the-Pooh and scratched him around the ears and cheeks, as if he were a big slobbering dog.

"Thank you, Baloo." She smiled dopily.

They packed the kids back in their saddles and waved goodbye to their bear friend as they made their way out of the flower field and back to the others, waiting at the edge.

As soon as they stepped out from the flowers, the numbness dissipated and they felt the tension emanating from the others. Reality seeped back as they turned to see Baloo foraging peacefully in the field.

George and Annabelle looked silently at each other.

"W-what happened?" Annabelle whispered.

George could see the event tumbling through her mind, as it was his. "I, I don't know." He held Eisen a little closer, a little tighter. "Something, though— did you feel that? Did you feel it?"

The audience waited, breathlessly hanging on every word.

"I felt so calm," Annabelle said, trying to put words to feelings. "Like, one moment I was screaming. I was so scared, George, in honest fear of the lives of our children. I thought for sure…"

"Yes, yes." Gwyn stepped toward her, taking her hand and holding it comfortingly with hers. "We could see it all from here. Both of you, and us— we were all hysterical, then everything changed very suddenly. When the twins stepped toward Baloo, that was the moment. And then you and Dennis and the bear—everyone looked like they had been hit with a… a…"

"It looked like they'd all just smoked a big batch of silly-weed," Griz blurted.

Everyone looked down the trail to see Granny and Cappy labouring their way up to join them.

George saw distress in Granny's eyes. "Is everyone all right?" She looked around to see everyone present and intact. "Jesus, Annabelle, we could hear your screaming all the way back at our place. Sounded like someone was—" She squinted at the flower patch, where Baloo was rummaging. "Baloo?..." He could see her doing the mental math. "Are the children all right? Is everyone all right?"

"Yes. Yes, Granny." Annabelle hugged Asana a little tighter and kissed her on the head. "The children are fine. It's a miracle, but they're fine."

They all made their way back to the village, recounting the entire event for Granny and Cappy. The twins carried on as if nothing out of the ordinary had happened, pulling and tugging on Mommy's hair and Daddy's beard.

Granny looked at everyone once she had all the facts. "Hmm, I see. So, this is the children's doing?"

George and Annabelle looked at each other, then nodded uncertainly.

"Yeah, I would say that it's the only explanation—that or the flowers are laced with something." George shrugged.

"How?" Granny continued. "How do the children know this? This isn't something we've taught them."

"No, you're right about that. We've had some suspicion that they've been communicating with each other lately, and possibly with the animals. But this was a lot more than just simple communication. This was something that hit everyone in the area."

"So how, then, George?"

He shook his head and lowered his gaze to the ground. "I don't know. I suspected there might come a time when the children would start to do new things on their own. I guess we're at that point. All I can say is that it was a very intense moment. I think the twins sensed that the bear was going to hurt Uncle Dennis. Maybe the children themselves likely don't understand what happened, or what they did. They just knew that they wanted it all to stop." He scratched his head. "*Pffft*, I have some deep thinking to do on all of this."

"I guess you do." Granny winked, then stepped up between him and Annabelle and smiled at the twins, pinching some chubby cheeks and poking at their tickly tummies for some giggles. "Quite the little charmers, aren't you?" She smiled. "I'm glad you're on our side."

When the Stanleys returned home that night, George went right to his workstation and cleared his chalkboard while Annabelle tucked sleepy children into their beds.

"I know that one could induce a feeling of, say, dopiness by changing the level of oxygen in the air, even if they could affect it by a couple tenths of a percentage point."

George caught a slight whimper from Annabelle and looked over to her. She was sitting in her chair beside the kids' beds, staring down at little blinking eyes. He rushed to her side and placed a hand on her shoulder, then squatted down to see that she was crying.

"Sweetie, what's wrong? It's okay, no one got hur—"

"They're so quiet, George… Aren't they? With everything else they've been doing, I never realized how quiet they are. I sit and think about it now, and they really don't even try to speak. Maybe a couple noises here and there. We should be celebrating their first words by now, like *Daddy*." She reached for his hand and squeezed it hard. "Or, or *Mommy*." The tears began to flow more heavily.

George drew her to him, holding her close to his chest. "Shhh, honey, everything's going to be fine. We'll work on it; we'll start working on speech first thing tomorrow."

"What have we done? Is this the right thing? I… I had no idea how big this was going to be." She sputtered onto his shoulder. "It's so big, and we're just beginning, aren't we?"

George held her back and looked her in the eyes. "Everything is going to be fine, Annabelle, I promise."

"It's all happening so fast. I feel like they're already slipping away. Like they don't even need me."

"Hey! Hey, sweetie, no, no… They need you so much. They need us both. Look at them." They both turned to the tiny, sleepy faces. "They're still just, babies, Annabelle. They're our babies and they need us."

She sobbed. "I feel like… like some sort of alien to them. They can't even talk to me. They can talk to each other, and all the animals, but they can't even say hi to me."

"Well, they're definitely not communicating with each other and the animals in English, honey. It's got to be something more along the line of communicating feelings, maybe more specifically than we can with words. It's really quite interesting."

She sputtered some more. "I don't know how you can be so calm about all of this!"

"Listen." He held her back again, looking into her eyes. "This is what you wanted, and now we're here—we actually did it. Now you have to be strong for them and teach them. Teach them everything you know and all that you respect about life. Annabelle, they got to this point because of you, because of us. They didn't get here on their own."

"Oh, George." She buried her face in his chest. "Did we do the right thing?"

It was a question he knew she would ask at some point, as he had been asking it to himself since the beginning. But he had trained himself over and over to answer it on a strict reflex, without even a hint of a pause.

"Yes, of course, sweetie."

The time to change direction had passed, so they had to stay confident and do the best they could with the path they had chosen. There was no undoing the done.

In the morning, George and Annabelle saddled the children onto Dennis and they all went down to welcome the sun. When they got to the spot, George took Asana and Eisen out of their baskets and set them on the ground as Mommy began her ritual. How those children worshipped their mother. They studied her beauty and, little by little, began to follow some of the more simple motions, raising arms high and bending down. So intent were they to follow Mommy that George was able to go meet with Granny for a cup of coffee.

As they sat and watched Annabelle and the twins, an intense sense of peace fell over everything and woodland creatures emerged from the forest and found a comfortable place to lay in the grass. Each closed their eyes and looked to the morning sun, feeding off its energy.

When the ceremony had finished, George got to work teaching the children everyday skills like talking—specifically, one very important phrase to a very special person.

***

A couple weeks had passed when Annabelle felt a tug on the blankets in the very early morning, then cracked her sleepy eyelids to two smaller sets of her own eyes looking back at her over precious smiles.

"Mama," Asana said.

Eisen followed immediately behind. "Mommy!"

They both giggled and clapped their hands, their chestnut curls bouncing with their jolliness.

"Oh! Oh, my babies!" She leaned over to scoop both twins up onto the bed. "Yes, yes! Oh, you make Mommy so happy!" She took turns chasing their jumping feet around the bed, tackling them and blowing on their squirming tummies as they laughed.

Then she lifted her head and looked toward the window, where George leaned against the counter. He lifted his steaming mug and smiled back with a wink.

The fact that communication was beginning to happen between mother and her children helped Annabelle get her feet planted emotionally again, and it rekindled her passion for what they had achieved.

***

Summer bath time in the ice-cold lake was always a challenge with the children. Once they were in, they tended to settle down and enjoy being sloshed around by Mom and Dad, but getting them to that point was all but impossible some days, especially with Princess Asana.

And now she had learned what seemed like her most favourite word to communicate to everyone: *No*.

"No, Mama!" She stood on shore in a pout with arms crossed tightly.

"Asaaaana." Annabelle splashed around not far offshore. "C'mon, little girl. The water's so nice."

"No!" Her little voice was stubbornly sweet.

"Asana," George called out with little Eisen floating in his hands, swishing around and giggling. "Look, sweetie, Eisen is having a lot of fun. Why don't you come in and—"

"No! No, Dada! Epen no! Epen is bad!" She marched down the shore a couple steps and picked up a pebble, then stomped to the edge of the water and threw it in their direction. She crossed her arms again.

"Asana!" Mommy scolded lightly. "That's not nice. Eisen is just having fun with Daddy. Why don't you come with Mom, huh?" Annabelle began to walk toward Asana with her arms out.

"Nononono! Noooooo!!!" Then came the screeching tantrums from the queen of *Nos*—tantrums so nasty they could bring an entire kingdom to their knees. And once she popped, there was no stop.

As was routine, Asana snapped, then Annabelle snapped and moved quickly toward Asana, which excited the fit even more.

But as Annabelle drew close, Asana suddenly stopped. Annabelle noticed her daughter's stare of disbelief into the water behind her. Then her mouth twitched and a smile appeared as she placed a finger between her lips and pointed with the other hand to the spot she was looking at. She giggled and said, "Epen, Mama, hehe."

Annabelle turned at the sound of splish-splashing feet as Eisen walked on top of the water right by her heading toward Asana, leaving George behind, slack-jawed, with both his hands frozen in place as if he were still holding his son.

Their gaze followed Eisen to the shore as he stopped just short of land and held his hand out to his sister. "Sana, come, Sana." He beckoned her with his little hand and stomped his little foot on the water.

Asana giggled again and took her brother's hand as she pressed one toe to the surface of water, then committed a little more weight, and then stepped both feet out. They turned back toward their parents and, hand in hand, walked right past them, out to the depths.

George and Annabelle never panicked. They looked over to each other with surprise that faded to loving smiles, and they swam to each other and embraced with a kiss. Then they turned to watch their two children, hand in hand, walking on water.

As the twins got out a little deeper, some fish began to jump beside them and they both bent and looked down with wonder, laughing and pointing and slapping at the surface.

***

A month later the village was buried in snow. And though the villagers had never labelled the holiday season as *Christmastime*, it was still full of merriment, gifts, and decoration. With a limited power supply, the lights had to be kept to a minimum, but with the children at an age to better appreciate the holiday, Granny had been trading goods with some contacts in town in order to gather a very large supply of Christmas lights.

"I don't imagine we'll have the power to run them all—maybe only for a moment—but gall-dangit, I'm gonna spoil me some grandchildren this year." She smiled as she tossed out bundle after bundle of lights from her shack.

The village erupted with cheer and everyone put in extra effort to give the children a special experience. And the twins were a big help in getting things set up while honing their skills. They lifted things to hang here and there, cutting the time required in half and doing it much more safely.

Then everyone went into the woods to find the perfect tree, with a harness set up on Dennis so he could tow it back to the village centre. George would have liked the children to levitate it back somehow, but he couldn't quite explain his wants to them. They did help pull it out of some rough terrain when Dennis struggled, and every time they helped with anything, they were celebrated and encouraged.

A wide path had been dug around the entire village, so they looped around the village and strung lights on either side of the path, stopping at every building along the way to dress it up. When everything was in place. Cappy, George, and Griz went to sort out the plugs in the shed.

"Well, I think it would look splendid—everyone put in so much work—but I don't see how we're ever going to get enough power to make them glow," Cappy frowned. "We've been socked in with cloud for weeks now. And half the time, the panels have been covered in snow."

George looked at his sullen face, then back to the village, where darkness had settled and moonlight glistened on the snow. Everyone stood with anticipation. He smiled at Cappy. "I have a feeling everything's going to be just fine, Cappy." George gave him a playful slap on the shoulder. "Have some faith, plug it in." He winked.

So Cappy did just that, and the lights burst bright in a holiday rainbow of colours.

Cappy looked out the shed door. "Well, I'll be damned."

Everyone stood stunned as the wonderland came to life. Then they clapped and cheered and hugged among the warm glow of the Christmas spirit.

They joined hands and walked the loop, admiring how everything had turned out. Cappy and George kept the impossibility of it all a secret between themselves, shared as a sly smile.

So it seemed that life in Beelieve would be a little warmer, a little more colourful, and just that much more wonderful within the glow of the children.

Winter melted to spring. Birthdays came and went with the seasons, and every year the children became stronger. They learned to power the village and help the flowers and crops grow. The bees began producing more, and their harvest had never been as splendid in all its history.

As the children grew more comfortable and confident with their skills, the villagers relied more and more on them to help get things done. The risk of one of the traders or someone else passing through witnessing some strange happenings increased. They'd often do a quick double take as they caught something hanging in mid-air that just shouldn't be, only to have it fall to the ground as they paused to watch, and then they would shake it off as a trick of the mind.

But rumours of the strange occurrences became widespread as the children grew older and Annabelle needed to make more trips to town due to the bountiful harvests.

"My dear, how nice to see you!" Mrs. Baumhauer said as Annabelle and Dennis pulled up to her shop. She set down the hose she was watering the flowers with and the two hugged.

"Isn't it a lovely summer day?" Annabelle asked.

"Yes, yes indeed." She looked toward Dennis. "Ah, and again no children with you? My goodness, they must be all grown up by now. Tell me, why don't you ever bring them to town to see me, huh?"

"Oh-ho! Well, yes, they've definitely grown, and they're both so full of energy, we just think they'd be too much of a handful for the trip right now. We're working with them to understand the manners of society, so hopefully not much longer. I'm as excited to show them off as you are to see them."

"Oh my, yes, Annabelle. I'm sure they're quite the little darlings. As beautiful as their mother, no doubt. And what with all the talk of them through town?"

"Oh…?" The comment gave Annabelle a curious pause. "Talk? What kind of talk of the children?"

"Oh, *pfft*." Mrs. Baumhauer waved her hand, then leaned in and lowered her voice. "Nothing, my dear, honestly. Just the mumblings of a small town starved for gossip."

Annabelle tried to hide her curiosity as she cleared her throat. "Silly gossip, yes. What kind of stories are we hearing?"

"Oh, nothing of credit. Just rumours travelling down from the hills with the transients, y'know, speaking of the twin children in the magical village. Mysterious happenings, floating objects, and talking to animals."

"Oh? Oh-hoho." Annabelle felt her jaw clench. "My, those are tall tales."

"Yes indeed."

The conversation paused, and there was a hint of tension in the air as the ladies busied themselves looking through Annabelle's wares.

Mrs. Baumhauer looked up. "But, you know, it doesn't help when Mr. Mulland keeps going off about the piles of produce you've been delivering. I think he's just jealous, is all. But having him go off about it to customers all the time only gives fuel to the fire."

"Mr. Mulland?" Annabelle looked to her friend, doing less to hide her concern. "He's having these conversations with his customers? The locals?"

"Oh yes, I'm afraid so." Mrs. Baumhauer pursed her lips, then reached over and gave Annabelle's shoulder a friendly rub. "Don't fret, my dear, it's just the ramblings of an old man. What with all the media on the fancy phones these days, the saying 'Give it five minutes to blow over' has never been more true."

Annabelle grinned. "Yes, I suppose."

***

George set down his paintbrush and watched from the loveseat as the children played with Munch. Munch had taken an interest in spending more time with the twins after George explained that those who spent more time with them had a better chance of learning some of their skills. All of humankind had the same ability as the children, their minds were just closed to it.

151

Munch had even made the twins flashy capes like his. Blue for Eisen and pink for Asana. And the three of them wore them as they chased one another around the village.

To keep his mind active while still giving him some much-needed time away from his theories and calculations, George had been getting some guitar lessons from Griz and had also taken up painting.

His work was very basic and he would never be the next DaVinci, but it was original to him. He loved the mixing of the colours and the feeling of brush on canvas. He loved letting his mind drift back to special memories and capturing them in such a personal way. His mind drifted back a couple days previous to when he and his family were walking through the flower field. The twins had a relationship with each other that was much deeper than anyone below their ability could grasp. They were children, but at times—watching them together, how they looked at each other—one could see a deeper intelligence. And the older the children grew, the more questions they had.

"Why can't you, Mama?" Asana had asked while holding on to one of each parent's arms and running and swinging between them. The higher she had gotten, the louder her giggles and the more her little curls bounced around her beautiful smiling eyes, while Eisen made the best of running and launching with Dad's other free arm.

Annabelle met George's grin with the same question.

"You and Dad. Why can't you do things like me and Eisen? Like move things, and walk through things, and— like we do, Mama?"

"I thought," Eisen had blurted between heavy breaths as he launched again, "I thought you and Daddy could do all of everything we do. That's how you teach us."

"Weeelll…" Annabelle took some time before digging in. "Yes, that is how we taught you. But, well, we kind of tricked you."

Asana stopped running. "A trick, Mama?"

Eisen stopped too. "Tricked us? So, you lied to us?" His voice was riddled with disappointment.

Annabelle shrugged her shoulders at George, who picked up the conversation. "Well, it wasn't really a lie. See, Mommy and Daddy knew the way things in the world really worked—at least, we had a pretty strong thesis."

"A wha-huh?" Eisen's face looked like he was calling Dad's bluff. "Tesick?"

George chuckled and picked up his boy. "Thesis—sorry, bud." He reached up and mussed his son's hair. "Dad and his big words, huh? A thesis is a science thing, like a plan. So, basically, Mommy and Daddy had proof that people could do all of the things that you kids can do. But we needed to raise you kids to really believe that you could do these things in order for you to be able to do them. So, we set up all of these... games, I guess, to help you know that you could do them. Aaand, now you can." He smiled at his boy and twirled a finger around in the air till it came to land on the tip of Eisen's nose.

"Mama, you lie to us!" Asana sweetly scolded her mother.

"Well"—Annabelle smiled at her little girl—"I don't really feel that it's a lie. Because how is it a lie if it's the truth?"

Both children jerked their heads and scrunched their faces at their mom.

"Really," she continued. "You two sillies can do all the things that we taught you. So how is it a lie?"

Pudgy cheeks scrunched even tighter, till they gave up.

"Mom is tricks us, Dad."

"Haha, yes, son. Don't ever try to fool your mom. She's a smarty-pants."

George snapped back to the present as he heard footsteps getting louder. He looked over to see Annabelle and Dennis marching toward him. His wife looked unsettled.

George sat up. "Honey?"

Annabelle stepped right up to him. "There's talk of the children in town."

He pushed his glasses up the bridge of his nose. "What? Talk of what? The children haven't been to town in years. What could they possibly be talking about?"

"The traders, the transients..." She waved to the hills. "Some of them have seen some things, I guess. Now there's rumours going around town about the children being magic, or having powers. Mr. Mulland's also suspicious of all the award-winning produce we've been growing."

"Okay, okay." He raised his hands to calm her down.

Annabelle plopped down beside him with a huff. "What do we do, George? We can't let this continue."

"No, no, you're right." He stroked his beard. "So, I guess we get the children disciplined up and then we start taking them to town."

"What?!" Annabelle glared at him.

"Well, yeah—we take them to town. We'll all go together."

She continued her disapproving stare.

"Listen, the best way to squash this is to let everyone see the children for themselves. See that they're nothing out of the ordinary and then the talk will die down." He gave her a hopeful smile. "Listen, I think it's time anyway. Of course the people in town are beginning to wonder. The children understand that they're different. I think we can have a good talk with them, and they'll be good. But don't panic. It's just word of mouth for now. We should be thankful none of the people up here carry cellphones." He chuckled.

They immediately went to work training the children up for their big return to town, making sure that they knew they were not to use any of their special skills while around anyone they didn't know.

Within a few days, George and Annabelle felt they were ready to chance it, believing it was necessary to get the children to town as soon as possible in order to halt the rumours before they got even more carried away. They went together as a complete family so they could maintain control and cover up any incidents that may need covering.

It was the first time the children had been to town in the time they could remember. They loved the trek through the woods, asking as many questions as if they were visiting a different planet, which for them wasn't far from the truth.

"What do they wear, Mama?" Asana asked.

"They wear clothes, silly."

"Like you clothes, Mama—you and Daddy?"

"Well, yes, kind of like me and Daddy, but a little different."

"What about all the buildings, Dad? You said there's so many big buildings that go waaaaaay up!" Eisen flopped his head back, looking into the sky.

"Haha, yes, son, there're a lot of buildings. I think you'll both be pretty excited to see everything. But the buildings aren't really that big here. In the big cities where lots of people live, there're buildings that go almost as high as the clouds."

"Whoa," the twins gasped together, looking to the sky.

"Big cities?" Asana asked. "How big? How many people live there?"

George shrugged. "Well, there's big cities all over the world, with millions of people living in them."

Eisen gave his father a doubtful look. "I don't know, Dad, that's a lot of people."

"How much farther, Mama?" Asana would persist in asking. And Eisen would follow that up with "How much longer, Dad?"—more and more so, the closer they sensed they were getting to town.

With the preparation for the trip to town focusing on "special skills," Mom and Dad had forgotten that many of the day-to-day living aspects of human life outside of Beelieve would be unfamiliar to the children. When the first vehicle drove by as they took their first steps into civilization, George and Annabelle immediately looked back at the children and had to stop for a healthy laugh at their expressions of disbelief. Their little eyes widened as they looked at all the brick, concrete, and asphalt, and at more people than they had ever seen before, who were strangely dressed and bustling this way and that in their daily life, most of them talking or typing away on handheld gadgets. For the Stanley children, Disneyland had nothing on this small mountain town.

The day was full of marvellous discoveries for the twins. Annabelle and George took them through town and introduced them to the everyday people. First up was Mr. Mulland, who was so excited to meet the children that he showered them with sweet treats and pinched chubby cheeks. Next up was Mrs. Baumhauer, who was quick to have her suspicions of witchery squashed when she saw how fascinated the children were with the running water from the bathroom faucets. The children spent most of their visit turning them on and off, hot to cold, and flushing the toilet repeatedly, until George put his foot down.

Annabelle always took the lead while George followed behind, watching the twins for any quick sleight of hand or even a focused look at anything shiny. The way that they did things had become second nature, and at times he could see they struggled with the urge. He imagined it was similar to taking away someone's vehicle or smartphone. There were only a handful of times when George felt he had to intervene with a harshly whispered, "*Tsst!*" or "Uh-uh!" before his children made an unconscious move.

Because they were twins in every sense of the word, and being as beautiful as they were with little brown curls bouncing and innocent eyes wide with excitement, there was no lack of attention from familiar acquaintances and passersby in town. They spent the better part of the day there to make sure as many of the regulars saw how not-magical the children were to convince them there was simply nothing out of the ordinary about them.

They even stopped for a couple ice cream cones. There were many laughs as the children went bonkers over them, and a bigger mess none had ever seen.

Many quick pictures were snapped of the loving family.

As the sun began to descend, the Stanley family walked to the edge of town and stepped back into the trees. Alone again in their realm, curious questions began. But the reaction wasn't what George and Annabelle had expected.

"How, Dad? How does the water come out of that… thing, Dad?" Eisen asked.

"Oh, you mean the faucet?"

"Yes, the faucet."

"Well, it's kind of complicated, really. They have to get a source of water."

"A what?"

"Source—so, like the lake. The lake is a source. Then they have to filter it and bring it up to drinking quality at a plant, then they use gravity or pumps to push the water to every faucet."

"Every faucet, Dad? Like the Ms. Bum lady?"

The parents shared a snicker.

"*Baumhauer*, buddy—but yes, like her faucet. Every building in town has at least one."

Eisen choked on his juice. "Wha… every house has faucets? All the buildings?"

"Yes, son."

"What are all the tappy things, Mama?" Asana asked.

"The tappy things?" Annabelle looked curiously back at her daughter.

Asana mimicked someone tapping on a smartphone.

"Oh, yes, those are phones—or *smartphones*, they now call them. They use them to communicate with… well, anyone from around the world. They can either type messages to each other or actually talk on them so they can hear each other's voices and have conversations. They can also get a lot of news and information."

Eisen scrunched his face at George. "How they do that, Dad?"

George went into a long, detailed description of how cellular service worked. Usually his in-depth explanations put people into a catatonic state, but both children hung on his every word.

The next question was about why everything was hard, referring to the sidewalks and streets, which cued George into an exhausting explanation of how vehicles and road systems worked. Then cars and trains and planes, the last of which he'd had to explain to the children every time they saw them flying over the village. The question-and-answer session took them all the way back home and into the evening, till it was tuck-in bedtime.

"I think it's all dumb!" Eisen blurted while bouncing on the bed.

"Eisen!" Annabelle scolded while trying to wrestle pyjamas onto him. "Where did you learn such a word?"

The interrogation drew an immediate look from Asana—clearly a strong warning that he had better not reveal the source.

"Uh… oh, I'm sorry, Mama. But it sounds dumb."

George found the comment interesting and sat down on the bed beside the children. "Why do you think this, Eisen?"

"'Cause, Dad. Why they do all this—get water from faucets, have all stuff underground, and roads? And tappy things, and statenlites, and things for talking?" His breath became huffy-puffy as he continued his bouncing around, while Asana sat calmly in her mama's lap, listening to the discussion.

"I can have water." Without even stalling in his jumping, Eisen turned to the washbasin and focused, and right before their eyes, the air in the basin began to bubble and froth, and the basin began filling with water.

George rushed to the bowl. When he looked back in shock, Eisen giggled.

The little boy turned to Asana. "Go, Sana, show them!"

Asana sat up in Mommy's lap and gave a sly smile before looking to the bowl, and within seconds, the air inside it began to steam, then bubble and boil.

Eisen laughed. Then he stopped jumping, gave a concentrated look at his father, and in the blink of an eye, he was gone.

"Eisen!" Annabelle gasped as a hand shot to her heart.

Asana giggled and reached for her mommy's hand. "Is okay, Mama."

In the space of another blink, they heard a distant shriek from Gwyn and Munch. "Holy accraba!"

Another blink, and Eisen was standing beside George, holding one of Munch's magic capes. "See, Dad, we don't need roads and cars."

Annabelle and George looked to each other, then to their children, then back again to each other. It had come to light just how much the children's skill set had advanced while given more freedom for their own self-development.

In another blink, Eisen was back bouncing on the bed. "We don't need faucets or tappy things, right, Asana?" He looked to his sister, who blushed.

"Asana and I can talk with each other always. It don't matter if she is here, or at Granny and Cappy's house. Is easy, right, Sana? And we can talk to aminals too. Bet people can't use tappy things to do that!"

George hurried back over to the bed, peering at his children. "You can communicate with animals?"

Both children nodded. "Uh-huh."

"'Cept, it's not the same as talking to you and Mommy. No, it's different." Eisen raised his face to the ceiling and rubbed the bottom of his chin the way his father did when he was in deep thought. "It's like, not with words, but how you feel. I don't know, but it's good. Is same when Sana and me do to each other. Is better 'cause we don't need all the words. Words are silly things."

George and Annabelle listened to the children's stories and explanations until their little eyes grew tired, and then they tucked them into bed.

George grabbed his pipe and he and Annabelle stepped into the starlit night and took a seat. She leaned back and pulled her feet up, hugging her knees close to her body.

"I knew it!" George whispered through a puff of smoke, pounding his fist on his knee. "I knew they were communicating telepathically. I knew it!"

"But how, George? How's it possible?"

"I've been working on a theory since that incident with Baloo. And what Eisen said tonight backs it up. It can't be through any type of written language—of course not. It's feelings and, like, emotions."

Annabelle looked confused as George continued.

"Okay, so, we talk with words, right? I mean, not just with words, but with body language also. But what if you could feel a person's... current state of emotion? Like, say there's a person you meet in the street who's going to... rob a bank, maybe. He could dress normally, put on a nice smile, talk respectably to everyone, and no one would think anything of it. But"—he shook a finger in the air—"if you could feel him, feel his adrenaline, his anxiety, his dishonesty... If you could close your eyes and communicate through emotion... no one could fake that. It's like their aura, right?"

Annabelle looked as though she was starting to grasp the concept.

George turned toward her and placed a hand on hers. "Words... when you think about it, they *are* silly. They can be totally inaccurate. Think about now, in today's world, where it's hard for people to speak to each other for fear they may offend someone. Even though all these people are likely good people, they pick the wrong words to express themselves, and boom! Someone misinterprets what they're trying to say, and everyone jumps on them. At this time in history, everyone is expected to be politically correct, but we're using words that exist in grey areas and ultimately have zero meaning. Our written languages limit our communication." He looked up at the stars. "Imagine it: being able to communicate effectively with anyone in the world. Erasing all language barriers. They're communicating with animals! They're still so young, Annabelle, and look at how skilled they are. And it's not just them—we should all be able to do what they can. They look at our modern world as if we're the Flintstones. The way we do everything is so primitive, when you see it through their eyes."

Annabelle chewed her lip, locked in a trance. "People wouldn't need phones. They wouldn't need cars, plumbing, electrical lines all over the place." She nodded slowly, piecing together the bigger picture. "They wouldn't need—"

"Anything." George looked at her. "People could survive with nothing. No need for any of it. No mining, no manufacturing, no economy. The world as we know it would be extinct. The people in power in this world do not want it, Annabelle. They don't want this knowledge out in the world. It would completely dissolve their way of life. Anyone with power would lose it."

George could see it sink into her, as if a physical weight had been added. She looked at him. "Yes… I understand it now."

"I wasn't sure how far this would all go. But even if they don't progress any further, what they know now is a huge step forward, for all human life… or a massive catastrophe, for the ones at the top of the food chain."

Annabelle sobbed, "George, our babies. I… I want to tell the whole world—imagine if everyone had these skills, the world would be such a beautiful place—but… our babies! Oh, George!" She leaned in and he wrapped his arms around her.

"We'll figure it out, honey. But for now, let's just enjoy having this time."

George and Annabelle snuggled together beneath the stars.

The seasons passed to years, and before they knew it the children had turned four, and then five.

Even with all their specialized skills, the twins still enjoyed working and learning in the primitive fashion: cooking with Granny, knitting clothes with Stella, helping Cappy blow glass jars. They also helped Griz carve out a giant wooden arch burned with the village emblem to welcome people. And, of course, Munch was after any of the children's free time to help him with magic tricks.

Oh, how their skills advanced. Some evenings when everyone had gathered for a family dinner, the children would put on a show to display new things they had learned. On one such night, things got a little carried away.

The twins were playing by passing back and forth small flickering lights between them, like little fireflies. They had done it before, and it was entertaining for everyone to watch the dancing lights illuminate their faces.

On this night, the children had shown an increased mastery of the skill. And they began to giggle and laugh as they always did. Then the excitement seemed to become contagious to the others watching, including George and Annabelle. Everyone started giggling and became dizzy, almost paralyzed with happy laziness. One of the balls of light began to grow, taking on a shade of green.

It grew to the size of a baseball, floating and darting between the children's palms. The air appeared electrified as the children's curly hair began to straighten and stand on end while the ball grew even larger. The children's eyes bulged as their laughter intensified.

Then the ball stalled mid-point between them. They continued to focus and move their hands. The ball grew and grew, till people were busting their guts with laughter, more and more until…

BAM! WHOOOOOOOSH!

The ball exploded into a ring of light, which spun out to the forest and disappeared, carrying enough energy to knock over the careless or unexpecting.

Deep silence fell over the entire forest. Then, slowly, sounds began to return.

Everyone wakened from their trance of giddy ignorance, blinking and looking to each other as if they had just been returned by aliens.

Munch sat up, shook his head and wiped some debris from his shirt, then looked around. "Well, that was all good fun, wasn't it?" His emphasis on certain words indicated that he was asking a question.

He stood and everyone else followed, one by one. Their movements were slow and investigative as they turned their hands over before their eyes, as if their bodies were new to them.

Granny broke the silence. "I feel pretty damned incredible!" Her hands dropped to her side and she looked sturdy, as if she had just eaten her spinach. Everyone smiled agreement, and mumbling began to spread through the crowd.

"Whooooo!" Granny shouted, pumping a fist in the air, quick and commanding, as if she had dropped twenty years… or forty.

One by one, each of the others followed her, saluting. And before they knew it, everyone was alive and full of spunk. The chatter was constant, and they began to toss around ideas about what they could do with all their energy in the middle of the evening, and then off they went to the lake for a late-night swim, with Dennis in tow.

George and Annabelle watched the mob walk down the path, singing and laughing, running and twirling, climbing and jumping off various structures like a group of out-of-control teenagers.

They waved their children over and then crouched down to check on them.

"My babies," Annabelle said with a smile, brushing grass and leaves from Eisen's curly hair, his eyes wide as he watched the crazed mob disappear into the darkness. Annabelle followed his stare, then looked back to her boy. "They've all gone crazy, I think." She grinned. "What did you two do to them? What was that, what you just did?"

"I don't know, Mom." He looked a little dazed. "We just did the little lights.

Then everything went way bigger. It was like we couldn't stop it. Like it was too fun, too happy."

George stood beside them with Asana in his arms. He placed his free hand on Eisen's head. "Yes, we felt that same thing. Maybe not as intensely as you two, but it was definitely interesting. You've never done this before… ever?"

They both shook their heads.

The excitement drained as quickly as it came and left them feeling an equally intense exhaustion. Mom, Dad, and precious children felt their eyes grow heavy.

Annabelle reached for Eisen's hand. "Okay, gang, let's call it a night."

George carried Asana as they walked the path to home. He looked up at the stars, focusing on the man-made stars blinking across the sky, and felt an unease.

In bed, Mom and Dad changed floppy children into their jammies.

Asana reached for Annabelle, wrapping her arms around her neck and kissing her dearly on the lips as she pulled her down into the bed to snuggle. "Mama, you think everybody is okay? You think the happiness left when they went swimming?"

Annabelle let go a big yawn and fell into bed with the rest of her family. Mom and Dad were on either side, with two children who were getting too big for family snuggles squished comfortably in between. "Yes, they're fine, my sweetie. You know old Uncle Dennis is over there checking on them."

"Uncle Dennis," squeaked a tiny voice from a face smashed into the mattress, hiding below floppy curls. "Can Uncle Dennis swim, Mama?"

Annabelle shared a smile with her husband. They both reached down to rub sleepy heads.

"Of course he can, honey."

"Okay… I love Uncle Dennis, Mama."

***

"Sir!… Are you seeing this, sir?" said a young graduate, waking from his doze on his first nightshift at the seismology institute.

His mentor across the lab woke as chimes began to sound in correspondence with blinking lights. He wobbled over to his apprentice's station, wiping at his glasses and placing them on his face. He cleared his throat and straightened his lab coat, then bent over the young man's shoulder to have a look at the computer screen. "Hmm, that's… well, that's very interesting."

"Is it an earthquake, sir? Should we be putting out a warning?"

"Hmm." He looked more closely. "I don't think this is an earthquake. I've honestly never seen this before." He pointed to the screen. "Look here, the amplitude is too weak to be of any concern, really. But look at how high the frequency is. I'm honestly surprised our equipment picked this up. It's right on the edge of its capabilities—very interesting indeed. How many sensors picked this up?"

The apprentice clicked a few buttons. "Whoa. It looks like hundreds, sir. Look."

"Yes, I see. Okay, good catch, young man. Now, you need to go through all the data and try to figure the… well, epicentre, if it has one. Once we get a rough location figured out, I think we should notify the eyes in the sky."

George woke the next morning and walked toward the vanity. He brushed the hair from his eyes and scratched his beard. Then he wiped the hair from his eyes and scratched his beard. The third time he wiped his hair from his eyes, he began to take notice of his need to constantly wipe the hair from his eyes, and then he touched his beard and realized its fullness. Things were feeling a little strange as he began to gain his morning senses. They got stranger yet when he had to brush his hair back yet again in order to see in the mirror.

"AHHHH!" he screamed, and simultaneously, he heard other shocked cries echo from the village.

He panicked, checking everywhere on his body as best he could with his hair constantly obstructing his vision. His whole head and face were covered in long, bushy hair, his beard tickling the tops of his toes—all that could be seen were his eyes and nose. And his body hair was testing the limits of the stitching on his jammies. He had turned into a werewolf.

"George?" Annabelle groaned from the bed.

He turned to see that his family were all little balls of hair beginning to stir. The werewolfism had gotten them all.

One scream came after the other as everyone scanned each other from hairy head to furry toe.

"Holy accraba!" sounded from afar.

Annabelle's breathing became laboured "George, what… what's happened?"

"I don't know, honey." He opened the door and peered at the outside world.

"Oh… Oh, my."

They all got out of bed and made their way to him. Annabelle looked like Rapunzel as she tried to gather up her hair enough to make the walk across the floor, but the children needed to be freed from it first—he never saw her find the end to it. Though her face had been spared, her eyebrows auditioned for a spot on *The Muppet Show*. The children couldn't see at all and reached for each other's hand to navigate the short distance. Their curly hair flopped all around them to the floor like it was a "Cousin Itt" reunion.

A whimper came from somewhere deep beneath. "Mama, what happened?"

"I'm not sure, sweetie. It's just hair, everything should be okay." She reached up and squeezed her eyebrows. "Mommy hopes."

When they reached the doorway, they all pushed their way outside, then parted their locks and peered into a changed world.

Everything as far as the eye could see had gone through a growth spurt overnight. 'Spurt' was putting it lightly. It was like they had stepped into Jurassic Park. The grass stood as high as an adult, the leaves on the forest trees blocked any passage, and vines had crept over everything, leaving only the windows and doors open. The chirping birds were so plump with feathers, it was a miracle they could fly, and it was the same with the bees. Some were the size of golf balls, and George could hear their wings struggling beneath their new weight, as the lure to harvest the giant flowers was too much for them to resist.

The vegetables looked almost too heavy for one person to carry. And the silly-weed—well, there was enough stock to keep a hippie happy for a lifetime. And when Baloo poked his fluffed-out face from between the stalks, he looked like a Baloo-the-Pooh times two.

They watched the others emerge from their dwellings with the same sense of wonderment as they slowly walked the path around the village beneath the morning sun. To their right, they saw Granny making her way up the hill—and looking normal. When she reached them, she scrunched down on her haunches with lips pursed and one eye squinted shut, then lifted a scolding finger to the twins, who leaned back and grabbed onto Mommy's leg.

"You two. I've been up for hours now, trimming myself back to normal. There's enough hair at my place to stuff a mattress—two, if you count the clippings I took off your Cappy. Now, which one of you is responsible for this?"

The children wasted no time thrusting a silent finger at each other.

Granny laughed and stood up with a hand across her tummy. "That's precisely what I thought." She winked at the children. "I'd be pinchin' me some chubby cheeks if I could find them on you two." She placed her hands on her hips and looked across the village. "Well, I guess we'll be harvesting today… and for the next several." She turned back to the family and gasped, a hand shooting to her mouth as she began to laugh again, pointing toward the loveseat.

Dennis gave a self-conscious grunt, then stepped out from behind the swing to gasps from everyone.

"My goodness, Uncle Dennis!" Annabelle exclaimed. "Our poor Uncle Dennis! My gosh, you must be so hot?"

The children burst into laughter and tripped and stumbled over their locks to get to their uncle and give him a big hug. They had trouble reaching his physical body through the amount of fluff that had grown on him. He couldn't even see, he was so puffed up.

"Well, I guess it's safe to assume that any animal within a"—George placed a hand over his brow to shield the sunlight as he looked over the land—"whatever-mile radius this reaches is suffering the same."

Everyone in the village came together at Granny's place to have themselves trimmed back to normal, which took the entire day. It took Cappy four hours to get Dennis looking normal again, and the mountain of hair that had gathered could have clothed the entire town.

When everyone was trimmed, the work on the rest of the village began. They cleared the path of grasses and weeds and cut back tree branches and intrusive vines from the structures. Then they made their way through the field of giant flowers to locate the beehives, which were found to be oozing with fresh honey.

There were many questions, especially from the traders and people in the hills. Tales of mystical lights flashing through the forest and the rapid growth of hair and plants had stretched far beyond their borders. But from what they could tell, they hadn't reached town. Everyone in Beelieve swore to all that they had no idea how it happened and that they were just as surprised as everyone else.

Granny and Cappy returned home early the next afternoon to prepare dinner and a warm washbasin for the villagers to enjoy at the end of a very hot and hard day of work. Everyone was soaked through with sweat because the humidity had spiked with all the fresh plant life.

After everyone had washed themselves, they sat one by one and looked with disbelief to the children.

Stella finally broke the exhausted silence. "It's incredible." She waved the children over, and they followed obediently and stood bashfully before her. She took one of each of their hands and shook them gently as she looked them lovingly in the eyes. "I know you two can walk through things and levitate things and walk on water. But I never realized how big of a deal this would be until today. Do you realize how precious your gift is?" She looked around the area, nodding softly. "All of this—what you've done—could feed millions. It could change life for hundreds of millions, maybe even billions of people who don't have access to food." A tear beaded from her eye as she pulled them both into a hug, squeezing them dearly. "You are so very special," she whispered. "Understand how important you are. Do good things with the gifts you've been given. Teach us, teach the world." She held them back and smiled before wiping at her eyes.

Although the Stanleys had put in much time and effort to prove their children were no different than anyone else, George and Annabelle were certain that news of this would filter down and reignite some suspicions.

With a harvest full of peppers as big as pumpkins, carrots as thick as tree trunks, and five-pound cucumbers, they decided to take only the smaller of veggies to town—which would still be looked on as obscenely large—and chop up the rest for canning.

There was so much honey and silly-weed that they required multiple trips into town with Uncle Dennis loaded to maximum capacity. And even with them holding back the trophy items, their crop was still the talk of the town.

"Hmm." Mr. Mulland tossed the carrot in his hands a couple of times, gauging the weight. Then he looked the Stanleys over one by one, stalling on the two children leading the mule. "Still no fertilizers, hmm? All organic still, are we?" He lifted his gaze back to Annabelle.

She blushed. "Oh yes, Mr. Mulland, we swear to it. There was a bit of a… well, a strange happening of some type up our way, just the other nigh—"

"Yes, yes, I've heard of this *happening*, as you say." His investigative eye turned back to the children. "I'd say all of the town has heard of it by now. Many of our visitors from up your way been telling all sorts of tall—or maybe long and hairy—tales of strange happenings."

"Yes, I would bet there has been. We had the same thing happen. It looks like it affected a large area. No one at our village witnessed anything out of the ordinary. Just woke up to everything being… well, more than it was before."

"Yes, more… much more, I would say, by the size of these vegetables."

She cut the conversation short and they made their way to see Ms. Baumhauer, who also informed them of the stories from the hills.

"They say there was a shooting light in the night—blinding, like a wind. It swayed all the trees, then it was gone and they thought nothing of it till they woke the next morning. Some say they were trapped and had to cut their way out of their homes. Peter's Barber Shop was lined up all day. He has so much hair, he doesn't know what to do with it all." She gave them all a suspicious look, ending at the children. She paused, then looked back to George and then to Annabelle. She reached out and pulled Annabelle close, wrapping her tightly in her arms. "I'll do what I can here for you, my dear. I don't have the slightest idea what's happening where. But it seems there's always some story coming down from your way, always about these children. You know I'm on your side, right?" She held Annabelle back and looked in her eyes.

Annabelle nodded.

Ms. Baumhauer went to George and gave him a hug and a kiss on the cheek, then she went to the children. "Oh! Such good-looking children, I can see why so many are talking of you. So blessed, hmm." She reached down and slipped them a chocolate bar apiece, then pinched a cheek each. "You two angels take care of your mom and dad for me, okay?"

The children broke a blushing smile.

The journey back to Beelieve was mostly silent, but George and Annabelle could feel that the other one was thinking the same thing: it would only get harder for them to keep the children a secret.

Back home by twilight, the Stanleys changed for sleep and then gathered on the bed in a circle, cross-legged.

Annabelle and George looked to each other, then they made everyone join hands.

"Okay…" George looked back to Annabelle.

"Yes." She grinned at the children. "Mommy and Daddy need to have a talk with you two about… well, people. Some people who may be looking for us and maybe aren't really good people."

"What do you mean, Mama? What people aren't good people? I love all people in Beelieve." Asana looked to her brother, who nodded.

"Yes, well…" George butted in, "see, the world is a really big place, and unfortunately, there's some people who aren't very nice. You two know how you're different from everyone, right?"

The children nodded.

"Well, we think there are many people who would be happy and excited to meet you two and see everything that you can do. In fact, most everybody in the world would be really excited to meet you."

"Yes," Annabelle said, taking over, "but then there are some other people in the world—really not very many people, but some—who might not like what you two can do. It's kind of like that with everybody. Some people like you, and some people don't, and that's okay. But because of how super-special you two are, there may be some extra-bad people who might be looking for you. We really don't think this, but we just wanted to have this talk with you because you're older now, and you're getting big and so smart and you understand so many more things, just like Mom and Dad, right?"

The children lifted their chins with pride and nodded.

Asana smiled. "Yes, we understand lots, Mama."

Eisen dropped their hands and jumped to his feet. "Don't worry, I can protect all of us against the bad guys!" He snapped his fingers and a softball of energy developed in his hand, flickering different colours.

"Jesus!" George held his hands up to his son. "Yes, Eisen, that's really great, but please, just…" He reached up and placed a hand on Eisen's shoulder. "Calm down, we don't want you to get anybody, okay?" He pulled the boy back down to a seated position and looked sternly at both twins. "You two, you understand that your skills are very special and you are not to use them for bad, like to hurt people, right?"

The children's chins dropped. "Yes, Dad."

"Only use your skills for good, right!" George waved a finger toward them till they both acknowledged his words.

"Okay, everyone, just calm down," Annabelle said. "All that we're wanting you two to do for us is to pay attention to strangers who may come to our village and to the people we see in town, and use your feeling power."

"*Skill*, Mama," Asana corrected.

"Ah, right, *skill*." She smiled at her daughter. "Use your skill to feel for bad people. You can do that, right?"

The children looked at each other, then nodded.

"So, if you see someone in town, and they have bad feelings for us, you two will be able to tell, right?" George asked, searching for confirmation.

The children nodded again.

He clapped his hands together. "Okay, great. So, again, we don't want you to harm anyone in any way. We just want you to feel out these people who don't have good feelings for us, and then tell Mom and Dad. Can you do that?"

The children smiled and nodded again.

"Okay, so you just do that, and then Mom and Dad can take care of things, right?" He held out a fist for each child to bump, and they responded enthusiastically.

"Aaaaand"—Annabelle smiled down at them—"if anything goes bad in town, you two need to get back to Beelieve, right! You use your transporting pow—*skill* to get you guys back here right away, no matter what. Even if something is happening to Mom or Dad, something bad. You get back here instantly and tell the others. Do not, *ever*, try to do anything that may be dangerous yourselves. Mom and Dad can take care of themselves, and Granny and Munch and everyone here will always know what to do. But the most important thing for Mom and Dad is to know you're both safe, okay?"

The children's expressions gave off a strong vibe that they didn't like where the conversation had turned. But George and Annabelle were convinced that it was a conversation needing to happen.

After a pause, the children both agreed, then everyone hugged and had some tickles to break the tension before snuggling into bed.

The snuggles coming from the children were a little tighter that night.

"Mama," Asana squeaked, "I don't never want to leave you, or Dad, or Beelieve."

"I know, sweetie. We're not planning on going anywhere." Annabelle kissed her daughter's head and squeezed her tightly.

From that night on, George and Annabelle helped the children advance their skills to the next level. They taught them about how life worked beyond Beelieve, as well as how to use their abilities in more practical ways than fancy light shows and magic tricks.

George also began calculating what exactly had happened with the sphere of light that made everything grow.

He stroked his beard while looking at his chalkboard. "Maybe accelerated particles of nitrogen?" he mumbled to himself. He turned to see two sets of blinking eyes above rosy cheeks standing beside him, dressed in jammies. He smiled as his face flushed with emotion.

In the morning, he woke to find their yurt empty. He stepped outside and saw three silhouettes against the morning sun, arms spread as they balanced and stretched, welcoming the energy. With the children present, he knew furry woodland creatures would slowly make their way to see them, and an obvious bout of jealousy would be seen coming from their stubborn Uncle Dennis. When they finished, they would sit with Granny, and the ladies would teach the children things about the great circle of life.

Their afternoons would be spent helping others around the village do their chores. They would learn about food and how the land works as well as building structures and weaving fibres.

True as it was that the children could do most of it by pure will, George felt it was equally important for them to feel life, to see it up close and personal. Learn the roots. See where they have been so they could lay a path forward.

In the evenings they would spend time with Dad. He schooled them first about the makeup of all matter in the universe and what particles to manipulate to pull water from the air, focus energy from the sun, and create vacuums and pressures. He would set out problems for them to solve using only their special skills.

Over the next couple of years, the children increased their abilities to almost god-like status. But when free time came and they played, they were simple children—who could run on water.

***

"C'mon! Please! I… I'll do anything. Anything you need!"

It was the summer after the children's ninth birthday. George grinned at Annabelle as they listened to Munch beg after inviting himself over for morning tea.

"Well…" George looked back to Munch. "There's not really much we need from you, Munch. I mean, I'm not implying that you're not a talented man, because you really are. I'm just trying to think of what I could possibly need you to do for me, and I honestly can't think of anything."

"*Buh!*" Munch shot a hand up into the air and looked as if he were going to respond, but then he just leaned forward in his chair and slammed his head down into his arm, which was resting on the table, while the other shook a clenched fist.

George took a casual sip from his mug.

"You do understand that Nelson is hosting the Provincials this year?" Munch strained to lift his head and brush the hair back from his eyes. "I don't need much from them, George." When he didn't get what he wanted from the man, he turned to the lady, pleading, "Annabelle!"

"Oh, the Provincials? I don't really follow hockey," she said to mock him.

"Magic!" he bellowed, as if wounded. "The Provincials for magic. The winner of this competition… well, they will be rewarded… greatly"—his tone lost concentration—"somehow, I, I'm sure."

"You don't know what the prize is? Is there even a prize?" George asked.

"Well, I… there must be a prize. No doubt it's riches beyond our imagination, and a chance to compete…"

"Nationally?" Annabelle assisted.

"Yes! Of course! National competition!" His finger shot up triumphantly.

"Ah, like hockey." She smiled again.

"No… damnit!" He slammed his fist down as George and Annabelle hid their smiles. He cupped his hands together. "Please, I know how sensitive this subject is for you, and normally I wouldn't dare ask. It's been how many years now, with the children and their abilities, and not once have I asked." He stood and walked to the window, staring out to the distance and letting the dramatic carry through his posture and voice. "Now, after fifteen or so years have passed, I finally have the opportunity for my vengeance against my most formidable of foes, Hernance Swizzletizz the Seventh, *pffffft*!" He looked at a fist he clenched to his side. "Just the sound of his name… the Seventh… the nerve. Who has ever been a Seventh? He thinks he's royalty? *Bah*!"

"Hernance?" George coughed tea out his nose.

"Swizzletizz?" Annabelle followed, hardly able to contain herself.

"Yeeaaas, the Seventh." Munch remained focused out the window, ignorant to the silent laughter in the background. "Just his name alone." His body shivered as he turned from the window, his expression stating clearly that he was reflecting on very painful memories. "It was out on Salt Spring Island. A one-time chance that the summer camp would be touring on our country's soil. I had been saving every nickel and following the schedule dates for my opportunity. The 'How to Do Magic, For Dummies' camp. Highly critically acclaimed, of course, according to the reviews."

"Oh, of course, *snfft*." George raised his arm to his face, his eyes swollen and nose running from holding back the laughter.

Annabelle couldn't even face them. With a sputtering tremor, she stood up and crossed her arms and turned her back.

"Oh, how I remember the snickering and the teasing as their parents dropped them off, one by one. Pulling up in their fancy vehicles." He turned his head and lifted his chin.

"W-wait… Munch." Annabelle's curiosity gained her enough control to turn to him. "Their parents dropped them off for the summer? Fifteen or so years ago you would have been…"

"Eeeh, early forties-ish." He tilted his hand to indicate "give or take."

"And h-how old were the others?"

"Well, I would guess… some were mid-teens—I'm sure one was shaving." Munch finally took notice of their amusement. "Well! We weren't all born into privilege, now, were we!"

George and Annabelle did their best to calm themselves, and Annabelle rolled her hand over to indicate he should continue.

Munch gave them a stiff glare, then turned back to the window. "How they mocked me. *'Old man Munchie made a crunchie in his undie…'* I heard their whispers. They thought I didn't, but oooooooh how they cut." He paced with slow recollection. "The day arrived to create our stage names. I announced myself as The Ggggreat and Marvellous Marvin Munchousin! And he said, 'Hernance Swizzletizz'—subtle, yet brilliant. Marketing genius, really. I'm sure his parents paid a healthy price for someone to come up with it. I said, 'The Sixth!' He shouted, 'The Seventh!' We all knew it was a lie.

"But I took their horribleness toward me and used it to fuel my passion. I buried myself deep in my studies, oblivious to all and any distraction: the armpit-farting noises when I walked by, the shaving of my eyebrows as I slept, and the spitballs!… Oh, how I loathed those wet, gooey, sticky wads.

"I was the top of the class—the never-ending scarf from the sleeve, the quarter from behind the ear, and 'Got Your Nose'—I made them all look like amateurs. So, on the day of the final exam, I decided to step it up a notch—way up… rabbit from the hat." He whirled around to face them and shot a finger in the air, with eyes steeped in mystery.

By this time George and Annabelle had settled into chairs, exhausted from the gut-wrenching laughter.

"But Hernance and his brood, they wouldn't have it. I could smell their jealousy from across the cafeteria. While I was performing my opening acts on stage, the little bullies secured my poor little bunny's feet to the bottom of the hat with plastic ties." He bowed his head and raised a hand to his brow, shielding the horror in his eyes. "I reached in and grabbed it by its ears. It was supposed to simply pop out, with no harm done. But it resisted—*'Whaaa,'* it wailed. I panicked, of course—it was final exam, you can imagine the level of pressure." He looked to them for reassurance. "So, I pulled my bunny again—*'Whaaa'*—harder I pulled again—*Whaaa!* It would cry louder, then I would pull my poor bunny harder, and louder yet it would cry. You can imagine my embarrassment. In all the excitement I had slackened my attention to any other happenings. The look of shock on the faces of the audience—all the parents had been invited, of course. It wasn't until I went to run off stage in my shame that I noticed my ability to

174

move my legs was limited." He sobbed and turned back to the window. "During the struggle with my bunny, I failed to take notice that they had… had… they'd pantsed me. Everything—underwear and all—right down to my ankles." He exhaled loudly. "All the time I was pulling on my poor bunny, my winky was bobbing and flopping at every member of the audience. There was even a media representative there who happened to snap a picture of it, then had the area in question censored and posted on the front page of the daily news of every city in a five-hundred-kilometre range."

George and Annabelle had both hidden their heads in their crossed arms on the table, knowing their amusement would be a direct insult to their friend.

Munch came over to sit across the table from them again. "I have recently gotten word that Hernance will be competing in this competition. He has continued to build up a name for himself over the last decade, but I, I know I have the skills to beat him now. Really, George, Annabelle… I wouldn't need much from the kids, just maybe a little extra kick with the lights, and maybe a little pyrotechnics. They could dress up and come on stage with me and Gwyn. Be part of the show. Surely they would love this?"

George and Annabelle looked to each other, fidgeting a bit. To this point, they had never let the children participate in anything risky enough to expose their abilities. But they had seen the light shows before, and some were pretty spectacular for a small, temporary stage in downtown. And they had also promised each other to loosen the leash on the children somewhat. Let them have a bit more independence. Surely with their abilities, they could take care of themselves better than most.

George raised an eyebrow to Munch. "Pyro and light show, nothing more. You have to understand the importance of this, Munch, and how bad it would be for everyone if those children got found out?"

Munch was straining to hold back his smile, but his eyes blurted his excitement as he brought his hands together on the table. "Yes!" He nodded rapidly. "Yes, nothing more. I swear! Oh, please!"

"Well, we'll have to ask the children…"

And as if on cue, the youngsters walked through the door, their once-small frames now turned long and slender.

"Oh, hey, kids." Annabelle gave them a look that told them there was something exciting in the works. "Uncle Munch here is needing some special help with his magic show. Sooooo, we've considered it—and there will be strict rules—but would you two like to play a part in his show? Up onstage and all?"

The twins looked at each other only for a split second, then raised their arms and cheered their uncle. "Yes! Oh, cool, Uncle Munch!" And they ran around the table, hugging and thanking everyone.

It would be an attempt at Munch's biggest show to date. With the magical Provincials showdown happening that year, the town was expecting an even bigger rush of tourists than usual.

Griz was busy for weeks before the event, with Munch standing over her every move, barking orders and directions until she would bark back, turning Munch into a fit of pleading apologies.

Every day for the entire week prior to the festival, every capable villager was weighed down with anything they could carry. Poor Uncle Dennis was loaded up to towering heights, like a scene off some sarcastic animation. Not all of it was for Munch's show: Stella also had a large supply of arts and crafts she had been building over the year, and Granny and Cappy had extra wine, honey, potions, and concoctions for this extra-special festival.

After all the hard work, everyone relaxed and enjoyed all the festival had to offer. The expectations as far as tourist population had been far exceeded.

"I've never seen it like this before," Annabelle marvelled as she, George, the twins, and Uncle Dennis squished in their shoulders to weave their way through the streets. Having their uncle in tow didn't make things any easier. Although the children were too big to ride on him, they still brought him everywhere.

As much as the population of normal, everyday tourists had grown, there was also a substantial increase to the witch and wizard population. As well as George could estimate, approximately one in every five tourists were in support of some magical community. And some of the outfits were much more razzle-dazzle than anything he had ever seen Munch wear.

"Freaks," Munch mumbled as he peered around the square they had developed in the usual intersection of town. "Very few of these people are actual magicians. Be concerned if any of them want to saw you in half, or make you disappear, *snnnrt* haha!" He slapped his leg. "They're just enthralled by the glamour of it all—fakes, wannabes."

"Well, I think they all add a certain bit of excitement," Annabelle smiled. "So"—she peered around the crowd inconspicuously—"which one is your nemesis? Hernance Swiggy-de-de?"

Munch looked unimpressed by her obvious mock of his community. "Swizzletizz, the Seventh."

George and Annabelle looked away for a snicker, then resumed. "Yes, of course."

Munch gave a light nod into the crowd to his left. "There he is—the clean-shaven one with the black, slicked-back hair. Gotten a little plump since I last saw him." Munch chuckled.

George and Annabelle peered casually through the crowd, filtering through the options until a line of sight parted to reveal a man fitting Munch's description, dressed in the obviously high-end fashion of the magic world—like a plus-sized David Copperfield. He had a small stand set up and was shaking hands and signing autographs for quite an impressive line of fans, with the smile and swagger of a seasoned politician.

It could be that they stared a little too long and a bit too obviously because he twitched his head in their direction for a second, then back and again, holding his gaze longer, till he squinted directly at Munch. He grinned, then held up a finger to his anxious fans and stepped in their direction.

"Uh…" Annabelle and George both turned their eyes away as Munch, who had his back turned, looked at them quizzically.

"Huh, what?" He turned just enough to see his foe walking straight toward them, wearing a weasel grin. "Oh, sh—"

"Hello?" Hernance raised a palm to them. "My god, is it… could it be?" His voice was loud enough to draw attention. "Munch? Crunchie Munchie, is that really you?" He leaned to the side, trying to get a better look at Munch, who had his back turned to him.

Munch winced and turned slowly toward Hernance, making sure to convey his disappointment to his friends as his eyes passed over them.

"Ah-haha! It is, after all these years." He raised his chin, then his arms and voice as he twirled to the crowd. "Ladies and gentlemen, please lend us your attention so I may introduce my dear friend, the average and something to watch—when you have nothing else to watch—Mervin Mudhousin! Ah-ha-ha-ha!" He slapped Munch on the back. "My, my, Munchie, how you've aged. I mean, you were old before, but my god, man. I've heard whispers that you were still flaunting your cheap cup-and-ball tricks in these parts. Hiding in the hills. Avoiding the spotlight, Munchie? Afraid your talent isn't up to hanging with the rest of us? I would say that's an accurate assumption."

Though the children had led a life sheltered from the politics outside Beelieve, they were old enough to pick up on sarcasm. And though they had been taught love for their fellow humans, they didn't appreciate anyone messing with their family. They could feel the arrogance of this new person, and they could feel his hurtful intentions toward their uncle, whom they loved very dearly. They could feel their uncle Munch's shame and hurt, just as they could feel the anger begin to boil inside of them as they looked to each other.

The man lifted Munch's cape in his fingers. "What's this, old boy? You—haha—you still in the game? Wait, wait, you…" He looked to all the different stages around the square. "Are you performing? In this? Today? Are you?" He bent over and slapped his leg with a dry, boisterous laugh. "You think you can keep up, old man? Remember to keep your pants on for this one, Munchie. There's children present."

Munch suddenly pulled his wand from its sheath and pressed it right up against the side of Hernance's nose. "You!" His body trembled with rage, and spittle flew from his words. "I, I am competing today, and you will see my full potential, Hernance the — the awful human being! Mark my word that tonight is the night I will send you crying back to your mommy and daddy!"

Hernance wiped Munch's wand off his face. "Careful with that, you brute. You may clog a pore and cause me a pimple, hahaha!"

Munch turned to the crowd, raising his arms high overhead. "Ladies and gentlemen, tonight you will all witness the greatest display of magic in the world! Tonight I, the Great and Marvellous Marvin Munchousin the Seventh, will be unanimously crowned the greatest magician of all time!"

George and Annabelle winced at the proclamation. Even though they had high hopes for Munch, they knew his acts were far from above average. The children would no doubt put on an excellent show of lights and fireworks, but it couldn't be enough to win the competition.

But... George and Annabelle were left out of the silent conversation happening between the two who had the most say of anyone on how the night would roll out. The twins sealed the plan with a subtle nod between them, and the night was now sure to be an event to remember.

Being that Munch was a long-time resident and friend to many of the townsfolk and organizers, and as a result of his much convincing that his show was worthy of closing the night out, he had been allotted the last spot, even though according to the rankings of the magic world, Hernance's show held the highest acclaim.

And for the small mountain town, the shows were indeed spectacular. The performances started in the early afternoon with up-and-coming amateurs putting on shows at various corners of the square—simple-level tricks like "Pick a Card," "Sleight of Hand," and "Guess a Number." But once darkness began to fall, four major acts were to take place on their own separate stages.

After the beginning half of the first major show, the audience knew these were no longer amateurs, and it far exceeded all of the Stanleys' expectations. As the night continued, they began to grow nervous for their friend.

Then came the time for Hernance's show—the show that by rights should have been the finale, based on reviews. And he was sure to let everyone know this at the beginning of his performance.

The stage was dark at first. A simple, lonely tune being whistled over the speakers was all that was used to draw the crowd's attention. When everyone had turned in wonder, two loud cannons burst, sending a single ball of energy into the sky, which then popped into a blinding white light that lit up everything in the square as if daytime had reappeared in an instant. When it had burned out, the show began with more pyro works and some catchy beat music, and a half-dozen scantily clad female dancers welcomed his majesty to the microphone at centre stage.

"Ladies and Gentlemen..." Hernance looked over the crowd as he adjusted the microphone stand. "I regret to say that this is usually the closing act for the evening, but apparently there's someone in the area with some dirt on someone in power around here, who had me bumped to now. But, on the bright side, you'll be rewarded with a few laughs while you're packing up after my show."

Hernance's show was many things. Visually stimulating, yes. The tricks were slight adaptations of baseline tricks that had developed over generations. The music and dancers and the stage and props were all very captivating and, honestly, a league above the rest. Hernance was more of a showman than an actual magician, and in the end, what his performance really proved was how brilliant you could be when you had wealth to back you.

Throughout his performance, he got his verbal jabs in on one of Beelieve's most-loved residents, who was hiding in silence behind his own stage while the rest of the village stood in the crowd, building up their own grudge.

They all knew how hard Munch had been working on his shows, and this one even more so. But they all realized there was no way he would be able to compete with Hernance. The night looked to be another devastating blow to their friend. Perhaps the one that would have him hang up his cape permanently.

The children could feel everyone—all of their thoughts and feelings, their despair for their friend. As the time for Munch's show drew near, they went behind stage to find Munch and prepare for the performance.

They found him sitting in the dark, on the wooden steps that led up to the stage. His face was buried in his hands, and Gwyn stood beside him, rubbing his shoulders and whispering support. The children knew he was crying and could feel his broken heart, and it energized them in ways they had never felt before. Anger was an emotion they hadn't had much experience with. They didn't understand how its passion could fuel poor decisions.

Gwyn stepped back with a sympathetic smile for the twins as they approached with Uncle Dennis on their heels. They each placed a hand on one of his shoulders. He lifted his head and, oddly, his spirits lifted, like the flick of a switch.

"It's time, Uncle Munch." Asana smiled at him. "Everything's going to be fine."

Munch looked at her, seemingly a little off from the strange turn of emotion. "Well, I… I think you're right. Everything is going to be fine."

Eisen nodded to him. "Yes, Uncle, c'mon. We have a show to do."

They all put on their outfits. Munch and Gwyn were dressed in their typical show wear—Munch with his flashy black and dark purple ensemble and Gwyn following the same colour scheme in something a little more form-fitting and cleavage-baring. The twins broke the trend with all-white suits and matching capes with black accents, and they wore masquerade masks to conceal their identities.

They waited backstage while Hernance's show finished, the roaring applause and cheers lasting for several minutes as he and his cast returned to the stage for several bows.

Then the crowd's cheering turned to mumbles as they stood, lost for direction, waiting.

In the night sky, thin wisps of clouds moved in to dim the half moon, and with a faint snap of fingers from Munch's stage, every single light extinguished and the entire town went black. All went silent.

Two small but brilliantly bright balls of light appeared, hovering over the stage. They illuminated the pale faces in the front row and cast a razor-defined silhouette of anything standing between them. On stage, to each side of the lights, one could make out the outline of the children's masked faces and their cupped hands beneath the hovering lights.

All was silent…

Then the balls flinched and moved inward, toward each other in the centre of the stage. Their glow cast out another figure: a darker, bearded figure holding a crooked wooden staff.

He reached for the lights, which moved with him and then away. A drumbeat began to play in the background, growing louder with the twirling ballet between mage and light, until the drums hit their apex and then stopped, silent, as Munch crouched into a caped ball on the floor.

The lights hovered above him, then slowly moved out over the crowd. Softly popping and sizzling like a pair of sparklers, they moved above everyone, shedding a ghostly light on their faces as they passed. At the centre of the intersection, they split, one going left, the other right, floating slowly down the street a few blocks until they stalled, sputtered, and fizzled as if they had run into something. Then the light began to spread, giving shape to their obstacles. The light extended up and out, colouring one end of the street in the shape of a giant mountain lion, taller than the buildings and wider than the street. At the other end, an equally large grizzly bear was revealed.

As both creatures looked toward the audience, they gave a sharp snort and a growl and their eyes blazed red.

The entire crowd gasped and a few screamed, and then breaths were held. The creatures of light stared each other down, groaning and snarling. Then the lion let go a loud, sinister, trademark growl as the beastly roar of the bear met its fury. The two raised their haunches and charged at each other, straight toward the crowd, destined to clash in the centre of the square.

The audience was frozen with fear as the monsters charged. The second before they hit the crowd, Munch's voice boomed from the stage. Standing with his staff raised, his body exploded into light and he grew equally as large as both animals. He leaped from the stage and swung his staff down hard as all three came together at the same time, and the whole scene burst into a rainbow of whistling streamers and confetti that rained down harmlessly on everyone.

On stage, still in a pose with his staff in the air, Munch reached his hand up, and all the light assembled into a ball in his hand. He held it before his lips and blew softly, it dissolved to glitter and spread to ingnite the town lights once again.

The audience went crazy, clapping, cheering, whistling.

Annabelle stood, not clapping. "Thaaat'ssss a little overkill."

George was not impressed in the least. "A little? Really?"

"What do we do? We need to get the children off the stage, we need to stop it!"

"No!" George grabbed her arm. "We can't, we'll draw attention to them. This looks bad enough. I hope that's all they do. I think we have to just go along with this as being part of the show." He nudged her and began clapping. "Smile!"

Annabelle followed his lead, reluctantly.

The show fell back into its scheduled routine, with little bits of flare mixed in here and there but minus all the little hiccups that were normal in one of Munch's performances.

***

On the sidelines, Hernance fumed at the spectacle.

He was truly baffled by the stunts this buffoon was pulling off so seamlessly. Like sawing people in half, and not even using the normal props. He didn't even look properly set up for some of the disappearing tricks, *so how?* Munch also wasn't his old stumbling and bumbling self. There was a strange air of confidence to him. Hernance had seen nothing different about him when he'd reacted to their meeting earlier—still the insecure, feeble old man, trying to be something he wasn't; yet it would appear now that he was.

He looked for secret lights, trap doors, and someone operating a drone. Surely Munch would need something mobile to move the lights all the way down the street, and those apparitions, well, it had to have cost him millions—money he knew this wasted old man had no access to.

There was a code among the magic world that no magician shall ever expose the ways of another to the audience. But there was no way Hernance would be beaten by someone so below him. And so he watched, and waited for his opportunity.

As nothing seemed out of sorts with the way Munch was acting—though he hadn't tripped over his own feet yet—Hernance began to focus on the others. Gwyn, the only other reasonable option, seemed out of rhythm with everything happening on stage, as if she had missed rehearsal. And judging by the stunned look on her face, he deemed there no way for her to be masterminding anything beyond burning the toast.

He walked slowly through the shadows and went behind the stage to see who was controlling the pyro show. When he got there, he found no one.

No one?... How is it possible? he wondered. It wasn't possible, in no way. He bent over and searched the ground for the cords and cables needed for the fireworks and light shows. There were some cables—cables hooked to nothing.

He stepped softly up the backstairs of the stage and found an opening in the rear panelling to continue watching the show. With all other options considered, he glanced at the children... *The children...*

They held no props and were never directly involved in any of the tricks, and so no one was paying them any special attention, but out of everyone on the stage, they were the most focused. Focused intensely, wherever the action was taking place. Their eyes turned and redirected every time a light switched or a spark burst. Their arms and hands were concealed beneath their capes, and after watching only a little while longer, Hernance knew they must have controllers hidden.

So he waited for just the right time.

At the end of the show, Munch walked out on thin air over the crowd, stepping up as if he were climbing a flight of stairs. Smiling and waving to everyone, he began to toss handfuls of candy to the crowd as they cheered and praised him.

"Oh, thank you! Thank you so much, everyone!" In his voice, one could hear it was the most glorious moment of his life.

Hernance had no idea how the imbecile was pulling it off. But he was about

184

to find out, and expose Munch for the fraud he was.

He ran onto the stage, grabbed the microphone from its stand, and jumped right in front of the children "AH-HAAAH!"

Startled, the children dropped Munch from the air, onto his fans.

"*Ooooph*!" was the sound he made.

Hernance turned with a sinister smile to address the crowd. "Here! Now you will see this man is nothing but a fraud! He's no magician!"

He pointed to the children, who were taking one slow step back after another, looking at him with fear.

"I, Hernance Swizzletizz, will now reveal just how he is fooling all of you. It is hidden beneath the capes of these children!" He grabbed onto the girl's cape and threw it open—to find nothing… nothing but little hands. "I… well, I…" His irritation spewed. "Where is it, you little… *GAHH*!" He began to yank at her cape, turning her around, searching in madness.

She shrieked. "Mommy, Daddy!"

The boy stepped toward the man, the expression on his face saying he'd had enough. "You!"

Hernance turned to him. "What! What do…" His eyes widened as he saw the kid's arms start to surge with glowing red light.

"YOU LEAVE MY SISTER ALONE!" The little boy raised one hand to Hernance, and in a blast of red, blew him clean off the stage and several yards into the crowd.

The audience gasped, then fell silent.

The boy ran to his sister and took her by the hands.

Both twins turned to the crowd, where everyone held perfectly still, watching.

In a blink, they disappeared into thin air, and the stage lights fell dark.

The crowd erupted around George and Annabelle, who went straight into panic mode. They turned around and saw Uncle Dennis running down the road, into the darkness, and went on an emotional search for their children while the stunned crowd waited for something else spectacular to happen.

Outside the square, the streets were dark and mostly deserted, other than a couple over-celebrated, stumbling individuals.

Where the twins had disappeared to was anyone's guess. It was possible they were back in the village, but there would be no way to get Annabelle back there until they had overturned every possible rock along the way.

"Oh! Those children! What did they think they were doing? And Munch! How dare he do this behind our backs… with our children!" Annabelle stormed down the street beside George, arms straight and hands clenched into fists of rage.

"Annabelle, we don't know any of the details yet. Just stay calm for now. First thing is to find them. They know they're in trouble, and probably scared to death."

"Oh!" Her fists relaxed as she burst into trembling tears. "George, our babies, where could they be?" She hugged her arms around herself against the chill in the night air.

There weren't many places in town where they believed the children would feel safe, but they checked any possibilities. Mr. Mulland's store was the longest shot, then Ms. Baumhauer's, but all the lights were out and everything was locked up at both places. They checked Granny and Cappy's wagon, then the storage yard. Nothing, and there was no Uncle Dennis to be found anywhere either. They knew that it was likely that when they found him, they would find the children.

Annabelle stood sniffling in the dark street as more stragglers began to file out of the square.

"Annabelle, c'mon." George beckoned to her as he started along the route that would lead them to their forest trail. "We have to keep going."

She looked up and down the street. "What if they didn't go that far, George? For all we know they could've transported somewhere not far from the stage?"

George huffed. "Yeah… Damnit!" He turned around slowly, looking in every direction. "Well, we have to decide on something."

"Okay, they'd probably go somewhere they know we'll be. So, let's go to the entrance of the forest, and if we don't find them there, maybe we should split up? One of us continues on to the village, and the other circles back to the square?"

"Yeah, I… I don't know. Sounds like as good a plan as any." He reached his hand out to her. "C'mon."

They walked briskly down the street, and as their direction drew away from the public pathways, they were hoping to run into some of their own from the village. Maybe someone knew where the children had gotten. But by the time they hit the train tracks, they had yet to run into anyone.

They stepped into the forest and stopped for a look and a listen. It took time for their eyes to adjust to the limited light.

There was something. A sound—a scuffle in the dirt, but not human.

Annabelle squinted. "George, look, it's Dennis."

Sure enough, over by the treeline stood the old mule, snorting and scuffing his feet in the dirt.

"Dennis? Uncle Dennis? Hey, buddy." George took a cautious step toward him, not knowing exactly why he was there. As he walked across the clearing, he kept his eyes peeled for the children.

"Hey-ey, there, big guy." George reached out for him and smiled when Dennis welcomed his touch, nuzzling his nose into his hand.

Annabelle stepped up behind Dennis and scratched him down the neck, the way he liked.

Neither of them could find any injuries or anything out of the ordinary with Dennis. He was just standing and waiting, the way he always did for the children.

"Okay," Annabelle said, raising her voice to the shadows, "Asana, Eisen, time to come out. We know you're here somewhere."

A quiet, snuffling whimper came from the trees. "You're mad at us." Asana's voice quivered.

George and Annabelle both exhaled a heavy weight.

"Oh, thank god," Annabelle sighed as George pulled her close and rubbed her back.

"Well, kids," George said, "that was a lot more than we said you could do."

"He's a bad man!" Eisen blurted from somewhere in the shadows.

"Who?" Annabelle asked. "Who's a bad man?"

"That man, that bad guy," Eisen called out. "He said bad things about Uncle Munch. He hurt him, we felt it… like you told us we should feel the bad people. He's a bad man, and when he hurt Uncle Munch, we got really mad."

"Ah, you mean Hernance," George said. "So, when you heard that Hernance teasing Uncle Munch, you got mad, and that's why you did what you did? That's why you did a lot more than Mom and Dad told you, you could do?"

"That guy hurt Uncle Munch really bad," Asana said. "He's a really bad guy. We could feel it, he's gross."

All Annabelle was focused on was getting the children to come to them. She could decide their fate afterward. "I see, well, why don't you two come here and talk to Mom and Dad about it."

"Nuh-uh," Eisen responded. "You're mad."

"Honey, we were frightened. We didn't know what had happened to you two. We were so scared, and really, we just wan—"

"Nuh-uh," he repeated. "You're mad, we can feel how mad you are."

"Yeah," Asana said. "You're really mad, Mama."

Frustrated and realizing that there was nothing she could do to hide her emotions, Annabelle let it fly. "You two get out here now!" An echo carried far through the valley. "Do you understand what kind of trouble you've caused for us?! Do you realize how careless and irresponsible you've been?!" Her body went stiff and her fists clenched again.

Sobbing came from the trees. "Mom, no, we're sorry… Please, please don't be mad at us, Mom. We were just trying to help."

"I can't believe you two defied our direct orders! You know how important it is for no one to find out about—"

"*HUFFFFF-GRRRRNT.*" Heavy breathing interrupted the scolding.

Annabelle turned, and she screamed, her eyes popping as she stumbled backward into George, who was already doing his own backpedalling.

"Jesus!" he gasped, grabbing his wife and pulling her a healthy distance from the giant moose that had managed to sneak up behind them.

Dennis moved back a few steps but remained surprisingly calm, not challenging the behemoth in any way.

"Mom, Dad, don't worry…"

George and Annabelle looked toward the trees and saw two little faces poking out from the darkness, their complexions pale in the moonlight.

Each twin held a steady hand up to the animal and began to step toward it.

"A-Asana, Eisen—no!" Annabelle whispered hastily, waving them back to the trees without drawing too much attention. "Go back!"

Asana looked at her. "It's okay, Mama. She's safe. She's here to see us. She needs our help."

"Kids, please, these aren't cuddly, friendly animals," George warned.

"It's okay Dad."

The parents watched as both children entered the clearing and slowly and carefully stepped up to the moose. The closer they got, the more assuredly they walked, until they were standing right in front of the animal. The moose was so much larger than the twins, it could end both of their lives with a simple stomp of the foot. But it never so much as flinched as the children walked right up to it. It bent its head down and the children rubbed its nose, and all three spent a moment in one another's intimate presence.

"We have to go, it needs help," Eisen said decidedly.

"Wha?… No, nuh-uh." Annabelle shook her head and reached a hand toward her children. "No way you're going anywhere with that thing."

"We're going, Mom, she needs our help. Everything's fine." Eisen smiled at her as he walked over and then touched his hand to hers.

Instantly, a feeling of warmth and comfort spread through Annabelle. Her fear vanished and she and George stood straight, moving away from each other but keeping their hands joined as they went straight over to Dennis and grabbed his reins.

George looked at the children. "Okay, we're ready."

Though she was present and awake through the whole journey, if you were to ask Annabelle afterward, she would say that it all felt very much like a dream.

The moose wasted no time leading the way along a path only fit for a moose, pushing its way through dense brush, heavy bog, and even over a river crossing. For a normal person, the trail would be unthinkable, but with the twins, everything just seemed to work. When they needed things to be moved, those things moved, and when they hit water, they just walked right over it. It was as effortless as walking down a sidewalk.

It seemed as if they had covered a massive amount of ground in about a half-hour's time. Annabelle had no idea where they were but didn't feel concerned.

They hit a small clearing, and everyone stopped. A helpless cry came from the treeline on the far side.

Asana gave her hand a casual wave, and the area lit with a warm glow. There, lying on the ground and struggling to get up, was a baby moose. It appeared to have suffered an injury to its back legs. It squawked and squealed, struggling with fright at everything developing.

Asana evaporated and appeared instantly before the frightened baby. She held her hand on its forehead. "Shhh, little baby. Everything's going to be okay." She smiled sweetly.

Mother moose stepped up to the pair and nudged reassuringly at her calf.

Standing back with Dennis in tow, Annabelle squeezed George's hand. Both of them transfixed as they watched their daughter cradling the baby's head in her lap. Her touch gentle and her words soothing. The way her face glowed in the light, anyone would swear they were looking at an angel.

Eisen was standing between them all, focused on a point in the darkness within the trees.

"I see you," he said and grinned, as if in a game of hide-and-seek. He took a few slow steps toward the trees. "I said"—he raised his hand and took a breath— "I see you." As he exhaled, certain areas within the treeline began to glow, one by one, and a pack of wolves was revealed.

The alpha stood the closest, growling with bared teeth.

"Eisen!" Annabelle shouted and stepped toward him.

George grabbed hold of her and pulled her back. "I think he's got this," he whispered in her ear, keeping an eye sharply trained on everything.

Dennis squirmed and brayed, while mother moose gave a loud snort and tensed her massive body for a fight.

"Easy, Uncle Dennis, shhh," Eisen whispered. "It's okay, everyone, not tonight. There won't be any fighting here tonight… How's baby moose, Asana?"

Asana remained in her place, completely at ease, and her tranquility passed into the young one resting its head in her lap.

Annabelle and George stayed still, except for their heads, which twitched in every direction, trying to keep tabs on everything. But then, like so many times when the children were doing what they do, a heavy calm set about the place. Everyone—person or beast—relaxed completely.

George and Annabelle stepped into the centre of the action and found a log to rest on. The wolves stood their ground, but they didn't seem at all interested in starting any trouble.

Eisen walked slowly around the area with a smile that was both wise and childish, seeming to hold all parties in peace while Asana went to work.

She moved out from beneath the calf and knelt beside it, gliding her hands gently over its body and whispering soft encouragement as it lay still and silent, its chest expanding and contracting with every breath.

Mama moose stood by, waiting calmly and patiently. The wolves began to walk around the clearing, sniffing around. One even came right up to Annabelle, who reached her hand out so it could have a smell.

But nothing happened under the watchful eye of Eisen.

He looked back to his sister while still pacing the perimeter. "How is it, Asana?"

"It's hurt. It's hurting in its back legs. I think maybe something is broken. I just need a little bit."

Eisen nodded casually, continuing his patrol.

Asana settled down, cross-legged, by the calf's hindquarters. She closed her eyes and took a deep breath, then placed her hands on the animal and began to rub very gently, moving her hands all around. Mama moose gave a short snort and laid her head over Asana's shoulder.

Asana's breathing intensified into long deep draws and equally concentrated exhales. The air felt electrically charged, and the leaves and grass and even everyone's hair leaned toward her.

After only a moment, it subsided.

Asana rose to her feet and brushed the earth from her legs. "Okay, c'mon!" she said to the calf. "You're all fixed now, give it a try." She reached down and gave the newborn a playful slap on the rear, then giggled.

The baby gave a soft whine, then began to move. It positioned its front legs first, then lurched and leaned on them. It gained its rear legs beneath it and began to push up, slowly at first, then straight up to a full stance. It gave each leg a kick, wiggled its bum, and took a few steps. Its confidence grew quickly and it gave a little hop and a jump.

Mama moose gave Asana a nudge, and the little girl reached her arms as far up the moose's neck as she could and gave her a hug.

Mama wasted no time joining back up with her healthy baby, and the two stepped off into the darkness.

The wolf pack perked up as they watched the mama and baby leave. Eisen raised his hand back to them. "Shhh," he hissed. "That's not fair, wolves. You have to give them a head start. I think it's time for all of you to have a nap for a while."

Annabelle felt the air start to change again, becoming heavy and cumbersome. One by one, each wolf eased itself to the ground and fell asleep.

Annabelle and George could hardly stay awake themselves, till Asana came to get them. On their way out of the clearing, they found Uncle Dennis fast asleep on his feet and snoring.

It was deep into the night by then. Everyone was tired and walked in virtual silence. Keeping their heads down for the most part, Annabelle and George held hands. Though they could not communicate telepathically, a lot was communicated in the way they held to each other and through the occasional look.

Reaching home, Annabelle felt that the walk should have taken longer. She could not recall passing any of the landmarks.

She and George tucked the children in with a smile and a kiss. Nothing more was said about the misstep at the magic show.

Moments later, Annabelle and George curled into bed together, looking into each other's eyes.

"They're so beautiful," George whispered.

"I know…" She chewed her lip.

"I know they messed up at the magic show, but… we can't hide them forever."

She nodded. "We shouldn't hide them, not anymore."

"We have to go. We have to take the next step." He squeezed her hand.

A tear ran down her face and her jaw clenched. She closed her eyes and nodded again. "I know."

She sobbed, and George was quick to wrap his arms around her and hold her close, long into the night.

First thing the next day, Munch was at their door with apologies.

The children got involved in the conversation, assuring George and Annabelle that Uncle Munch had no idea what they had planned and admitting that they had put him into a bit of a trance to give him the boost in confidence he needed for such a performance.

George and Annabelle just smiled and nodded, telling everyone that they were forgiven.

But times had changed for the Stanleys in their little piece of paradise. They distanced themselves from the others and never mentioned their plans to leave to anyone. They decided they needed to figure out the when and how first. And they agreed that the children would be kept away from town until the situation could be properly assessed, and so Annabelle went it alone for the next few trips.

Mr. Mulland was quite cold toward her. Conversation was limited, his body language was suspicious, and he even began to lowball her merchandise.

Ms. Baumhauer was as welcoming as always, but she was deeply saddened by the turn of events and had words of warning for Annabelle.

"Oh, my dear, you didn't bring the children? I think that's for the best, for now. That magic show they were involved in, I think almost everyone in the audience captured some of it on their fancy phones. I heard they put a lot of it on the social sites online. Apparently it's gone viral, whatever that means?" She waved her hands with a roll of the eyes. "Talk of all you villagers isn't that positive around here right now. I would even warn you about coming here on your own, Anna."

A group of teenagers yelled out from across the street. "There she is! Look! The witch!" They snapped some pictures.

Annabelle blushed and turned away.

She heard more whisperings around her as she briskly made her way back to the path. She could feel their stares when they stopped and pointed.

She made the trip a couple more times over the next few weeks, but the experience only worsened and she gave up, with Stella taking her place.

The summer was hot and dry, and the happiness felt dampened in Beelieve. The others could see it in the Stanleys, and some carried the weight of guilt for it.

The children continued to use their skills to help the village grow a bumper crop. No longer making the trips to town, George and Annabelle were left to the gardens, working away the days sweaty and dirty.

On one evening, the storm clouds began to build in the west, carrying the promise of much-desired moisture. But Granny became uneasy as she watched the thunderheads grow.

When the clouds approached the other side of the valley, flashes of lightning stabbed violently to the earth and the thunder rolled heavy as a landslide. As the storm stretched out over the lake, a violent wind swept up from the valley, tossing around anything that wasn't tied down and sending Uncle Dennis into a nasty fit.

The villagers gathered on the crest by Granny and Cappy's. The wind caused them all to hunch down.

Granny looked to them all. "I think it's best we take shelter."

Everyone began to funnel into Granny's place, while Annabelle, George, and Uncle Dennis circled back for the children. The twins had joined hands and were standing silent, watching the storm as the wind flattened their curls.

George placed a hand on Eisen's shoulder and yelled through the noise, "Eisen! Get your sister, we have to go inside!"

Neither child acknowledged him.

George squeezed his shoulder harder. "Eisen! C'mon, it's time to go! Enough fooling around!"

Still nothing.

Annabelle grabbed hold of Asana. "Asana Stanley! You get moving inside right n—"

Both twins simultaneously pointed down into the valley.

George and Annabelle turned just in time to see sparks fly in the tinder-dry forest below as a bright flash of light retreated to the threatening clouds. Only seconds later, a ravenous flame shot into the air as a snarling roar carried on the wind.

George's heart held for a second. "Oh… God help us." He grabbed hold of Eisen's arm. "C'mon, let's go! NOW!" He pulled hard, to the point where Eisen was starting to drag, while Annabelle was attempting the same with Asana.

But the more they pulled, the more they felt the children gaining weight.

The twins looked at both parents. "No, we have to help us," they said very calmly.

George peered at the valley below. The fire had now engulfed the entire ridge along the lake. With the strong wind blowing uphill, it would be on them in minutes, or less.

Distant yelling and screaming came from behind them—and they all turned to see a dozen or so people running into the village from the hills.

"Help us! Save us!" a woman called from the group as they rushed toward the Stanleys.

With no time to spare and no other options to think of, George pointed them toward Granny's.

As the last of the villagers filed inside, Granny turned back to George and Annabelle while she struggled to hold onto the door. "The children, get them inside!"

George looked at the children, then waved for her to go inside.

More flashes of lightning crackled around them as the storm drew overhead. The wind tore at everything and sharp beads of rain began to burn into their skin. But George and Annabelle couldn't budge the children, and so they stood beside them.

The door to Granny's crashed open and everyone ran out, ducking and holding onto each other, screaming and crying. They looked up at the flames towering all around them, blocking their every move.

They fled up the hill, to the centre of the village. The children began to step backward toward them as they continued to stare down the fire, with George, Annabelle, and Uncle Dennis holding loyally by their side.

The flames grew taller and louder as they crept to the crest, and right before they arrived came the stampede of every animal in the area: deer, moose, bears, foxes, wolves, rabbits, squirrels, and birds of every feather came to the clearing and gathered behind the children.

This time it was Asana who held the peace while Eisen tended to the situation.

She turned to everyone and took a deep breath, spreading her arms to the side with palms raised to the sky just as the flames arched high over their heads.

Again, an intense calm pressed into her audience. The screaming, the crying, the terror—animal and human—all relaxed and they sat down quietly.

"Get it, Eisen! Get it!" Asana yelled back to her brother.

It had become an inferno of biblical proportions, and the village was their ark.

The flames swirled in vortexes, raging into a sky so thick with smoke that the sun was blocked out and the entire village sunk into sinister darkness.

"Uh-huh!" Eisen yelled back.

George looked to Annabelle, then to their children. Fire suppression was something he had trained the children to do… on a small campfire. But all fires required the same formula for existence. He stepped up behind Eisen and put his hands on his shoulders, then bent down to him and whispered, "I love you, son. You've got this."

As he whispered the words, he watched as the front line of flames diminish considerably. They were still massive and menacing, but Eisen was having an effect.

George bent to him again. "That's it, you've got it. Remember, breathe and focus." He felt Eisen take a deep breath, and the flames died a little more. In the background, the fire still roared on unaffected, but anything threatening the village was weakening.

Annabelle stepped next to George and spoke softly. "How… What's he doing?"

"He's suffocating it. Just like we practised. He's removing the oxygen from the air."

Eisen's confidence grew as he killed the frontline of the fire. But it was still spreading quickly in the background, and Eisen followed it as it made its way around the village, leaving a distinct border of ash.

Every person and beast sat quietly, their gazes following the young boy around until eventually, the flames had passed around Beelieve and continued their natural course up the mountain.

With the danger gone, the sedative state lifted from the group.

The animals sniffed around some, then slowly found their way back into the wilderness. The people slowly stood up and looked up the slope to the fire, then back to the children.

One man in white robes looked to the sky. "Thank you, Lord, our Saviour!"

A woman threw herself to the ground before the children, bowing to their feet. "You! You are angels of mercy! Thank you! Thank you for our lives."

All people present, including the village residents, took their turn thanking the children.

As George and Annabelle watched, they held each other and shared a kiss.

At first, George was tempted to try to have them all swear secrecy about the happening. But he knew it would never hold. Events like this would continue as the children grew and became more involved in life. Now, the Stanleys would have to speed up their departure.

Knock-knock-knock!

The sound on the door startled General Mathis as he leaned back in his chair to have a sip of his morning coffee. People calling on him for any reason had become a rare occasion over the last years. His position in the tank had been in continual demotion. His current title, if he were to have one, would be "General of Shipping and Receiving of Any Materials of Unimportance—and Looking for George Stanley." He had begun to take his workplace misery home with him, till eventually, even his wife had left.

George Stanley… how the name burned in his mind. The hardships that man had caused him with his stunts. The general had turned over every rock in an attempt to find him but had never succeeded in finding so much as a crumb of direction. So, there he sat, collecting dust as everyone else advanced their positions. He figured George Stanley had probably been killed not long after he left. If that were the case, the general would remain where he was until retirement.

He grunted, then sat up straight in his chair and shuffled some papers on his desk. "Yes?" he called out.

A balding man with heavy spectacles meekly poked his head in the door. "Uh"—he pushed his glasses back up his nose—"General Mathis?"

The general raised an eyebrow at the little man. "Yes, you can come in."

"Oh, uh, thank you, sir." He pushed the door open and straightened his tie. As the door opened, a similar-looking and equally timid man was revealed. "Yes, um, sorry… Sorry to bother you, sir. I'm Stuart Dickens, and this is my associate

Simon Withers."

The general's brow raised with curiosity. "Yes, hello… How can I help you?"

"Yes, sorry."

The two men sidled awkwardly into the small office and closed the door behind them. Stuart approached the desk, setting a binder down before the general. "We, uh, we're from the geographical seismic division."

"*Hmph*, never heard of it." General Mathis laced his fingers and set his hands down before the binder.

"Yes, well…" Stuart laughed nervously. "You likely wouldn't have heard of us, our divisions don't really deal with… hmm, sorry." He tugged at his tie as the general stared at him.

The general was losing interest, fast. "Yes, so, how can I help you?"

"Yes, well, we had a special circumstance—or event, I guess—unfold a while back. A seismic event, north of the border, sir. One of really peculiar frequency, something we've never seen before. So, we made some calculations and narrowed the source down to a general location and then watched. Over some years, we picked up other random events and started to pay attention to the news feeds in the area. It's pretty remote, so there wasn't much to watch. But recently there have been a few remarkable events. We've been relaying the information to our superiors as we've gathered it. They tossed us here, then there, and—well, you know how the system works… or doesn't, hehe."

"Yes, go on."

"Then, we finally got some interest from a Harper Munroe."

"Harper!?" The general's interest renewed. Harper Munroe had been his superior when he had just joined the division. It had been years since he had heard that name mentioned. Harper had apparently moved so far up the secret ranks, he was beyond the general's reach.

"Yes sir, General. Anyway, when Mr. Munroe sat down with us and we told him about everything we had been following, he suggested that this may be of some interest to you."

As Stuart opened the binder, the general leaned over and stared closely.

Stuart flipped through the pages slowly. "See, the seismic event was very strange, as I mentioned before. Just in the range where we could actually detect it. But it was obvious that it wasn't an earthquake, so we called in some favours and had the area put under some loose satellite surveillance, and we had a few little pops or whatnot from time to time. We continued to research the frequencies and found that the only likely cause—even though it was a long shot—was a change in matter densities."

"A what?" The general's eyes shot straight to Stuart.

Stuart smiled. "Yes, I know, right? Really far-fetched, but it was as if something was changing the density of the molecules in the area. We honestly thought it might be some sort of secret-weapons testing. That's how we got to talk to someone as high up the ranks as Mr. Munroe."

Stuart flipped the pages in front of the general; the first few were a garble of seismic readings that someone without intimate knowledge would never understand. "And, yeah, well, anyway…" He looked back to his assistant. "You have it ready?"

The young man nodded eagerly and handed his phone to Stuart.

Stuart glanced at the screen and placed it in front of the general with a smile. Then he reached down and tapped the PLAY button.

The general was vaguely amused as he watched, and then he gave Stuart a quizzical look.

Stuart pointed to the screen with another smile. "It's a magic show in the local town, Nelson, during one of their annual festivals. The video went viral— over a million views."

The general watched the entire clip again, showing little reaction other than a shrug of his shoulders. "So?"

"Seems pretty extravagant for a small-town magic show, don't you think?"

The general took a moment to reconsider, then nodded. "Sure."

"Did you pay attention to the ending?" Stuart dragged the play bar back enough to show the ending again. "See, at the end, they focus in on the children. This video piqued our curiosity, so we had a couple investigators rent a place in the area and pose as tourists. Got them to snoop around a bit and see what they could find out. They're still there now, actually."

"And?"

"Well, what they discovered is that the children come from a family that lives in a village up in the hills—hippie folk. The area is crawling with them." Stuart flipped through his binder until he came to a satellite photo. "So, we got a rough idea of where the village was located, and they had a bit of bother finding it, until recently. A nasty storm went through the area and started the forest on fire.

And…" He flipped till he found the page he was looking for. "There! They call it the village of Beelieve. Notice how the entire area around the village is burned to the ground. The fire was massive. Took down everything in its path. But somehow it went completely around this little village, which has virtually no electricity and zero running water."

The two scientists were gaining the general's interest, and he nodded for them to continue.

"The people in town were a little skittish when our people started asking questions. But one store owner let it slip that the children belong to the Stanleys."

The name sent the general's blood to a boil and his face flushed.

Stuart flipped through the last few pictures. "So, we got our friends to zoom in as much as they could on some of the village residents. Mr. Munroe was under the impression there was a chance you might recognize someone."

As Stuart hit the last page, the general felt a fire burn in his gut. He looked closely. The hair and beard threw him off, but the height and build fit. And those eyes… the eyes never lied. *Hello, George Stanley…* said a vengeful voice in his mind.

After a moment of silent flipping through the photos of George and his wife and children, Stuart finally spoke. "Well, General, do you recognize anyone?"

The general was surprised to feel a little choked up. A chance at redemption had finally come, after all the years. "*Ahem…* Yes, indeed I do." He took control of the pages, flipping back and forth. "I'm gonna need the names of your contacts on the ground, in the town." He peered up at Stuart.

Stuart smiled and nodded eagerly. "Yes, sir. If you pass me your email, I'll send you all the information I have."

They exchanged contact information, and immediately after the door closed behind the scientists, the general picked up the phone.

"Yes, General Mathis here. I need satellite surveillance over an area in Canada. I also need monitoring on any and all internet cafés in that area. Scroll back through the search history as far as you can… What am I looking for? I'm looking for someone setting up to leave town, someone in contact with local authorities, someone setting up a new email address. Tap into the computers' cameras, I'll send you a photo of the individual in question."

He hung up the phone and sighed heavily. He wrung his hands together in front of him as he looked at the wall, thinking. Thinking about all the years he'd sat idle in that dank office, and who was responsible.

40

George passed through Nelson early the next morning. He walked as swiftly as he could without drawing too much suspicion. He wasn't as well known in town as Annabelle, so few people, if any, ever paid him any attention, other than the few suspicious glares from Mr. Mulland when George couldn't manage to avoid him.

He had been making a trip to one of the internet cafés every few days over the last couple of weeks. At the start of his endeavour, he had set up a new email under a false name. He didn't like the idea of communicating in such fashion, but he had little choice.

The man he was in conversation with, a lawyer out of the States, was well known for handling exceptional cases such as with his family. If they were going to leave now, after all the happenings of late, they were going to need protection—physical and legal.

On his last visit to town two days previous, he had uploaded some videos from his camera and sent them to the lawyer for review. This day would be the follow-up.

George sat down and glanced subtly around the room for anyone suspicious. He had heard the stories about strangers asking questions about them around town, but he had yet to encounter anything out of the ordinary.

He logged into the private chat room. To date, both George and the lawyer had been chatting under false names: George as *John* and the lawyer as *Dave*.

John: *Hello?*

Dave: *Good morning, John, how are you and the family holding up?*

John: *As well as can be expected, I guess. Did you get a chance to review what I sent you?*

Dave: *Yes, I did. It's very interesting. I'll admit that I was skeptical at first. I do have some training in detecting doctored images, but these seem legit.*

John: *I promise you everything is accurate. Can you and will you help us?*

Dave: *Yes, John, I've decided to take on your case. I would like to get you and your family out of there and to safety as soon as possible. It may seem a bit sudden, but I'm planning on arriving in town tomorrow, at our previously discussed destination. I'll be bringing security with me. We'll stay in Canada for the first few nights, till I can decide whether it is better for you to remain there or return to the States.*

John: …

Dave: *John? You still there?*

John: …

Dave: *John?*

John: *Yeah, I'm still here. Sorry, it's just a lot to take in.*

Dave: *I understand. But I think it's best if we make this happen as soon as possible. With all the happenings there lately, I'm concerned for your safety. You're right to think that there will be very powerful people interested in you and your family.*

John: *Yes, I understand.*

Dave: *What you and your wife have created with those children is going to change the world, for the better. Right now, we have to keep you safe. I know it's tough, John, but it's time.*

John: *Yes.*

Dave: *Okay, then, at the scheduled spot, at the scheduled time tomorrow?*

John: *Yes.*

Dave: *Good, everything is going to work out fine, one step at a time. We'll see you all in the morning*

John: *See you. Thank you.*

The chat ended and George took a moment at his cubicle. He removed his glasses and wiped at some tears. Finally, he exhaled, sat up straight, and gave himself a shake. He placed his glasses back on, logged out of the computer, and headed for the front door.

He saw them on the sidewalk as he came out: a man and woman dressed casually, but looking a little too artificial together. They were standing right in George's path. He was suspicious, but he was suspicious of everyone, so he put his head down and assumed his usual pace. But as George walked around them, the man took a step back and bumped into him.

The man turned immediately and smiled. "Oh, man, I'm really sorry for—" He lifted his sunglasses and squinted at George as the woman looked around the side, taking her own interest.

The man pointed with a smile. "Hey! Oh, wow, you… Are you the guy? The one they talk about around here? The one with the magic family?"

George said nothing. He quickly turned and continued down the sidewalk.

But the couple followed him. "Remember, honey? The family from the video, with the magic children? I think he's the father."

George picked up his pace, but the couple matched it. His voice grew less happy and curious, leaning a little toward the threatening.

"You remember his name, honey? Uhhhh, what?"

"George," the woman answered, her voice flat and jagged.

"That's right, George Stanley. Where you going George?"

George picked his pace up even more, crossing the street at a light jog.

The couple were now obviously in pursuit of him, calling out his full name. He tried to ditch them around a couple corners, but they weren't having it. His only hope was in the forest. When he hit the tracks, he burst into a full-out sprint and began to put some distance between them. Then he cut hard into the trees and looked behind to see they hadn't made the turn yet. He found a patch of trees to duck behind. He stood silent, and listened.

He heard their feet skidding in the dirt as they cut around the corner. Their breath was laboured. He could tell they had stopped in the clearing.

"What? Where did he go?" the woman huffed.

"Ahhh, damnit!" the man shouted. "I don't know. Stupid forest."

"Should we keep going?"

"Keep going? Where? Look around you. The people in town said this place was impossible to find. No… let's just head back and report in."

George listened to their feet shuffle over the ground and waited until the sounds of their voices grew distant before he dared to peek around the tree. He waited a bit longer before stepping out and continuing his journey.

***

General Mathis answered the phone. "Yes?… Uh-huh, great! Send it through immediately. I'm sitting in front of my computer right now."

He had just been informed that they had tracked down what they believed to be his target while searching the internet feed of a café and found a conversation in a private chat room between a Dave and John who seemed to be in the exact position the general had mentioned.

They had followed the lead through cyberspace and linked it to a couple email accounts. In one of the messages several videos were linked: videos of young children displaying very exceptional talents.

When the email came through, the general sat glued to the screen. Two children, who looked like twins, were transporting objects though the air, teleporting themselves, and walking on water, then laughing and playing and falling into the lap of a young woman, who swallowed them both in her arms and smothered them with kisses and tickles. All smiling and laughing in the summer sun.

That's where he was. George Stanley. All this time, skipping around in the mountain fields, making love to his wife, and, somehow, raising extraordinary offspring. They were a beautiful family.

During all the years that had passed, he was there, living life to the fullest. While the general was stuck in his depressing windowless prison.

He picked up the phone and hit a speed dial button that connected him to his superior. "Yes, it's Mathis. I've reviewed the data and confirmed it's him. Wife and kids also… Yes, they've been very busy… The children are the only ones with any skills, from what I've seen. There's no report of any of the others having abilities… Oh yes, they're very advanced… Uh-huh… Yes sir." The general hung up the phone.

George was sweating aggressively and obviously frustrated when he made it home, just before noon.

Annabelle stood from the bed. "George! What happened to you?"

"Where are the children?"

"They're playing outside."

"I was followed. Chased. Back in town, after I left the café. A man and woman began to ask questions about the magic show and the children. I tried to walk away from them, but they followed me. Even when I ran, they followed me down the train tracks and right into the forest. But I hid from them and they left. These weren't tourists, Annabelle. They knew my name—my full name. And the way they talked—they're not tourists."

She wrapped her arms around him. "George, my god, are you okay?"

"Yeah, I'm okay. But we have to leave first thing in the morning, all of us. I was second-guessing it myself, until I met those two. I have it set up with the lawyer. He'll meet us at the spot. He's bringing security and he's going to keep us safe."

Annabelle's eyes widened and her jaw fell. "I… I…"

"Nope." George shook his head at her. "No more stalling, Annabelle. This is for our safety. For our children's safety. We've held on here way too long."

She sat heavily down on the bed. She looked around their home as she slid her hands gently over the blanket, then broke down in tears.

George stopped packing and rushed to her side, pulling her face into his chest as she sobbed. "I know, honey, I know. Everything's going to be fine. But we're not safe here anymore, not any of us. Our being here is putting everyone else in danger. It's time to do the responsible thing."

She pushed herself back and wiped at her eyes. She nodded. "I know… I know."

At that moment, the door squeaked open and two sad faces stood in the doorway—three, if Uncle Dennis peeking around them counted.

George gave them a questioning look. "Kids?"

Little chins quivered. "We're leaving? We're leaving Beelieve?"

There was no point in hiding anything from them. George nodded. Annabelle did the same.

Both children burst across the room, leaving Dennis in the doorway, and jumped into their parents' arms.

"No, Mama!" Asana sobbed. "Why do we have to go?"

"Yeah, Dad," Eisen burbled.

George and Annabelle couldn't help but break down a little. It was the only home they'd ever had together.

"It's not safe for us here anymore, kids." George kissed the top of his son's head.

"But Mama," Asana continued, "we can't leave. Leave Granny and Cappy, Gwyn and Uncle Munch, Stella and Griz, and"—both children looked to the door—"and Uncle Dennis?" They both broke free from their parents and rushed back to their furry elder, squeezing him tight and smudging his fur with their tears and runny noses.

"Asana, Eisen," Annabelle called to them. "You knew this day was coming. We told you a long time ago. None of us want to leave, but for right now, we have to. For the safety of everyone, including Uncle Dennis."

Still wrapped tightly around Dennis's neck, Asana turned her face back to her mom. "We can come back, right? Come back someday, when it's safe again?"

Annabelle and George looked to each other, then Annabelle turned back to her daughter. "Well of course, honey. Of course we'll come back some day. Once it's safe, we can come back whenever we want. And we'll all still be together, you and Eisen and Mommy and Daddy. We're going to go live in a big city for a while. You'll get to see all the tall buildings, and busy highways, and all the people. It's going to be an exciting family adventure."

"Really?" Eisen loosened his grip and turned to his parents.

Asana also let go and she and her brother made their way back to the bed.

"Big buildings and lots of cars? Like Lamborghini cars, Dad?"

George chuckled and ruffled his boy's hair. "I'm sure we'll see a Lamborghini sometime, for sure." He winked.

The twins crawled up beside their parents and the curious questions began to roll. Slowly but surely, Annabelle and George could see their grip loosening on the tiny mountain village they had known as their home for their entire life.

Annabelle looked at the wooden frame around the door, where they had carved the children's height on their birthday every year, then at the section of canvas wall where she and George had let the children dip their hands in paint and put their colourful paw prints everywhere. There was even a blue snout print from a certain relative whose curiosity had gotten the better of him. Then her gaze moved to the part of the room that had been their play area when they were young, now turned bedroom with their two single beds. Her eyes moved to the woodstove that popped and hissed during the peaceful winter nights, when the snow outside was as high as the roof. Annabelle quivered when she pictured her home empty and lifeless.

But there was limited time to dwell. Annabelle looked to George, who smiled at her. They reached for each other behind the children, who were rattling off questions about life in the big city. When their hands found each other, they gave a loving squeeze. They understood that they were both ready to take the next step together, as a family.

"Okay!" Annabelle clapped her hands. "We leave first thing in the morning. So now we have to go tell everyone, and then we have to have a party!" She grinned.

The children's chatter stopped instantly, their eyes bulging as their smiles widened. They jumped to their feet. "Oh yeah!" they shouted and ran to the door, pushing Uncle Dennis out and following behind him. They called back, "C'mon! We have to celebrate!"

The twins skipped around the village, calling for everyone to meet at Granny and Cappy's. After everyone had gathered they made the announcement, and there were many sad faces and enough tears to raise the lake.

They'd all known it was coming. It was just never certain when. Griz and Stella rushed back to their place and returned shortly with a couple presents. Stella had made Asana the prettiest of dresses: light, with a floral print running down the front, then tracing around the perimeter of the bottom. And for handsome young Eisen, there was a shirt and pants made of the same material, with strips of small native totem art running down the seams.

As the twins modelled their outfits for the crowd, Stella turned away, unable to contain her emotions.

Griz presented them with two small boxes. When opened, they each found a small wooden medallion of the Beelieve village symbol attached to a necklace. Griz was in tears, as much as she tried to remain strong. She looked at the children and pointed to the welcome arch they had erected together. "These are to always remind you of your home, your roots. Don't ever forget us." She could barely make a smile when the children ran into her arms. She gave them a tight squeeze, then let them go and went to comfort Stella.

Gwyn and Munch came next. Munch was arguably the biggest mess of them all.

"Oh, I feel so responsible for all of this," he said, his face and beard heavily tear-stained. "I don't think you can ever know how strong a hold you have on our hearts. I know that the next time we see each other, the world will have changed, and we will be free to put on the biggest performance in history."

The children went to hug their Cappy and Granny, taking turns sitting on their knees, though they had grown quite large for it.

"You two." Granny hugged them close. "There was only supposed to be one of ya, hmm. I knew before you were born there was something extra special about you, and look at you now. Going to save us all."

The twins then went over to Uncle Dennis, who was starting to show his age and had been very quiet since the announcement back at their home. Even now, he stood with his back turned to them. But they stepped on either side of him and wrapped their arms around him.

Asana whispered in his ear, "I'll miss you most of all, Uncle Dennis."

"Me too, Uncle," Eisen whispered in his other.

Sad announcement aside, the sun was beginning to set, so the celebration began. Wine and silliness flowed freely. Stories were told, tears were shed, and laughter was spent.

The children entertained the others as usual by showing some of their new skills. With the bonfire crackling into the night, they took turns fuelling it and then diminishing it to almost nothing, then bringing it back again with nothing more than a wave of the hand. It was getting to the point where they almost didn't even have to make the gesture anymore.

As each one had flanked the flames, the others had settled into their chairs or spread out blankets to lie on the ground. The festivities had taken their toll, the darkness had settled, and eyes became heavy and yawns contagious.

Gwyn reached to Annabelle's hand and gave it a squeeze.

Annabelle looked at her and saw her eyes were tearing again as they watched the children.

"I'm sorry, Annabelle. I just can't imagine how this place will feel tomorrow, after you all leave us. It's going to be a very different place."

Annabelle smiled at her, then lifted her hand to her lips and gave it a tender kiss.

Suddenly, the kids stopped doing tricks and backed away from the fire. They looked up.

Annabelle sensed immediately that something was wrong. And she knew they felt it too.

The sound of the crackling fire had been enough to mask it, till they were upon them. There was a sudden gust of wind, and the children froze in fear.

George looked up, then screamed "RUN!" from the depth of his gut just before the area became flooded with blinding light.

The military assault was quick and efficient. So much so that it had even evaded the children's detection until it was too late.

Stealth choppers swarmed in, and before anyone could react, multiple concussion grenades rained down with sonic booms and blinding flashes that left everyone stunned and broken.

Soldiers dressed in pure black rappelled to the ground. Annabelle watched from her stunned state as they cast nets over the adults, while two separate teams crouched with guns raised toward her children. They then wedged themselves between the twins and were able to push them farther apart in their debilitated state.

Two more soldiers raised their rifles and each child buckled as sedated darts struck their legs. They dropped to their knees, crying in terror.

Annabelle watched as her husband pushed himself to his feet as best he could, tripping and stumbling forward, screaming, "Leave them alone! You bastards! They're just childr—"

She watched him latch on to the back of a soldier, just as another stepped up quickly behind him, kicking a heavy boot to the back of his knee and buckling him to the ground. The other soldier turned around and slammed the butt of his rifle into the side of George's head, and he fell lifeless.

"MOMMY! DADDY! NOOOOOO!" The children's helpless cries tore at Annabelle's soul.

Sounds all around her of people moaning, crying, and pleading.

Uncle Dennis charged at the soldiers as they moved closer to the children, braying and kicking and spinning in madness. Another man in black raised his rifle, took aim, and *POP-POP*. Uncle Dennis's body fell to a heap, one of his hind legs twitching.

"NO, MOMMY! NOOOOOOOO! UNCLE DENNIS!"

Annabelle moaned as she rolled over in agony. Grabbing at her heart, she reached her other hand toward her children. "Go!... Go, my babies. Go…"

A soldier crept from behind in the darkness and pounced on her son's weakened form with a net. He buckled beneath the weight.

She could see the tears in his eyes, the fear. He reached his little hand toward her. "Mommy…."

"Go, Eisen!" she yelled to him. "Go! Don't let them get you, honey. You have to go, go and never come back. Show them! Show the world! Show them— AHHHHGHHH!" She let go a gurgling cry as a large, broad-shouldered man appeared from the darkness and hit her with a taser.

"Now, kids," he said, "don't do anything stupid. Something that might get Mommy and Daddy hurt." He chuckled through his smouldering cigar.

As her seizure subsided, Annabelle turned her focus back to Eisen. "Go! Now!"

"Mommy… I love you!" Eisen began to glow, causing the soldiers around him to pause. Then in a crack of light that sent the ones holding him flying thought the air, Eisen vanished.

"GOD-DAMNIT!" The broad-shouldered man clenched his fists and looked to the soldiers picking themselves back up. "Can't you dipshits do one simple thing? They're children, for fuck's sake!"

He reached down and tasered Annabelle again.

Her body jerked and twitched, but she had no energy for sound anymore, only froth bubbled from her mouth. She fell out of consciousness.

***

"Mama!"

Annabelle opened her eyes to the darkness of her mind. Slowly, Asana appeared, walking toward her.

"Mama, what do I do? Why are they doing this?"

"Asana! My baby… Can you hear me? Is this real?"

"Yes, Mama, it's real. I'm here, I can hear you. What do I do?" Tears rolled from the little girl's eyes as her head twitched toward the muffled voices of the soldiers in the conscious world.

"Asana, honey… you have to go now. It's not safe here anymore."

"But you and Daddy, and Eisen… Where did he go? U-Uncle Dennis, Mama." Asana sat and hugged her knees, sobbing.

"No-no, sweetie…. Shhh. Everything's going to be okay. But you have to leave now. It's time to be a big girl. Everything's going to be all right. You're so big and strong, and so smart, Asana—you and your brother. It's time for you to go now. Daddy and Mama and everyone will be all right. We'll find each other again, I promise. Nothing can keep us apart. But you can't let these bad people get you, Asana. If they get you, everything we've done will be lost… Don't let them get you."

"But where do I go, Mama?" Her crying grew heavier. *"I'm so scared. I don't want to be alone."*

Annabelle paused, doing everything she could to stay strong. *"Go… Go to where they need you the most. Go to where they need hope. That's where they need you, Asana. Go to where they need… to believe."*

"But… I'm scared…"

"I know. I know, sweetie, but we have to be strong. Look at me…" Their eyes locked. *"You can do this, baby. I will find you… I love you so much."* Annabelle's voice crackled with the weight of her breaking heart.

She felt her eyes blinking as she returned to the conscious world. The sounds of shouting voices caused her to turn her head toward her daughter, who had collapsed on the ground. The soldiers jumped on her and pinned her down.

Asana's eyes appeared groggy as she and Annabelle reached out their hands to each other and they looked across the darkness at the other one last time…

"Go!... GOOOOOOO!!!" Annabelle screamed with her last breath of life.

The air hissed as the little girl began to glow. With another flash of light,

Asana Stanley disappeared.

Defeated, Annabelle's head dropped lifelessly to the ground.

***

The general squatted down beside an unconscious George and smiled. "Well, hello George Stanley. Fancy running into you here, haha." He stood and looked around. "Load them up and search the village for the children, and anything else of interest."

"General, sir! You may want to come look at this."

Mathis walked up the slope to the Stanley residence. He stepped in the door and was greeted by the warmth of family togetherness: cozy beds for nighttime stories, colourful handprints on the wall, and paintings of silhouetted children and mother praying to the sun, dancing with the bees, and riding their mule.

He took a walk around, then turned back to the soldier with a wicked smirk. "Take those," he said, nodding to the pictures on the wall, "then burn it down." He stepped out the door and addressed the others. "Burn it down. Burn it all down!"

***

The thumping roar of spinning blades brought Annabelle back to a mild state of awareness as the helicopter she was in lifted from the ground. Piled in a heap of bodies, her head hung just far enough over the side to have a view of the village burning around Uncle Dennis's lifeless body. Tears ran from her eyes, and she clenched them tightly shut.

In her mind, she journeyed to that place she yearned for. That place in the warm glow of the wood-fired stove, with happy faces and curls bouncing on the bed, and with a handsome, spectacled man solving worldly riddles with a piece of chalk.

But no one was there when she arrived. Dark... empty... cold, she walked the ghostly room, dragging a finger along a dusty tabletop. The measurements by the door, the play area, the colourful handprints—all gone. As if none of it ever happened.

She went to the door and peered out into the night sky. A tear trickled down her cheek. She closed her eyes and searched her mind for any hint, any sign, that they were safe, that they were warm, that they knew how much they were loved...

But there was nothing.

QUANTUM AVIDYA

END